CW01044913

A Measure of Trouble

A Measure of Trouble

Alex Warren Murder Mysteries Book II

Zach Abrams

To my wife who has supported my efforts and suffered my obsessions while writing.

Chapter 1

The paperwork would have to wait. Detective Chief Inspector Alex Warren had honoured his good intentions and arrived early to clear out his trays but it was all for nothing. He'd barely started the task before his plan was interrupted. He replaced the receiver on the rest and sighed audibly.

He needed to think clearly but he couldn't get the old joke out of his mind, 'Man dies in a distillery, his body was a mess, but you should have seen the smile on his face.' This was no time for jokes though. Within the last few minutes, a man had been found lying face down on the floor of the cask room at the Benlochy Distillery. There was collapsed shelving and upset casks lying around him together with broken glass spread over the general area. The description was unusually clear for a reported incident, but the reason was obvious as it came from the security man and he was a retired policeman. Now Alex needed to get himself and his team thirty miles up the road post haste and, ideally, before the blood had time to dry.

Alex opened the door of his private office and peered across the dimly lit expanse of the open-plan area. Although his view was partly impeded by the baffle screens, he was aware of Detective Constable Donnie McAvoy at the far side of the room and he was the only officer at his desk. Donnie was coming towards the end of his nightshift and his space was the only one with its overhead light switched on; the rest of the office was in darkness. Alex instructed Donnie to alert the 'scene of crime' team and to phone round each of the day shift officers to call them in early or to send them straight to the distillery. He considered asking Donnie to work on but then thought better of it. Donnie was only a few months off retirement and he was an old-school type of cop. Alex wasn't confident how safe it would be to leave Donnie alone with one bottle, let alone set him loose in a whisky manufacturing plant. Instead, he would have the support of Sergeant Sanjay Guptar and Constable Philip Morrison. Being Moslem, Sanjay was teetotal, and whilst Phil didn't come close to a life of abstinence, he was dependable. Alex would have preferred to have his other Sergeant, Sandra Mackinnon, but he knew that would be impossible as it was her day off and she already had a full day's activity scheduled flat-hunting. Alex was acutely aware of Sandra's plans as they'd spent most of the previous evening talking about them.

It had been just a few weeks now, but Alex and Sandra were becoming an item. They were still keen to keep their blossoming relationship a secret, but it was increasingly difficult. Both were ambitious and loved their jobs and they knew it was impractical and contrary to policy for them to be a couple working in the same team.

Alex donned his scarf and gloves and pulled his Crombie-style wool coat tightly round him before exiting the building and braving the cold spring morning. The sky was already bright and blue with only a light scattering of clouds, but the icy breeze took his breath away.

Alex walked briskly round the corner to where he'd left his Santa Fe. He removed his coat but kept on the scarf and gloves waiting until the car warmed up. He first turned the ignition then boosted the temperature on the climate control and flicked on the switch for his heated seat.

Within a couple of minutes, he reached the motorway on-ramp at Charing Cross and already he felt warm and comfortable, his legs and back starting to tingle from the infused heat. Accelerating onto the M8, he turned the thermostat down.

Although familiar with the area and knowing its location, Alex had never been to the distillery before. Still early morning, most traffic was heading towards the city. Vehicle flow was unimpeded coming out of town, and Alex made steady progress first along the M8 motorway then cutting off along the A80 dual carriageway towards Stirling. His speed had to be curtailed on the narrower country roads. Besides being smaller in size, the surfaces were uneven and he had to manoeuvre around the frequent potholes. Alex had his windscreen wipers on intermittent to clear away the smurry spray thrown up by other vehicles, a result of the remains of the previous night's downpour which hadn't already seeped or drained into the adjacent fields. Even so, he arrived less than forty minutes after receiving the phone call.

Seeing the buildings in the distance, Alex pulled off the road and snaked his way along the winding avenue, lined with Scots pine trees, and through the tall wrought iron gates. He held up his warrant card as he drove past the security booth then followed the signs for the visitors' parking area, sliding into a space alongside a squad car. He alighted from his vehicle and strode across the cobbled courtyard towards the office reception, his lengthy gait covering the distance in seconds.

After scanning his identification, a young lady escorted him back out of the building and across a walkway. In front was a large plain wall about sixty feet in length and twenty feet tall, roughcast and freshly painted stark white. On top, a red tiled roof sloped upwards. Towards the rear was a substantial timber entranceway large enough for a commercial vehicle to enter but sunk within the large door was a standard-sized door for pedestrian traffic. Constable Winters was true to his name; his skin had a blue tinge from the cold and he was standing, shivering in the doorway where he'd been stationed to ensure the area was kept secure.

"Glad to see you, Sir. I've had a hell of a job trying to keep everyone out." Winters pushed the door open to give Alex access and followed him through. Inside was a large hallway lined with racks, each neatly labelled and holding large barrels spread at regular intervals. The lighting was dim but Alex could clearly see a broken rack about halfway down the room with several barrels lying askew on the ground. A prostrate body was set in their midst, otherwise the room was empty.

"They all wanted to come and see what's happened and some of the bosses are used to having their own way. I've been manning this door and Bert Ferguson, my partner's trying to keep everyone else together in the board room. Sandy Johnston's been a good help. He's head of security and he found the body. He was a sergeant in Central constabulary until he retired about eight years ago."

"What did you find when you arrived?" Alex enquired.

"Bert and I arrived at the same time as the ambulance. We were shown to this room and the body was lying there just as it is now."

Alex sniffed the air. Although no expert, he enjoyed the occasional dram, and the pungency was unmistakable. To his concern, the smell was emanating from Winters.

Seeing Alex's expression, Winters quickly explained, "As you can see, some of the barrels had fallen about and one of them split open and was spilling onto the floor. Sandy and I helped to right it. We couldn't let it spread across the floor and maybe destroy some evidence, and besides, it would've been a crime to have good whisky going to waste. See, that's it over by the wall."

Alex studied Winters' face to see if he was joking "And you've not touched anything else?"

"No, Sir, only what I had to. I didn't touch the whisky other than to help move the cask. I never drink spirits, I can't handle it. It goes for my stomach. I'm a beer man," he added. Judging by the man's girth, Alex had no reason to doubt the veracity of his last statement.

"What about the body?"

"He was lying like that when we arrived. Sandy said he'd already checked and he was dead. Even from a distance we could see he was right. His head's bashed and the eyes are unblinking, wide open with that startled look. The ambulance boys had a closer look but knew better than to interfere with anything. They hung about for a while but then had another call and reckoned they would be better trying to look after the living. That's when we spotted the barrel was leaking and

Sandy and I righted it, that's why my uniform's reeking. We ushered everyone out of this area and Bert and Sandy are keeping them all in the board room waiting for you to arrive while I've been keeping watch on this door."

"Who's all in there?"

"I can't be sure by now. Sandy had clocked in at seven this morning and he found the body shortly after that. He called in the emergency and we got here before half past. At that time, there were only a couple of other security men and three or four lads from the warehouse and production. But pretty soon all hell broke loose with other workers coming to start their shift. Shirley, the receptionist, arrived and we've let her stay to man the office but everyone else has been kept together. Sandy must have called the owners 'cause they arrived all at once and tried to take over but we've managed to hold them back so far."

"What about the dead man? Does anyone know who he is?"

"Yes, did I not say? It's Hector Mathewson. He's one of the owners and the Managing Director of the distillery."

"Christ, we'll be swamped by the media the moment this gets out."

Alex walked across towards the body but carefully stopped a few feet away. He crouched down for a better look. He took only a few seconds, but with his keen eye and experience it was enough to take it all in. As far as he could tell, Mathewson was aged in his late forties, of fairly average height, but muscularly built with broad athletic shoulders, about five-foot-ten and maybe one hundred and seventy pounds. He had a slim angular face, a powerful jaw with a shadow which fell short of designer stubble. His hair was thin and jet black on the crown with silver showing at the temples and on the re-growth. Alex guessed it had previously been tinted. Gravity had already affected his blood supply and most of his visible skin had a grey pallor. Alex reckoned he'd been dead for several hours. Unable to examine further until the technicians had done their bit, he stood again and walked back to the door.

He could hear footsteps approaching and, sure enough, the door barged open and he was greeted by the scene of crime team, all clad in white jumpsuits and bootees. As they had no discernable uniform, Alex gazed from face to face looking for Inspector Connors but was disappointed not to recognise him.

Other than Connors, he didn't know any of them well, but three of the new arrivals looked familiar, all being about the same height and build. The fourth, however, was different. She was an elegant, tall, young lady with long, dark hair, and chiselled features. Her complexion was ebony, contrasting starkly against her jumpsuit. She confidently approached him. "Morning, Chief. Is it okay if we get started now?"

"Who are you? I don't recognise you. Have we met before?"

"Only briefly, I was in Inspector Connors' office when you came in to see him last week. My name's Anne Dixon. I only joined the team two weeks ago. I was with the Met up until last month. I applied for a transfer and got the job here. I was delighted to have the chance of working with Inspector Connors; he's well respected on a national scale and it can only help my reputation to be associated with him. The move came about because my partner's a lecturer and was offered a tenured position at Glasgow University."

"Welcome to Scotland. What does he lecture?"

"Biochemistry, we met when we were both undergraduates at Queen Mary University in London, and he's a she."

"Sorry, I shouldn't be jumping to conclusions."

"Don't worry about it. It happens all the time and we're used to it."

"Well, I hope you're thick-skinned. Although times have changed and it's nowhere near as bad as it used to be, you could face a lot of prejudice coming up from London."

A startled look came over Anne's face. "You mean because I'm black or because I'm a lesbian?"

"No, no, neither, the Scots are generally quite tolerant where that's concerned." Alex replied unable to hide his smirk. "It's because you're English. The moment anyone hears your cultured BBC accent, you could have problems."

"Okay, you had me going there," Anne said and she lightly and playfully punched him on the shoulder. "Now better get started." She moved forward and pulled up her hood and tucked in her hair.

"Right, I'll leave you to it. I need to go and take statements and I'll check back with you later. Where's Connors today, anyway?"

"He has a day's leave to go to funeral. His wife's cousin I think."

"Poor sod, as if he doesn't see enough death, he goes to a funeral on his day off." Alex turned to leave and had PC Winters lead him across to the offices.

With perfect timing, Sergeant Guptar and Constable Morrison were approaching the reception. They were accompanied by Constable Mary McKenzie, the most recent addition to their squad. They were an unlikely looking trio. Sanjay, the most senior of the three, was also the smallest. Only five-foot-four in height, he wouldn't have met recruitment criterion until fairly recently, but what he lacked in height he compensated for in determination and intellect. His slight frame was crested with short, jet-black hair and he sported studious looking, thick-framed, black spectacles. Phil was nearly ten years older, having joined the police as a replacement career choice after his former employer migrated to Eastern Europe. Seeing them together was like looking at a 'Little and Large' contrast but neither having any similarity to the comedy act he recollected from years before. Only slightly smaller than Alex, with a sportsman's physique and a height of six-foot-three, Phil towered over Sanjay. Being moderately tanned, his skin tone was lighter but because of his overgrown schoolboy attitude and sense of humour, you could be forgiven for thinking him the younger of the two. Mary's country upbringing was evident from her wholesome appearance. A little bit taller than Sanjay, she was stocky without being fat and had a pale complexion contrasted by naturally rosy cheeks. She had a pleasant, full round face and shoulder-length, curly locks. Although young and enthusiastic, Mary was daunted at the thought of this being her first murder enquiry.

"Sanjay, Phil, Mary, you're just in time. We're about to get started interviewing witnesses and anyone who knows what's been happening."

"Can I volunteer for any stocktaking duties?" Phil asked. "With the emphasis on the taking, that is." A broad smile settled on his face.

"You'd better wipe that grin off before we go in. There's likely to be a lot of shocked and upset people we need to talk to, so you can start by adopting a more professional demeanour. I say adopt because I know it couldn't come naturally to you."

Phil feigned a hurt expression.

All five entered the board room and were met by a barrage of questions and demands. Everyone was asking what had happened and wanted to know the details. Alex held up his hands and called for silence. He explained the procedures they would be following. He wanted details of everyone present, their names, addresses and telephone numbers. Everyone on site at the time of the death would be interviewed first, as well as each of the owners, directors and senior managers. Everyone else would follow if and when necessary.

A short pudgy man came striding forward. He had a spherical head but the almost perfect geometry was spoiled by large protruding ears. His pate was topped by light brown lines of hair which were so sparse they appeared to be drawn onto his balding scalp by biro. The large ears gave the appearance of jug handles and his face was bright crimson in colour with the uneven texture of blotting paper.

"I want to know exactly what's going on and I insist you keep me up to date with every development. I'll let you use my office for your interviews, but I'll sit in on them."

Alex stood to attention, straightened his back and let the man see the full benefit of his muscular frame and six-foot-six of height. He did not turn his head or bend his neck, instead adjusting his eyes to literally look down his nose. With an expression on his face indicating he had just become aware of a nasty and unpleasant smell, he replied, "I don't think you understand that we are investigating a mysterious death. I'm in charge here and I can conduct this enquiry any way I chose. If you insist on getting in my way then I'll have you arrested and held in custody until I get round to speaking to you. And I warn you, I won't be in any hurry."

"You can't speak to me like that," the man blustered. "I'm a director and one of the owners of this business. I'm a local councillor and, besides, the dead man's my brother-in-law."

"I can speak to you any way I like. So far I've not lost my temper and I've been very restrained. I can assure you, Sir, you don't want that to change. Now, if you really have some authority then I suggest that other than the employees we identify, your security and other essential staff, all the rest of the employees are sent home to give greater opportunity for my team to gather evidence in the course of the day. Now what's your name?"

As Alex was speaking, the man's face was growing even brighter and the vein on his neck pulsed visibly. His hands were shaking with rage and his eyes looked upwards to Alex's face as if trying to burn their way through him.

"I'm Quentin Burns," he said, then he turned away and thumped his fist on the table as he sat back down.

A second figure approached Alex, but this one was more respectful. "Good morning, Sir. I'm Sandy Johnston, I'm the security supervisor and I was the one who found the body and called it in. I take it you'll want to talk to me, then I can help with the interviews if you like."

"I'm pleased to meet you, Sandy, although I'd have preferred different circumstances." He extended his hand and Sandy shook it enthusiastically.

"You're right. I'd like to interview you. We've still to ascertain the cause of death, but for the time being it can be considered suspicious. Winters has told me that you've been a great help already. You're a key witness and you can also brief me on who's who in this operation with a bit of background too. But you must realise you're no longer a cop and you can't be present when we interview anyone else."

"Of course, I'll do anything I can."

A schedule was set up planning the order of interviews and who would conduct them. A number of uniformed officers had arrived and were assisting with the organisation.

Rooms were identified where the interviews would be conducted. Hector's private office was left vacant to enable the scene a crime team to conduct a thorough inspection. If only to assert his authority, Alex decided to commandeer Quentin Burns's office and, accompanied by Phil Morrison, he selected Sandy as an obvious first choice and called him for the first interview.

Chapter 2

The executives' offices were all on the first floor above the reception, and Quentin's office overlooked the main gate. It was large and opulently adorned. All the walls were covered to ceiling height either by wooden shelving or wood panelling. Everything was a rich cherry-wood colour with the exception of the frames of the large windows which took up most of the wall facing the entrance door. These looked as though they had recently been replaced using white uPVC, although the ledges remained consistent with the rest of the room.

On the left wall to the side of the windows was a substantial timber fireplace and in front of the window sat an ornately carved wooden desk with matching armchair. The legs on both were scrolled and the desk's surface was protected by a plate glass cover. The set looked to be eighteenth century and Alex guessed they must be worth a fortune. In front of the fireplace were a further two, stout armchairs, also vintage but not of the same age or quality. The opposite wall was covered ceiling to floor with a bookcase filled with leather bound texts. Close to the remaining wall, beside the entrance, was a solid table surrounded by six chairs, not quite to the standard of the desk but nevertheless an imposing piece. Above the table hung an oil portrait depicting a man who had all the trappings of being wealthy, strong and influential. He was dressed in Victorian garb and had dark hair with flowing side-locks. However, his jug ears and round flushed face had a distinct resemblance to Quentin Burns.

"Is there any way of getting a cup of tea around here?" Alex called as he walked across the room.

"I'll get it sorted," Sandy offered. "Just give me a sec."

Alex sat at the table with his back to the wall. Phil took the seat to his left and Sandy returned and pulled up a chair facing him. Phil lifted a notepad and pen from his case then pulled out a portable recorder. Switching it on, he noted and confirmed all the standard information before the interview commenced.

"Right, Sandy, I gather you were the first one to find the body?"

"That's right, Sir. I'd only clocked on a short while before and I was making a regular tour of inspection. When I got to the shop I thought it a bit odd, a lot of the shelves were empty and looking a bit untidy, then I saw the door through to the cask room wasn't closed. It all seemed very strange because that door's always kept locked and it's standard practice for the shop to be cleaned, tidied and restocked every night.

"I went through the door to the cask room and that's when I saw Mr Mathewson lying on the floor. I was pretty certain he was dead but I checked for a pulse just in case. I felt nothing and his skin was cold so I reckoned he'd been dead for some time."

"Did you touch anything else?"

"No, Sir. I only checked his pulse then I moved away and called in '999.' Fred Winters and Bert Ferguson were here in a matter of minutes and I brought them in to see. We secured the door from the shop so there'd be only the one way in, then we took a look at the body, that's when we saw one of the kegs had a split and was leaking. Fred helped me right it and move it out the way so it wouldn't cause any damage."

"Yeah, we realised from the smell off his uniform. Did anyone..."

Alex's next question was interrupted by a loud knock on the door. Phil jumped up to pull it open.

The receptionist wheeled in an elaborate and well-laden tea trolley. She lifted bone china cups, saucers and side plates from the lower level and passed a set to each of them. A quality, silver-plated tea service was then placed on the centre of the table followed by a large plate piled high with butter shortbread and a second plate full of Tunnock's teacakes.

"Thanks, Shirley. That was perfect timing. We were just gasping for a brew," Sandy said.

"Would you like me to pour?" she offered.

"No thanks. We can manage just fine ourselves."

Shirley parked the trolley against the side wall and pulled the door closed behind her with enthusiastic words of gratitude ringing in her ears.

"This sure beats the sludge served in Styrofoam cups we get in the office," Phil said while taking the initiative and serving the tea. "Do you want a break, Sir?"

"No time. There's far too much to do. We can have our tea while we keep going." Alex carefully lifted the fragile teacup, the delicate porcelain looking incongruous, lost in his meaty hands. Much as he enjoyed the finer things in life, Alex would have felt more at home with a robust mug. Instead, he felt a little bit uncomfortable, with the dilemma of being keen to quench his thirst but being wary of crushing the crockery. He tried to refocus on the interview.

"Did anyone know Mathewson was here?"

"That's the problem. Security records show that he left at 3 o'clock yesterday afternoon when he drove out and his car's not been back in since."

"Did he live close-by? Could he have walked?"

"He's not that far away, maybe a couple of miles, but it's not been the weather for walking and Mathewson didn't go in for unnecessary exercise at the best of times. Not unless he was posing, that is."

"Are you sure it was him who left at three? Or could someone else just have taken his car out?"

"No, the records show it was him leaving. Besides, there were stories he had an important meeting in Glasgow."

"Yeah, what was that about?"

"Well, you know there's been talk about the business being up for sale."

"Sorry, Sandy, you're assuming too much. This is the first time we've been out here and it's to investigate a suspicious death. Don't assume we know about anything else that's been going on. But it could be relevant, so I'd like you to go back to the beginning and tell me what you know. I need as much background information as you can give me. How is the business structured and who's all involved. Most of it will be irrelevant but it'll help us build up a picture."

Alex's concentration became slightly distracted as out the corner of his eye he caught sight of Phil trying to stuff a teacake into his mouth in one piece. Inevitably he failed and the chocolate covering broke up, spreading glutinous, white marshmallow across his lips and chin, which he then struggled to lick clean.

"For God sake man, can't you show some decorum?" he exclaimed, but was unable to keep the laughter out of his voice. "Besides, don't you know where all those calories will end up?"

"Not much worry there," Phil replied. "When I'm not working, I'm forever running after the two wee ones."

The words were out his mouth without thinking and he regretted them immediately when he saw a brief flash of pain showing in Alex eyes. Alex's marriage had ended a couple of years beforehand and his two sons lived with their mother with Alex only having limited opportunity to exercise his custody rights.

"I'm sorry, Sir. I didn't mean..."

"Let's stay focussed. We've got a hell of a lot to get through. Right, Sandy, what can you tell us?"

"A quick history – the Benlochy Distillery was first set up here on this site in the first half of the nineteenth century. There's stories about an illegal still on this same site going back long before that. I don't know if it's true but it's something to do with the burn flowing past the door. There's also talk of a natural spring just the other side of the hill. Anyway, the distillery was created by Samuel Burns and it's been a family business ever since. His grandson was also a Samuel Burns and that's his portrait up on the wall."

Alex turned to again examine the picture occupying a large section of the wall. The subject was an austere looking man standing in front of what was now the main building. He was dressed in a dark velvet cape and holding a cane in his right hand and a book, possibly a bible, in his left.

"It's been there for the last hundred years and more." Sandy continued, "His great-grandson is Daniel Burns. It was always a good business but Mr Daniel really built it up over the last thirty years or so. He increased production and added another still. He modernised the place and built storage. He had the brand recognised as one of the best known, single malt whiskies in the world. There are three main marketing brands, the 12, 15 and 18 year old. But there's a whole load of other specialities as well, sometimes using different types of cask. Also there are bulk sales for supermarket and blend products. On top of that, we have whiskies which have been bottled in different years and they're sometimes supplied to collectors and clubs. The 12, 15 and 18 are the number of years the whisky is left to mature in the casks before it gets bottled because, unlike wine, it doesn't continue to mature in the bottle."

Sandy's pride in being associated with the product was obvious. Phil was fascinated with his explanation. Alex was already aware of much of what he was being told and, much as he too was interested in what he was hearing, he was aware it wasn't what he needed now.

"Thanks, Sandy. We'd like to hear more about the product but let's leave that part until later. Tell us more about the people for just now."

"Yes, of course, Sir. Sorry, I was getting a bit carried away. When Daniel took over, he owned or controlled most of the shareholding, but as part of the growth strategy he allowed in some outside investors. Even so, the family still controlled the vast majority. Some years ago he got involved in tax planning and a lot of the shares went into a family trust and others were distributed to his three children. Georgina is the oldest, that's Hector Mathewson's wife. Then there's Quentin who you met a few minutes ago and his young brother Stanley. They were each given an equal number of shares so they had some of the ownership, but Daniel used to be a bit of a tyrant and he kept absolute control himself."

"How do you know all of this? Is it public knowledge?"

"It used to be very confidential but it all came out a couple of years back when Daniel took ill. As I said, Daniel was a bit of a tyrant and he kept control of absolutely everything. Georgina worked in the business and used to look after the office. After she married, Hector came to work here too. He was an accountant, at least that's what he claimed but he didn't show much sign of it. He had no idea about controlling money but he certainly knew how to spend it. Georgina gave up working when her children were born and more's the pity because she knew what she was doing in a way that Hector never did. Quentin's always worked here and he's the director of sales and marketing."

"What about Stanley?"

"He never wanted to be involved. He's a lot younger than the other two. He wanted to go to university and study medicine and he had the grades to do it but Daniel wouldn't let him and insisted he come in and learn the business. He was smart too, but never fitted in. He and Quentin never got along. They couldn't stand the sight of each other, actually. After a few years, his father let him go off and travel. By then it was too late for him to take up the medicine offer and he wasn't interested in studying anything else. He's bummed around ever since. Every so often he comes back and does some work for a few months and then he buggers off again."

"What was the cause of the aggro?"

"I can't say for sure but Stanley was always the blue-eyed boy, his mother's favourite, and I think Quentin resented it. He always wants to be the centre of attention and he'd quite often create problems for Stanley or undermine his efforts and then tell everyone about how useless he was. He's a bully and Stanley was an easy target. His father's a bully too, but at least Daniel had real ability which goes some way to make up for it.

"Like I was saying, Daniel ran this place with an iron fist. But then a couple of years ago he had a stroke. It was a bad one and completely floored him. At first, no one thought he would pull through but he's an incredibly strong man. It took him months but he got back most of his mobility. He's got a limp now and uses a stick and his speech is a bit slurred but he's made a remarkable recovery. It's really weakened him though and sapped his confidence.

"When it first happened, the family got together. They knew they had to do something to keep the business going. As part of his planning, Daniel had set up a living Power or Attorney and the children used this to take over control."

"What about his wife?"

"Oh, she died a number of years ago so it was all down to the children. In theory they had equal say but Stanley still didn't want to be involved and used his influence to stop Quentin getting control. As a result, Hector, using Georgina's shares, became the managing director. Quentin was livid. He thought the company was his birthright and he also thought he was the natural successor as he knew the most about how the company functioned. There were some major squabbles but there was nothing Quentin could do. Even the investors backed Hector because they'd been led to believe he was a professional. Quentin had threatened to walk out but it was all bluster. Since then they've worked together okay but the atmosphere has not always been pleasant."

"This sounds a right hornet's nest."

"Aye, you could say that."

"Who else is involved?"

"On the senior management side there's a couple of others. Patrick Gillespie is the Company Secretary. He's in his seventies, probably about the same as Daniel and he's worked for the company all his life. He started as a junior clerk but he was given training as a boy and sent off to college to get his qualifications. He always deferred to Miss Georgina when she worked here but he really ran the office when Hector was supposedly in charge. He looks after all the office staff, the general admin, the accounts and the sales and export administration. I suppose in a modern organisation he'd be called the Finance Director or Chief Finance Officer but we're still a bit old fashioned here so he's just the Secretary. The other manager is Callum McPherson and he's responsible for materials control. He takes care of stock control, buying and inventory management.

"On top of that, we've got the children. Hector and Georgina have two and so do Quentin and his wife Fiona. Stanley's never been married and there's talk that he never will, if you know what I mean. As for the children, they're all pretty much a waste of space. They swan around here as if they own the place, which I suppose they do in a way, but not yet. They all take out a salary but they don't do very much. Quentin's oldest, Samuel, is the only one who even tries. He was named after some of his fore-bearers but that doesn't seem to have gone for anything as he's as daft as a brush. Quentin gets him to go on sales trips and to stand at our stall at whisky exhibitions, but pouring the whisky seems all he's good for, and drinking it, of course. He seems to have developed quite a taste for the product."

Phil had been taking his own notes to supplement the recording but he saw a natural pause to put down his pen and refill the teacups. All three slurped down the hot liquid and Phil took the opportunity to devour a thick slab of shortbread.

"Have you had no breakfast, son?" Alex enquired.

"No, Sir. I'd been planning to pick up a bacon roll before going into the office but Donny phoned to tell me about coming out here first thing. I'd thought of getting something to eat on the road out but I couldn't take bacon or sausage into the car with Sanjay. It wouldn't have been right with his religious beliefs."

"Very thoughtful," Alex added sardonically.

"Thanks for all that, Sandy. Now we know the main players and we also know that Hector wasn't meant to be in last night. We can easily check who else was meant to be here, but as the records don't show Hector Mathewson as being on site then there's every chance he could have had others with him who also weren't on record. We now need to get a better understanding of what's being going on. What can you tell me about Mathewson? What was he like? How did he get on with the others? You know the sort of things we're looking for."

"Well, Sir. To start with, that's easy, but it won't help you too much. I think you'd have difficulty finding anyone around here with a good thing to say about him. He wasn't liked and didn't get on with anyone. He was a bully, but that's no surprise, it was a pretty consistent family trait. But while folk were wary and even a bit scared of the other members of the family, at least they were respected. That wasn't the case with Mr Hector. He was only a member of the management because he married in, so he was never seen to have the same right to be here or be in command and, worse still, everyone thought he wasn't making a very good job of running things.

"The worst part has been all the rumours that the distillery was up for sale. The managers keep denying it but that's only been adding fuel to the flames. There seems to be loads of meetings all kept very quiet. If anyone enters the room while the meetings are on, then all the talking stops and nobody knows where to look."

"I thought it was a very successful and profitable business. Why should they want to sell it?"

"I really can't say, Sir. As nobody's prepared to talk about what's going on, they can hardly tell us the reason why. I'm sure the business is good and profitable but it's an awful big family to support, particularly when not many of them are making an effective contribution to running it and, added to that, they've got expensive tastes."

There was another loud knock on the door and a police constable Alex didn't recognise poked his head in.

"Sorry to interrupt you, Sir. The Medical Examiner, Doctor Duffie, asked me to request you to come down and see him at the earliest opportunity."

"Tell him I'll be there in a couple of minutes then come back here to sit in with DC Morrison." Alex turned his attention back to Sandy. "I think I've got the essentials but please stay a bit longer and tell Phil anything else which you think might be relevant. I'll be back soon."

Chapter 3

"Hi Doc, what have you got to tell me?" Alex enquired before the door had time to close.

"Alex, it's good to see you, too. Okay, you're in a hurry so I'll forgive you skipping the pleasantries. Nothing certain yet, but I've conducted my initial checks and I'm ready to have the body shipped out. I'll get the PM done this afternoon and should have a full report by tomorrow morning. My first impressions, if you want them, death caused by head's impact with a blunt instrument. Something's hit the side of his head with a lot of force. It looks like being murder as he couldn't have done that to himself. I reckon death happened sometime after midnight last night, but I'll know more later on, after the PM. There's a circular indent on the side of his skull and there was some tiny glass fragments next to the wound."

"What do you think caused it?"

"Hard to say at the moment."

"What about the broken racks? Could it have been an accident? Could he have fallen into them and they collapsed around him, with some of the debris striking his head?"

"I don't think that's too likely. The type of wound and bruising are not consistent with it. My guess is he was hit and went down. Maybe he fell back into the racking, and it was weak, causing it to collapse. More likely he just went straight down then the attacker pulled the racking over in a crude attempt to cover up or to cloud the issue. The

PM might tell us some more. So if there's nothing else, I'll get ahead and do it."

Alex stood back and watched as the body was carefully loaded onto a stretcher and carried out.

Having already broken from his interviews, Alex took time and enquired about progress from Anne Dixon. Her team had completed their initial checks and samplings from the cask room and were now in the process of examining the adjacent shop. Alex looked around admiringly at the rows of shelves stacked with a variety of bottles. The area was clean and modern with bright, halogen lighting reflecting off the polished floor and glass and metal shelving.

"What are your plans? And when do you expect to have anything for me?"

"I'm not going to rush this," Anne replied. "There's a big area to cover. When the body was found the door was open between the cask room and the shop. The shop's open-plan onto the café and the public toilets are beyond that. All of this but nothing else is contained in this building and I think we should check every part of it. I also want to go through Mathewson's office with a fine tooth comb."

"I didn't realise that was still one of the tools you used, with all the modern technology you've got."

Anne gave a wry smile but didn't take up the point. "We're likely to be at this most of the day. I've spoken to Shirley and told her to cancel any tours and visitor trips booked for today or the rest of this week. She didn't seem too happy and said she'd need to get the okay from Mr Quentin, but she went off to do it. I'll let you know any important findings as soon as we finish and will get the formal report out in due course, just the way you'd expect from Inspector Connors. I've not been here long, but he's taught me well."

Alex raised his hand as a farewell gesture and marched back to the office building. Sergeant Guptar was just showing someone he didn't recognise out through one of the office doors when Alex caught sight of him.

"Hi, Sanjay. I timed that well. How are you getting on?"

"Slow and steady, Sir. So far, all I'm doing is carrying out very brief interviews and taking folk's details. Just to see who was where and when and see what else they volunteer."

"What's it produced?"

"Not too much. I've spoken with everyone who was listed on site through the night. No one saw Mathewson or even knew he was there. But I've also found out that it wasn't unusual for him to come in at night and often without his car. Quite frequently the light in his office was seen on and it's not just because the cleaners forgot to turn it off. When security checked, they'd found he'd been in. One that I spoke to said he'd asked him how he'd got in without driving or being clocked by security and he'd gotten his ear bitten off for asking. I've got it all in my notes."

"Okay, that's good. It's not given us any answers but it's taken us a fair bit forward. Keep up the good work. I'll go back and see what else Sandy has to tell us."

Alex slipped back into Quentin's office and resumed his seat. Sandy was in full flow, talking about the various members of the Burns family and his discourse was hardly interrupted by the movement.

"I was just telling Phil more about all the different members of the remote family. As I'd said before, Quentin, Georgina, Stanley and Samuel are the only ones who actually work in the business, but the three other children as well as about twenty cousins are involved in the family trust and they all take money out. Some of them I've never seen. I don't think they even live in Scotland, Monte Carlo or somewhere like that, I think. Most of them turn up though from time to time if there's a family dinner or sometimes when there's a big promotion and they want to be seen with celebrities. When they do come, they always go away with a suitcase full of product. I suppose it's none of my business but it's a bit different for the workers. If we were to find any of them trying to sneak out a bottle they weren't meant to have, then they'd be out on their ear and collecting their P45.

"Oh, by the way, I've arranged for some fresh tea to be brought in."

"Sandy, I'd like to go back to what you were saying earlier. I've heard that Mathewson was in the habit of coming in at night."

"Yes, Sir. It had happened a few times before. We'd just find out he was on the premises. Either he'd be seen in his office or else walking about the yard or the shop and we didn't know how he'd got in.

"We tried to ask him about it but he just chased us. Even when we explained we only wanted to ensure the security was working. He'd have none of it. He was a law unto himself, a bit of an arrogant prick. He only spoke to us when he wanted something or wanted to tell us something. The rest of the time he didn't want to know."

"I'm guessing he wasn't too popular then?"

"Aye, you can say that again."

"How do you think he got in?"

"I truly don't know, Sir. We checked round all the walls and the perimeter fence and didn't see how he could have done it. There's the main entrance with the security gate and that's always manned. I suppose he could have walked through on an odd occasion without being seen but that meant he'd been able to slip past the man on duty. I could see that happening very occasionally, but it was more often than that."

"What about other entrances?"

"The store shed over there," he said, pointing into the distance, "has a doorway straight out onto the road, but it's never used these days and when we checked there was no indication that it'd been opened in years. The same applies for a gate in the fence on the far side. There's an old pathway that leads out to the woods but the gate has a padlock and it's covered in rust."

"There are no breaks in the fence or weak points someone could have climbed through?"

"No, Sir, we checked. The fence is all thick mesh and it's covered in razor-wire so no-one in their right mind would try coming over it. Where there are buildings instead of fence, there's the same razor-wire around the guttering so no-one tries to climb over, no sane person anyway. The entranceway and main courtyard have security cameras and PIR lighting, but we've never picked up anything to explain."

"It was a bit of a mystery, then. Was it only Mathewson? Or was anyone else able to miraculously appear and disappear?"

"As far as I know, it was only him. It wasn't that often either."

"You mean, 'It wasn't that often that you were aware of.' If he had a way of popping in and out whenever he wanted and without being seen then there's no telling how often he did it without you knowing."

"Aye, I suppose that's true."

"From what Winters told me, all the owners arrived at once. He thought you must have called them. Is that right?"

"Not exactly, Sir. Mr Quentin's always in early and very often he brings in Mr Samuel with him because they live in the same house. As far as I know, Mr Stanley's not here, I haven't seen him. He's rarely seen before midday. When Mr Quentin arrived, I told him what I'd found. Ally, Bert and I were just trying to keep a lid on things 'til you arrived."

"Did you know officers Winters and Ferguson before this?"

"Oh yeah, I've lived in this area for a number of years and, being an ex-copper, I know all the local boys."

"Okay, back to this incident. Has the widow been told?"

"No, Sir. When Mr Quentin heard, he wanted to phone her right away but I told him that he shouldn't and he needed to leave it for the police to handle. He seemed to think about it for a second and then backed down."

"Okay, I'd like to do this myself and I'll take Mary with me. Can you give me directions to the house?"

Chapter 4

Fifteen minutes later, Alex, accompanied by Police Constable Mary McKenzie, turned the Santa Fe off the road into the driveway of a large, modern, architect-designed villa, sitting alone on a wide stretch of land atop a small hill.

They climbed down from the SUV and crunched across the red blaize pathway, halting on the penultimate of the four approach steps before ringing the doorbell. They heard thunderous movement from within and the sound of loud barking.

A few moments passes before they heard, "get down, get down," and the metallic click of a lock turning. The door pulled open a few inches.

"Yes, can I help you?" They were addressed by a dour looking middle-aged woman. She was plump and her round, red face was accentuated by her long greying hair being tied up in a bun. She was dressed all in black, wearing a tight fitting sweater and leggings and she was holding a rag in her left hand.

Alex held out his warrant card. "I'm DCI Warren and this is PC McKenzie. We're here to speak to Mrs Mathewson."

The door was promptly opened fully and they were invited inside. Two young but large dogs circled and sniffed at them as they advanced. They were Rottweilers, speckles of dark brown interrupted their otherwise solid black colouring and they had broad muscular shoulders, square-shaped heads with alert but kind looking eyes. They looked well exercised, not an ounce of fat on either of them. Alex judged that standing on their hind legs they would each be taller than Mary and probably almost as heavy in weight. The housekeeper pushed the dogs away to clear a path and Mary walked briskly, clearly uncomfortable with having the powerful beasts so close. Alex, by contrast, extended his arm with a closed fist in introduction, allowing the dogs to become acquainted before stroking and ruffling their sleek coats. Alex and Mary were shown into the lounge and invited to take a seat while the housekeeper went to find her employer. The dogs stopped at the open door and lay down in a 'V-shape' pointing in, acting as sentries, keeping a close watch on the visitors.

The room was cavernous and very bright with floor to ceiling sized windows on two walls. In the far corner where the windows joined sat a heavily lacquered, boudoir-sized, grand piano. Vertical blinds offered it limited protection from the daylight. The walls were painted in a rich gold colour and the seating comprised of four, large, deep buttoned, chesterfield couches surrounding an oak, opium table.

Alex and Mary had only just settled onto a couch but bounced back onto their feet as steps approached.

The dogs also jumped attentively, standing apart to clear a channel to permit access.

"Good morning officers. I'm Georgina Mathewson. If you're looking for my husband, then I'm afraid you've had a wasted journey," the lady called as she walked through the door. The dogs resumed their sentry duties but this time in a sitting position.

The lady was tall, about five-foot-ten and very thin. The skin of her face was parchment white, almost transparent and it was punctuated by neat delicate features and powder blue eyes. She was dressed in a brightly coloured wrap, worn in the style of a sari. Alex judged her to be of similar age to his own forty-two years. She was far from the most beautiful woman he had ever met but her appearance was attractive, striking and most certainly memorable.

"Good morning, Mrs Mathewson. It's you we're looking to speak to, not your husband. Please take a seat. I'm afraid we have some very bad news for you."

She did as suggested and her eyes darted back and forward between the two of them.

"Is it Daddy? Oh no. What's happened?"

"I'm sorry to have to tell you that your husband was found dead this morning."

"Hector?" she exhaled long and slowly and Alex interpreted her reaction more as being one of relief rather than surprise. She regained her composure following the momentary lapse. There was a further pause as she looked enquiringly at their two faces. "You're a DCI and you've come to tell me this so I don't suppose it was a traffic accident?"

"No, you're right, it was nothing like that. His body was found this morning in the cask room of the distillery. The circumstances are suspicious and there's a distinct possibility it was murder."

Georgina said nothing at first. She sat impassively, staring straight ahead. They could see her eyes flickering, deep in thought as she collated the implications of what she'd been told.

"Where are my manners? Can I offer you a cup of tea?"

"No, Madam, we're fine. But I think maybe you should have one yourself. PC McKenzie can get it for you."

"That won't be necessary. I'll have Agnes bring a tray."

Georgina called instructions to the housekeeper. Alex looked on with interest. He wasn't certain if she might be in shock or if she was just a very cool customer. He had only limited exposure to the aristocratic classes and in all cases to date it had been with men. She was clearly used to being in control and no doubt had vast training and experience of how to behave in company. But, nevertheless, he'd just told her that her husband had been found dead, probably murdered, and she'd shown no emotion. Surely that was carrying the 'stiff upper lip' a bit far.

"You've had some shocking news. Would you like me to call your doctor or one of your family or friends to be with you?"

"No, I'm fine. I'll need to let the boys know what's happened. They're away just now. They're skiing in Klosters."

"How long have they been away? And when are they due back?"

"They've been gone about ten days, in London to start with and then Switzerland. They're due back tomorrow."

"We haven't released anything yet but it's only a matter of time before there'll be a news report. Your husband was well known in business circles and it's certain to make the headlines. You'll want your sons to hear before the news goes public. We can arrange for the local police to visit them if you'd like."

"Certainly not, I'll call them myself."

"There are a number of questions we'd like to ask you and, if you're up to it, we'd like to try and do it now."

"Yes, of course. Please go on."

"It's believed that your husband's time of death was in the early hours of this morning. Can you tell me when you last saw him?"

"He came back from the office mid-afternoon yesterday. He changed and then went back out again because he had a meeting last night in Glasgow."

"Do you know who the meeting was with? And where it was?"

"Yes, he was meeting an American, Chuck Holbein, the CEO of Hanser, the international drinks conglomerate. They were having dinner together at the Rogano."

"Do you know what the meeting was about?"

"I'd rather not say."

"We've heard rumours that the distillery was being sold. Is it anything to do with that?"

Georgina gave a weak smile. "You may think that, I couldn't possibly comment."

As he was a fan of Michael Dobbs' books and in particular the 'House of Cards' series, Alex smiled back and nodded, acknowledging the reference.

"We'll maybe have to come back to that. Hector never came home last night. Did that not surprise you?"

"No, I hadn't even realised actually because we sleep in separate bedrooms. He snores so badly I couldn't possibly sleep in the same room," she replied candidly.

"Would you not have expected to see him in the morning?"

"It wasn't unusual for him to stay out. He quite often stayed at his Club in Glasgow, particularly if he'd been entertaining and had a drink. That way, he wouldn't have to drive home late and under the influence."

"Did he take his car into Glasgow last night?"

"Yes, he drove out and his car wasn't in the garage this morning. I know because I went out to the newsagent first thing this morning, myself."

"He drove out of the distillery yesterday afternoon but he didn't return later by car."

"So?"

"His body was found there. We want to know how he got there."

"Maybe he walked or maybe someone else drove him in."

"He'd still have needed to leave the car somewhere and we haven't found it yet. Security has no record of him entering and no-one saw him. Security say there have been several other occasions when they've found Hector on the premises with no record of how he'd gotten in. They asked him but he refused to explain. He sent them away with a flea in their ear."

"I'm not surprised. He wouldn't have been too impressed if they'd allowed him in without having a record of it."

"That's the point. They knew he was in but had no idea how he'd managed it and they were trying to find out."

"Maybe he used the tunnel," Georgina conjectured.

"What tunnel? I've not heard about this before."

"It's a very old tunnel and, if I remember correctly, it runs from somewhere around the shop area, goes under the hill then comes out on the far side. The land there is owned by my father, it's part of his farm. There's a small building on the far side of the hill, more of a shelter really, and there's a farm track that runs by it. The story goes that the tunnel was originally built as an escape route, back when it was illegal to make whisky. It was there in case the still ever got raided. Then later it was used to smuggle out product and hide it from the excise man, but that was a long, long time ago. Everything's legitimate now."

"How did you know about it?"

"When we were young, my brothers and I used to be taken into the still room when we weren't at school. We used to make our own games and we were always looking for good hiding places. I think it was Quentin who first found the tunnel. After that we played there all the time. It was cold and dark and not very tall but we used to have great fun. We asked father about it and he told us the history. But it was kept as our special secret. That all happened more years ago than I care to remember. I've not heard anyone mention it in years."

"Did you tell Hector about it?"

"No, not that I can remember, no, I'm certain that I didn't."

"How might he have found out?"

"I really couldn't say. I can't imagine father or Quentin would have said anything and Stanley was so young at the time I doubt he'd even have remembered. No, come to think of it, Stanley wouldn't ever go in the tunnel. He was too scared. He always was a bit claustrophobic. I suppose Hector may have come across it when the building was being refurbished a few years back. I can't think of any other explanation."

"We'll certainly check it out. Maybe once we find Hector's car then we'll have a better idea. What was it that he drove?"

"A Jaguar, it's an XK8, a blue one. I can get you the registration if you want."

"Yes, that would be helpful."

Georgina fished out the information and Mary scribbled it onto her notepad.

"We'd like to ask you some more delicate questions, if we may?"

Georgina raised her head impassively. "Yes, go ahead. We'll need to deal with this sometime, so may as well get it out of the way."

"Can you tell us about your relationship with your husband?"

"What's to tell? You probably know already or if you don't you'll easily find out so you're as well to hear it from me."

"Please go on."

"Hector and I have been married for twenty years. I was in my twenties when we met. I was working in the office and he was one of our suppliers. He had his own company and he sold us packaging. I was quite young and innocent back then and he seemed so suave and sophisticated. He was a good looking young man and I was flattered when he asked me out. Daddy wasn't too happy about it. He said I could do better and Hector would never amount to much. When I fell pregnant Daddy was livid. He threatened to throw me out without a bean. Hector said he'd take care of me and offered to elope, but then Daddy agreed to the wedding.

"Hector's business had problems and he closed it down. It was a limited company but there were some creditors who threatened to cause bother. Hector said to let them do their worst but Daddy paid them off. He said it was the only way to make them go away without it hurting the family reputation. Daddy gave Hector a job in the office, my job actually, because I took maternity leave and never properly went back."

"Did you want to go back?"

"I've asked myself the same question and I'm not really sure what the true answer is. I needed the time off to bring up the children and that was really what I wanted to do, at least while they were young. I missed being in the office though because I liked the interaction and the feeling of responsibility, and besides, I was really good at my job. Although Hector took over managing the office, he never truly understood what was going on. Quite often he had to ask me what to do or how to handle different situations."

"We were told he was an accountant. Surely he should have known how to run the office?"

"Yes, he claimed to be an accountant, but he wasn't really. He'd taken some bookkeeping courses and he'd bought a fake diploma from some American outfit who claimed to be a university, but he wasn't a qualified accountant or anything like that and he didn't really understand accounts. He needed a calculator to count his toes. He was useless at arithmetic and that didn't help."

Alex noted the bitterness in her voice. He was acutely aware that only a few moments ago he'd told this woman her husband was dead. She'd shown no emotion and now she was revealing his shortcomings. It didn't seem like a normal reaction. Perhaps she was in shock or maybe she was just very detached. In any event, Alex was happy to be gathering information. Much of it may be irrelevant but he'd gladly take it all for now and later he could sift through the dross looking for diamonds.

"After the boys started school, I offered to go back in part-time but Hector talked me out of it and Daddy agreed with him. It must have been the first time they'd agreed on anything so I could hardly fight it. I needed something to stimulate my mind. I wanted to be a person again and not just the boys' mother so I started working as a volunteer for the local hospice charity. To start with, I was working in their shop but then they moved me into the office and for years now I've been running it. It's just something I'm good at."

"And Hector was happy for you to be doing this while he continued to run the distillery office?" Alex enquired, trying to keep her a little bit more on track.

"Yes, he didn't mind. By this time, he wasn't too interested in what I was doing. Relations between us had grown rather frosty. Hector had wanted to be a bit more experimental in our lovemaking. I didn't mind a bit of adventure but his tastes and requests became more and more bizarre so I said no."

"What..."

"I'm not prepared to go into detail, but he wanted me to share our bed with other men and women. I flatly refused and it was only afterwards I found he'd being playing away from home. It wasn't that he was having an affair. It was nothing as dignified as that. He was putting himself about at every opportunity. It was only then that I discovered he'd been at it for years. He'd even tried to seduce my sixteen year old niece while I'd been pregnant with our second child. He didn't seem to care who he slept with, and when he couldn't find someone to seduce, he'd consorted with whores."

For the first time since they'd started talking, Alex could see emotion in Georgina's face. Her pale cheeks had become flushed and she was spitting out the words with venom.

"Once I knew what he'd been up to, I wouldn't let him near me. God knows what diseases he'd be bringing home. We had a massive row and I told him to leave but he refused to go. He did at least move into one of the spare bedrooms but he enjoyed his standard of living too much to give up on it without a fight and I didn't have the strength for one, not then. I looked to Daddy for support but he didn't want to get involved. Hector had always been a good father and Daddy was very big on the importance of family. He was brought up strictly as a Catholic and he doesn't approve of divorce. I suspect he's had his own secret relationships over the years. I thought it strange because Daddy had so strongly disapproved of Hector in the beginning and I was sure he still didn't like him, but they seemed to have formed some sort of reluctant acceptance of each other over the years. I don't know if maybe Hector had found out something that Daddy didn't want to get out.

"Anyway, in the end Hector and I just agreed to co-exist, living in the same house, and Hector kept on working at the distillery. I agreed to let him stay provided he never brought any of his 'friends' back to our house and on condition he was very discreet about his philandering.

"Quentin did try to get involved though. He wanted to get Hector out, but it was so obvious what he was trying to do. He didn't care about me. He just wanted to secure his own position as Daddy's next in charge and to do so at my cost. I never forgave him for that. That's why, when Daddy took ill, I supported Hector becoming managing director. It was more to stand in Quentin's way than it was true support for Hector."

Alex felt a vibration against his leg and realised it was a text coming in. He'd turned his phone to silent before leaving the car. He slipped the device from his pocket and sneaked a glance at the screen.

"R U OK for swim tonight," he read and realised his younger son Andrew was checking if their planned evening was still going ahead.

Alex returned the phone without replying but he made a mental note to text back as soon as he was clear of the interview. The reminder of his own disjointed family was a timely one, making Alex realise that relationship problems are seldom down to the singular fault of one party.

"Could you tell us where you were last night between the hours of eleven pm and four am?"

"I was in my bed. I watched a film on DVD until about midnight and then I went to bed."

"Alone?"

"Yes, alone," Georgina spat back, her face slightly flushed.

"Was anyone else in the house to corroborate this?"

"No, Agnes only works here through the day."

"And do you now have another boyfriend or partner?"

Georgina looked up sharply, "I hardly think that's any of your business."

"You have to realise that this is potentially a murder investigation. We need to identify anyone who could have a motive."

"I'll keep that in mind," she replied her head involuntarily slowly nodding but nevertheless yielding no further information.

"Well, I think that's as far as we can take matters for just now," Alex said while rising from his seat.

The dogs were immediately on their feet and escorted Alex and Mary to the door.

Chapter 5

Alex, taking advantage of the opportunity for a moment's privacy, pressed the remote to unlock his car and ushered Mary inside. Then he opened his mobile and pressed the speed-dial code for Andrew's number. He listened to six rings followed by the metallic tones of the outgoing voicemail message.

When his turn to speak came, he replied, "I opened a new case today and it could be a big one. I may be delayed but I'm still hoping to be able to pick you up before seven. Please be ready for me then and see if you can get Craig to do the same. That's the plan. I'll call back if there's any change." Concerned that Andrew might not check his messages, Alex also sent a text merely stating, "Check your voicemail."

Alex thrust the phone back in his pocket, climbed behind the wheel and turned the ignition in one fluid movement. "What did you make of that?" he enquired.

"It had a real wow factor. I've never been in a house like that before. My, how the other half live."

"It wasn't the house I was asking about, it was Mrs Mathewson. And I can pretty much guarantee it's nowhere near half the people who live like that, half of one percent more like."

"Sorry, Sir. She was a strange one. A real cold fish. I've heard talk of the wealthy hiding their emotions, the 'never let the plebs see your weaknesses bit,' but her reaction just didn't seem natural. We told her that her husband was dead, and yeah, true they weren't living as husband and wife, but I think we'd have got more reaction if we'd said one of her dogs had been knocked over."

"Yes, I'm sure we would."

"Do you think maybe she knew already before we went round? Maybe someone phoned her, or maybe she was involved in the killing." Mary was getting excited by her own speculations.

"You may be right and she already knew but I think it unlikely she was involved. If she had been, she'd probably have made a better job of feigning surprise so as to cover up. She's an intelligent woman and if she was involved she wouldn't have wanted to bring suspicion on herself."

"Unless it's a double bluff," Mary conjectured, her eyes sparkling.

"I think you've been watching too many 'B' movies," Alex quipped while his foot stroked the accelerator and he directed the car back towards the distillery.

Only a few minutes later, he turned his Santa Fe into the avenue and was surprised to recognise a familiar vehicle travelling only a short distance in front. The hardtop was on the blue Mazda MX5 as it had needed to be since the start of the year. It was Sandra's car. She'd previously driven a more functional Ford Mondeo but only a few months before she'd traded up to the flashy sports car. Alex was surprised to see her as she was meant to have the day off.

They pulled into adjacent parking spaces and were out of their cars in seconds, Alex's eyes studying every movement of Sandra's athletic and lithe frame as she climbed up from the roadster and moved towards him. The breeze caught her straight, jet black hair and it bobbed in the air behind her, leaving an unfettered view of her pretty face. The stern professional expression Alex had maintained for the investigation faltered and his eyes softened.

"Are you following me?" Sandra's appearance was lit up by a broad grin and her amusement was only heightened seeing Alex's quizzical expression.

"What are you doing here? You're meant to be flat hunting today."

"It's a long story and I can't wait to tell you all the details, but I was successful with the first viewing so I cancelled the others. What's even better is I can move in tomorrow morning. The letting agent's office was just round the corner from Pitt Street and I dropped in to tell you. That's when I heard you were out here. I thought maybe you'd want some help and I was kind of hoping that maybe I could work the rest of today and take tomorrow morning off instead?"

"It's okay with me, but Christ, the paperwork will be a nightmare to keep the admin records right. How about we just do it but leave the files showing you having today off? We can always do the forms later if anyone picks up on it."

"Fine by me." Mary was walking with them and Alex sent her on ahead, instructing her to get hold of Sanjay and Phil for a meeting, but also to give him a moment alone with Sandra.

"Now tell me about the flat."

"No, it will take too long but I'll tell you later. Something important though. We've got a bit of a crisis back at the ranch and you and the team need to know about it."

"Okay, you'd better tell me first then maybe bring Sanjay and Phil in on it too."

"It's about the case we broke last week. The armed robbery, you know? With the Asian boys who'd held up the string of garages."

"Yeah, we caught them with the weapons and the money, a slam dunk. What's the problem?"

"No problem with anything we've done but the deputy fiscal asked to have a word with Abdallah. One of the uniforms was sent down to bring him up from the cells and spoke to him inappropriately."

"What do you mean inappropriately?"

"I believe the expression he used was 'move your fat, Afghani arse so we can pin it to the wall.' As if that wasn't bad enough, there were loads of witnesses. Abdallah's made a formal complaint about racism and brutality. He's also now refusing to speak, saying English is not his language and we need to have a Dari translator present before we can interview him."

"You have to be bloody joking. The guy has a degree in English literature from Durham University."

"I told you it was a crisis and it gets better. Special branch have got wind of it and they want to take over, claiming there could be security issues. It wouldn't be so bad if it was just the local boys, but London is already taking an interest and they're talking about sending someone up."

"Okay, you'd better bring the boys up to speed too. Let's get in."

Fortunately, Sanjay and Phil had both just finished with their last interviews, and within a few minutes, the four of them were sitting around the table in Quentin's office, a fresh pot of tea in front of them. Sandra repeated what she'd already told Alex.

"I could maybe help," Sanjay offered. "I'm not fluent but I can speak quite a bit of Farsi."

"You'd be wasting your time. Abdallah speaks perfect English, every bit as good as you and me. He and his brief are just doing this to make a point. It's more a respect thing."

"Surely it can't interfere with a conviction?" Phil enquired.

"It doesn't change any of the evidence, but it sure as Hell clouds the issue. I'm just glad that, if it had to happen, it was one of the uniforms and not one of our boys. Truth be told, I think Donny McAvoy's capable of such a cock up, even with all the training on multiculturalism."

"Who was it that screwed up anyway?" Phil asked.

"It's one on the new young constables, just out of probation. Fulton's his name," Sandra replied.

"Bloody Hell," Phil rejoined. "He shares a surname with one of Scotland's greatest ever comedians, may God rest his soul, and he thinks he's got a right to make people laugh, not that there was anything funny in what he said. Please tell me his forename wasn't Rikki. Dick or, even better, Dickhead would be more appropriate."

"I think it was George, actually."

"Okay, there's nothing more we can do about it just now. We need to concentrate on today's investigation. Time's slipping by and we need to make progress. As we all know, the first few hours are always the most important, so I'm particularly pleased Sandra is now available. I've a number of things to clear back at the office, not least this Abdallah situation, so I'll need to be off early. Let's compare notes, see where we're up to and make a plan of action."

The next few minutes were spent bringing each other up to date on developments and information gleaned from the investigation and interviews so far.

Sanjay volunteered to brief Anne Dixon's team about the tunnel and to organise a search for Hector's car. It was decided that Sandra and Phil would go to find and interview Daniel, the victim's father-in-law, and Alex thought it time to speak to Quentin. He said he wanted ten minutes to get some fresh air and go through a few matters with Sandra, and meanwhile, Mary was instructed to wait until his return and then to fetch Quentin.

Alex and Sandra walked out through the security gate and followed a footpath which skirted the edge of a mixed woodland, just outside the perimeter fence of the distillery.

They took the opportunity to examine the integrity of the security arrangements as they went.

The day was bright with wisps of cloud interrupting an otherwise blue sky. The air was fresh and the ground still wet from the previous night's downpour. The branches on many of the trees were bare but there was a greenness from the sprinkling of conifers and a distinct clawing aroma of pine in the air.

Broken twigs and leaves from the previous autumn still carpeted the path, and their shoes scuffed over the top. The ground was sodden and the mulch squelched underfoot as they walked, with the occasional snapping sound when they trod on dried out twigs. Where the path was broad enough to permit it, they walked side by side, but as the path narrowed their hands made contact and without thinking their fingers entwined. They stopped in a small clearing and turned to look at each other.

"So, tell me about the flat," Alex enquired.

"It was the first one I went to view and it was just perfect. It's a first floor on Thornwood Avenue in Partick. It's newly decorated, magnolia and white, as you'd expect from a rental flat, but it's fresh and clean. It's in a red sandstone building and has double glazing and central heating with a combi boiler so it should be cheap to run. There's a full-sized kitchen with loads of storage, a cooker, fridge-freezer, washing machine, microwave and even a small dishwasher. There's a lounge and a double bedroom and the bathroom has a bath and an over-bath power-shower. Oh, and it has a security entry phone and there's on-street parking."

"It sounds just what you were looking for. It ticks all the boxes."

"The owner bought it to live in herself, but she was made redundant from her job and had to take a lower paying one. She couldn't afford to live in it and has moved back home with her parents. So she needs to rent it out."

"It's a shame for her but good news for you."

"It gets better. When the agent heard I was a police detective, he was really pleased. He admitted they've had a problem letting the flat because there's a tenant on the second floor who's been causing bother. There have been a number of moans about him but they've not been able to do much because nobody would make their complaint formal. He's been causing a noise nuisance and he's let his dog foul the back court, the pavement and even in the close. All the neighbours are up in arms about it, but they've been a bit scared of him and none of them would go official.

"Obviously, I'd have no problem dealing with it and I'm bound to have the other neighbours backing when I do. So we'll make sure he either cleans up his act or we'll get him out with an ASBO. The agents' offered me a short assured tenancy for twelve months at a third less than the normal rent and with no deposit. It suits him and the owner as it will get the flat rented right away and it's bound to solve their neighbour problem."

"That sounds terrific but are you sure you want to be dealing with these problems when you're off duty?"

"No, but you can deal with it for me," Sandra added with a laugh. "No, seriously, the guy's not a problem. I checked his record and he's just a petty thug and a bully. I'm sure I can scare the shit out of him. He'll be a lot more scared of me than I ever will be of him. As I said before, I get the keys tomorrow and can move in right away. You can be sure I won't be wasting any time getting to know the neighbours. Oh, and one other thing, if it all works out, then I will be given first option if I want to buy it."

"It sounds absolutely perfect."

They turned and walked back, hand in hand, until the path became more visible, then they adopted a more professional demeanour as they moved back towards the offices.

Chapter 6

Alex was already seated at the table when Mary returned followed by Quentin. He strode into the room, and whether it was to try to assert himself or purely from force of habit, he took the seat behind his desk.

Alex showed no reaction and didn't even look across. Instead, he called over, "If you'd like to join us at the table, please. We have all the equipment set up to work from here."

Quentin was nonplussed. Here he was, a director and part-owner of the business, in his own office and being instructed what to do by an outsider. He didn't know how much authority the police had under the circumstances and he was torn between complying with the request or making a stand and risking having to make a humiliating climb-down. At least none of his staff were close-by to hear or see what was going on.

"Of course, of course, just a moment," Quentin relented. He lifted and shuffled some papers on his desk, then placed a couple of items into a drawer. It was done as a face saver, to indicate he'd sat at the desk for a purpose. He then stood, walked across to the table and sat down facing Alex but was unable to meet his gaze.

"Good afternoon, Mr Burns. I'm sorry to have kept you waiting so long, but I'm sure you must understand these are exceptional circumstances. We need to speak to potential witnesses first and, of course, also the widow, your sister."

Although the apology was half-hearted, Quentin took it with good grace and acknowledged with a nod.

"You've seen Georgina? How was she?" he enquired, trying to sound sincere and showing concern for his sibling.

"Probably what you'd expect, shocked by the news but holding up fairly well." Alex lied but was curious to see Quentin's reaction; however, he showed none.

"Now how can I help you, Officers?"

"If I can start with the formalities and then by asking where you were last night and up until we met you this morning."

Quentin provided his personal details and confirmed he was at home the previous evening with his wife and children. As was his habit, he departed from his house at seven-fifty this morning, arriving just after eight o'clock, then was alerted by Sandy to what had been discovered.

"Will we be able to corroborate what you've told us?"

"Yes, I'm sure Fiona, my wife can confirm what I've said. I was working in the office on a new promotion for a 'Whisky Live' event in London. I didn't leave until about seven and then went straight home. Security will have a note of when I left. The boys were out and I dined with Fiona at about eight. We watched some television and then went to bed. I was up at seven and, as I said, drove in around eight. I brought Sam in with me."

"You said the boys were out. What time did they get home?"

"They were both out with friends. Frank was home at about eleven; I saw him come in. Sam was later, after I went to bed. I think it was about half past one. I heard the door close."

"A bit late wasn't it when he was to be up early for work the next day."

"Not a bit of it. He's a young man and full of energy. He regularly stays up late and is still up, full of beans, the next day. It doesn't affect his performance. Frank's just the same."

Alex considered how Sandy had described Sam's ability. Maybe it was just sour grapes, resenting the privileged classes, but maybe he was right and Sam's performance could hardly have deteriorated.

"Do you know where the boys were?"

"Yes, Frank had gone to the cinema and Sam was round at his friend's house, a lad by the name of Billy Farquarson. He lives quite close-by. I believe they were playing cards."

"Okay, we can check on all of that. I'd like you to tell us a bit more about Hector. I take it you first met him through your sister?"

"No, that's not right, quite the reverse actually."

"What? You mean you introduced them?"

"Not exactly. I first came across Hector back when I was at University. We met at the student union. I was at Strathclyde doing a BA at the Business School. Hector was at the Caly, Caledonian University, but it was a while back before it had university status. Glasgow Polytechnic it was then. He was doing an HNC or an HND or something like that. I don't think he ever completed it.

"We met in the bar and at gigs on a few occasions. I wouldn't say we were close friends but we got on okay.

"After that I didn't see him for a number of years. Again it was in a bar, strangely enough. I was hosting a dinner at Minsky's restaurant at the Hilton. I was there early, in the Connich bar with some business contacts and Hector was there too; he was waiting to meet up with someone. We got talking and he told me he had a company which made specialist packaging and he had a product line for the whisky trade. I told him he should come and talk to us and I took his number and set up a meeting for him to see me along with Callum McPherson. Callum has responsibility for buying and I look after the marketing so it made sense to see us at the same time.

"Anyway, he seemed to have some good ideas and we gave him a trial order and it worked well so we kept him on. As it turned out, his products and ideas were really good but his organisational skills were a mess and he kept letting us down.

"I didn't realise at the time that he'd met Georgina in the office and they'd started dating. If only I'd known, I'd have warned her off, but the first I knew was when I heard she was pregnant."

"How do you mean 'warned her off'?"

"Hector was okay as one of the lads but he didn't have any respect for women. He treated them like crap. He was fun to be with and he was fortunate enough to be quite good looking and had the gift of the gab. He never seemed short of a bob or two either so he had no problem picking up the girls or finding a new one when he'd let the last one down.

"The chances are Georgina wouldn't have listened to me anyhow, but I didn't get the chance. She was smitten by his charm and the result was she got pregnant. She trusted him. She was young, wasn't on the pill and she was inexperienced. Hector had claimed to use protection but I'm not so sure. I think he might have baited her. Well, when she found out she was expecting, he claimed to be delighted and he offered to marry her and that was that."

"I gather your father wasn't too happy."

"That's a bit of an understatement. He was furious. At one stage, I thought he was going to disown Georgina, but gradually he came round. I don't think he ever liked Hector but he brought him into the business after Hector's company went bust. He paid off his creditors, I think it cost him about thirty grand to do it, and he let Hector take over running the office, which had been Georgina's job. I say running the office but he didn't have much idea. Fortunately, we had Patrick Gillespie to keep things right."

"I gather that Georgina and Hector had a serious falling out some years ago."

"Ah, you know about that then?"

"We'd like to hear what you can tell us about it."

"I've already told you what Hector was like. He treated women like shit, but he claimed he was a changed man after he met Georgina. He kept up the pretence for a while but not that long. He'd have all sorts of excuses to be away from the house, meetings with friends, family, or there were Clubs he attended. In reality, he was away chasing skirt. I had a pretty good idea what he was up to, but he was fairly discreet and there was no evidence. Of course, Georgina had her head in the sand. She would hear nothing said against him, not to begin with at least."

"But that all changed?"

"Yes, that all changed. I thought it a bit strange at the time. He seemed to become bolder with his dalliances, almost as if he wanted to be caught. The crunch came when he asked Georgina to get involved in some of his sordid activities. He wanted her to join him in an orgy; he was as blatant as that.

"She was shocked and, of course, refused. Only then did she start to believe the rumours and check into them. She was horrified and she wanted to throw him out. I tried to support her and get rid of the bastard and I expected my father would have done the same. If anything, I was worried he'd have taken a gun to him. Not that I'd have been unhappy to see it, but I wouldn't have wanted him to go to prison as a result. Father surprised us all; he supported Hector. He told Georgina she'd just have to accept it. Since then, they've lived separate lives but stayed together in the same house. That must have been more than ten years ago now."

"Not a very comfortable way to live?"

"No, but I suppose they got used to it."

"And how did you get on with Hector? You had to keep working with him."

"To start with it wasn't very pleasant and there was a lot of hostility, but fortunately I didn't have much to do with him. What I do is pretty independent of admin as we have our own inside sales staff. There is the export documentation and currency planning, but I usually spoke to Patrick about that. Hector wouldn't have dealt with it himself, anyway. Over the years, we learned to accept each other and work together."

"And what about Georgina?"

"She had been dreadfully hurt and she became very bitter because of it. I tried to be supportive, but when she wasn't able to throw Hector out, she didn't want to know. She sort of climbed into a shell and blamed everyone else for everything. It was months before she'd even talk to me. Gradually, she came back into the real world."

"What happened when your father took ill?"

"You mean when he had his stroke three years ago? It was terrible. He was devastated by it. It affected his speech and his mobility. We thought we'd lost him. He was in hospital for weeks, but gradually, he clawed his way back. He was never the same, of course, but he got back his movement. At first he needed help to get about but now he can walk by himself with a zimmer or a stick. He has his speech back too, a little slow and a bit slurred, but he's so determined and he's managed it by sheer willpower."

"And what about the business?"

"That was so nearly a disaster. The old man liked to control everything himself and kept it all under wraps. When he went down, nobody else knew what to do or what was happening. It took quite a while to get to grips with it."

"What happened about control?"

"The investors wanted a managing director to be announced and both Georgina and Stanley supported Hector so that's what happened." Quentin tried to keep a relaxed tone but he was clearly agitated to be talking about this. He was blinking rapidly and there was a nervous twitch to the side of his eye.

"Wouldn't you have wanted the job?"

"I was prepared to do it but the others chose Hector. We all wanted what was best for the company."

"Weren't you surprised that Georgina had chosen to support Hector after what they'd been through?"

"No, not really. Over time they'd formed a working relationship for the sake of their children, and I suppose she thought it was in their best interests if Hector had the position."

"Maybe so, but I thought their children didn't get involved in the business."

"They're still young. There's plenty of time for them to change their minds."

"Yes, but isn't your son Samuel already involved?"

"You know he is, so why are you wasting my time with stupid questions?" Quentin was getting rattled.

"Okay, we don't need to pursue that just now. But can you tell us why Stanley would support Hector instead of you?"

"Wouldn't you be better asking Stanley and not me?"

"Don't worry, we will do. But for the moment we're asking you."

"Stanley and I haven't seen eye to eye for a number of years. That's all there is to it."

"And the reason?"

"There doesn't have to be a reason. Can you truly tell me that every family you know all get along?"

"Is it because you think he's gay?"

"How dare you! This has nothing to do with your enquiry. I'll be making a complaint about you."

"Complain all you like. We're investigating a suspected murder. You have a close relationship to the victim, and by your own admission, there was a lot of animosity between you. You've just told us about 'misunderstandings,' shall we say, you've had with other members of your family. I think we're entitled to ask for more information to determine why you've had those problems and ascertain what you're capable of doing to deal with them"

Quentin looked deflated. "I didn't kill Hector, if that's what you want to know. I don't have a problem with Stanley being gay, but I did have a problem with some of the friends he brought home. This was way before I was married when we all lived together in my parents' house. One of the bohemian friends Stanley brought home showed no respect for me, my family or the house. We had a big argument and I threw him out. Stanley was upset, claiming I had no right as he was his guest, and he's held it against me ever since. Is that what you wanted to know?" Quentin asked, angrily.

"That answer will do for just now." Alex remained calm and composed. He knew his lack of emotion was the best way to keep Quentin riled, and when he was riled, he was more likely to impart useful information.

"What involvement does Stanley have in the business now?"

"Practically none, nothing on a day to day basis. He doesn't have any executive duties. He is a director, in name, and he turns up at most of the monthly board meetings. On an odd occasion, he'll even read the briefing papers before he arrives, and when he does, it saves us having to explain every last detail to him. One thing he is diligent at, he draws his salary and he claims his expenses and his dividends. He never fails to be around when there's money being handed out."

There was an obvious bitterness in Quentin's words. Alex could see there was no love lost between the siblings.

"And where would I find Stanley just now? Does he have any other work?"

"Stanley? Work?" Quentin gave an ironic guffaw. "When he's not swanning off on his travels, he lives in a house in Newton Mearns, on the other side of Glasgow. He calls himself a professional artist and he has a studio in his house, but I doubt he's ever sold very much. He does some sort of modern art, painting shapes and squiggles in bright colours and then he tries to pretend there's some deep hidden meaning. He travels to France and Italy and Spain looking for inspiration, but it's never made any difference from what I could judge. He presents his work through some art groups but he's never been able to get any of the galleries to take him seriously. I know he spent quite a bit of cash hiring halls around the country to put on exhibitions, but I don't think it made any difference. The last I heard, he was trying to sell on the internet and he had a website set up."

"Does he present the work under his own name?" Alex had a keen interest in art and his enquiry was genuine, wondering if he'd come across Stanley before.

"Yes, he uses his own name and he signs his paintings 'S R Burns' for Stanley Robert. I think at one time he wanted to market as Robert

Burns or even S Robert Burns so he could get some benefit of any perceived connection with 'Rabbie,' but he was advised against it because he might have faced a legal challenge, so he settled for 'SR.' "

"Does Stanley live alone or does he have a partner?"

"He's had a series of different partners over the years, but I think he's been in a stable relationship for quite a while now, a chap by the name of Barry. I can't remember his second name."

"If we can maybe get a note of his address and phone number. Now, if I might change the subject. We understand that Hector was in the habit of coming into his office at night."

"Yes, I've heard that. I've seen him do so on a few occasions."

"It had upset security because he hadn't let them know he was in."

"Hmmm."

"How do you reckon he got in and out without them knowing?"

"I couldn't say."

"Do you think he might have used the tunnel?"

"The tunnel? Oh yes, it never crossed my mind. I remember it from when I was a child. I haven't been down there in years. But how did you know? Oh yes, Georgina must have mentioned it. I suppose he could have used the tunnel if he knew about it. Georgina must have shown it to him."

"She says not. She wondered if he might have just happened upon it, or been shown it."

Quentin looked perplexed. "There weren't very many people who knew about it. Father knew because he showed us, and me, Georgina and Stanley were the only other ones who knew that I was aware of. I didn't tell Hector, and if you're saying it wasn't Georgina, then that only leaves Stanley."

"Unless he came upon it by accident?"

"From my recollection, it was pretty well hidden. That's why it was so effective for smuggling over the decades. There was a secret panel in the wall of the cask room and another in the building on the other side of the hill. Mind you, I said the cask room but that was all remodelled to build the shop. Maybe it was discovered by the builders when that took place and they could have shown Hector."

"Where about would the entrance be now?"

"I couldn't say for certain but we could have a look if you'd like."

"It's okay, we can take care of that. We'd like to check out the tunnel from both ends. I take it we have your permission?"

"Yes, fine."

"Okay, I've just got a few more questions for you. We've been hearing there were rumours that the company was up for sale."

"Yes, there'd been a lot of rumours."

"What I'm asking is was there any truth in the rumours?"

"Well, not exactly. The business wasn't being marketed for sale but there had been an approach made to us and Hector was rather interested in pursuing it. Somehow, word leaked out and when it did there were some further approaches."

"You said Hector was interested. Are you suggesting that nobody else was?"

"Hector was interested in anything that would line his pockets. He had expensive tastes and he liked a flutter. He played cards, badly, and he managed to build up debts doing it so, yes, he would be interested in anything which would have given him a wad of cash."

"Would that really have helped him? I thought Georgina had the shareholding and not him."

"Yes, you are right but you have to remember that although they lived separate lives they were still legally married and Hector would have rights. There's a fair chance Georgina could have wanted to use the money to buy a complete split from him. Her children are grown and our father's no longer in a position to stage any effective objections. It follows she may not have been against a sale if it would achieve her independence."

"I presume the rest of the shareholders would object to it?"

"I can't speak for anyone else but I can give you my opinion. The outside investors have been very happy with the returns they've received, but if they were given the opportunity of an exit route and a big cash payout then who's to say how they'd react. Of course, they may not consider a payout as their best option, particularly in today's market. They'd be taxed on their capital gain and they'd then need to find another suitable investment to put their money in. Banks and insurance companies are giving precious little return at the moment so they might have a problem finding something safe which gives a reliable and high return on their investment. Maybe they'd prefer to keep their money where it is and continue to collect their dividends."

"I take it the rest of the family wouldn't be favourable though?"

"Well, father would be dead against a sale, but since his stroke, he no longer has a say. He had a living power of attorney which was invoked when he took ill and it's never been reversed. Georgina, Stanley and I have the say to act on his behalf.

"As for me, you're right, I'm totally against a sale. The business was set up by my family the best part of two hundred years ago and it's been owned and controlled by us ever since. As well as the family aspect, it's a traditional Scottish business making a market-leading Scottish product and selling it on a worldwide basis. It typifies all that's best about Scotland. We exist in Scotland. We employ local people and we pay our taxes, which are not inconsiderable, to help the Scottish and the UK economy. If we were taken over, then it would most likely be by one of the international consortia. This part of the business would be stripped to the bare bones and any profits would probably be taken offshore so the country would lose most of the tax revenues so as to pay off shareholders in America or Japan or Saudi or somewhere like that. Scotland would lose out and local people would lose their jobs. I certainly wouldn't be supporting a sale."

"You're sounding as if you're a Scottish Nationalist."

"Who, me? Certainly not, I'm not SNP, I'm a Tory through and through. I'm very pro-Scotland and I'd like to see us have a fairer share of the pie. I'd even like to see more powers devolved from Westminster to Holyrood, but that doesn't make me a Nationalist or a Separatist. No, I'm a Unionist and a Tory, a fully paid up member of the Conservative Party and a local councillor to boot. If you want to talk about

Nationalism, then it's Callum McPherson you want to talk to and not me. Callum's all for an independent Scotland and we have great debates together. We argue all the time and it can get quite heated and loud. Some folk think we're fighting but it's nothing like that and it's all in good humour."

"Does Callum know about the sale discussions?"

"He's not meant to. True, he's a senior manager but it's only the board that have been kept informed about what's really going on. Patrick Gillespie is his uncle, and as Company Secretary, he attends the board meetings, but I'm sure Patrick won't have said anything. Having said all of that, and as you've told me yourself, there are lots of rumours going about and I'm sure Callum will have heard those. He'll have his suspicions, but he's never asked me, point blank, about what's going on."

"Could he have asked Hector?"

"Yes, I suppose that's possible."

Alex glanced at his watch and realised the day was slipping away and he was due back into the office. "I'd like to thank you for all your assistance. I'm sure we'll need to talk again but we have enough to work on for the time being. We'll keep you informed of developments as best we can."

"When will we be able to get the operation back up and running?"

"I can't say for certain yet. We still have a number of people to speak to and our technical people haven't finished yet. They shouldn't be too much longer, then we can give you back free use of the site as a whole, but we're likely to need access to people and some of the facilities for a few days to come."

"And my office?"

"You should have that back by the end of today, but we might want to keep Hector's office for a further day or two."

Chapter 7

Sandra watched Sanjay's car disappear along the adjacent farm road before turning her Mazda into Daniel Burn's driveway. The pathway was broad and covered in asphalt of a higher standard than the outside roadway. In front of the house, the path split to surround an ornate fountain topped by a sculpted central figure which wouldn't have looked out of place in a public park. The house itself was an imposing stone built villa, well over a hundred years old. Off to the left and recessed back from the path, there was a significant stone built garage, large enough to hold several cars. Sandra parked her roadster to the side of the fountain leaving ample room for another vehicle to pass. Then she looked at the facade and let out a low whistle. The building was three storeys high and symmetrical. An entranceway protruded from the centre, and on each side of it was a room fronted by a four-sectioned, bay window, and beyond this was a further large room with windows to the front and side. Sandra couldn't judge how deep the house went but she was able to see turret-shaped towers extending to both sides rising above the main body of the house. The windows on the first and second floors mirrored those on the ground and, as if someone found the house too small at some stage, dormer extensions had been added to the roof-space, perhaps for the servants, she mused.

Sandra and Phil approached the main entrance, climbing the five marble steps towards a heavy timber door. Before they reached the bell push, the door was pulled open. Looking down on them was a man aged in his sixties. He was, tall, slim and muscular, dressed in a white shirt and dark suit. He had a military bearing, standing with his broad shoulders pulled back and his chest prominent, lungs fully inflated. His pallor was grey and his face expressionless.

"Yes?" he enquired dryly.

"I'm Sergeant Mackinnon and this is Constable Morrison," she replied holding out her warrant card. "We've come to speak to Mr Burns."

"Walk this way," the man replied then he turned and marched back through the entranceway.

"Not without an operation," Phil replied in a whispered voice to Sandra, while stifling a giggle. She shoved his arm as a minor admonishment but couldn't restrain a smile in response.

They walked along an oak lined hallway which led towards an opulent and gaping stairway leading to the upper floors. There were several display cabinets sitting against the walls giving the impression of a museum. The contents were various collectibles and objects d'art, mostly treenware. Before they reached the stairway, they were shown into the first room on the left.

"Please take a seat in the drawing room, I'll ask Mr Burns to join you," the man stated as he moved deeper into the hallway.

"Drawing room? Is this a game of 'Cleudo'?" Phil asked in an undertone.

"Shut up and behave yourself," Sandra whispered back.

As they looked around, they saw several, large, horsehair stuffed couches positioned against each of the walls and a number of low level tables interspersed throughout the room. The couches looked ancient and comfortable. The floors were polished oak with Chinese rugs adding to the opulence. The walls were decorated with a rich flock paper and were further adorned at regular intervals by landscape paintings in ornate, gold coloured frames. Two of the tables each had a centrepiece of a French bronze statuette and a third had a small collection of Caithness glass paperweights and ornaments. They sat down together on one of the sofas set against the back wall, facing the windows.

They heard a simultaneous rolling and scuffing noise as the door opened and a rather sick looking elderly gentleman shuffled in supported by a zimmer frame.

His eyes were sharp but his back was stooped leaning over the walker. Even so, they could see he was taller and slimmer than Quentin. He was clearly older and his face was wrinkled, the skin sagging a bit from his cheeks and neck, but otherwise they were looking at Quentin's double.

"I've been expecting you. I'm Daniel Burns. You must be Sergeant Mackinnon," he said, holding his hand out towards Phil.

Phil jumped to his feet. "No, Sir, I'm Constable Morrison. This is Sergeant Mackinnon," he added, indicating towards Sandra.

Burns withdrew his hand and gave a curt nod. He abandoned the zimmer in the centre of the room and slowly staggered unaided towards an armchair and flopped down. All this was carried out without acknowledging Sandra's presence.

"Thank you for seeing us," Sandra commenced. "You said you'd been expecting us, so I suppose somebody has already told you about the purpose of our visit?"

Burns cast an appraising eye over Sandra, lingering a moment too long over her legs, and then turned back towards Phil to give his answer. "Hector's body was found in the distillery. Yes, Quentin phoned me. Could you hold back any questions for a minute until Therese serves the tea?"

They could hear a rattling sound becoming louder and heavy footsteps echoed off the wooden floors marking her approach.

Therese entered the room carrying a tea tray laden with cups, saucers and a silver tea service. She was young and pretty, probably aged about twenty. She was tall with long shapely legs and she had Mediterranean features. Her body was slim and curvaceous. She was wearing what could be best described as a French maid's fancy dress costume. The front was low cut, giving a clear view of her ample bosom, and the skirt was short with black fishnet tights underneath.

She rounded the table so she was facing the guests then slowly and carefully leaned forward to place the tray on the table and dispense the tea. Phil was treated to an uninterrupted view of her cleavage and Mr Burns a close up view of her legs and rear.

Phil looked down at the floor to avoid embarrassment but Burns was less self-conscious and was clearly enjoying his view. As Therese stood to leave, he smiled, patted her rump and said, "Thank you very much, that was very nice."

She smiled and gave an appreciative wiggle as she scuttled out the door. He turned to Phil and winked, "She's a good girl and takes very good care of me."

There could be no ambiguity. Therese had been deliberately acting in a very provocative way. The only question Sandra and Phil couldn't answer was whether it was of her own volition or whether she was following instructions.

Seeing Sandra's stony glare, Daniel added, "I'm no longer a young man, but I can still take pleasure from looking at and touching beautiful things." As he spoke these words, his hand gently caressed the bronze on the table to the side of him. It was a quality piece standing eighteen inches tall and depicting a voluptuous half-naked girl. Daniel's fingers lingered over her breasts as he stared straight back at Sandra as if in a challenge.

"Who all lives in the house, now?" Sandra enquired.

"This house was built for my ancestors and my family have lived here for over a hundred years. I own it now. I'm a widower and the children have their own places so I am the only one left. I have two full-time live-in staff. Travers, who let you in, looks after everything in the house and manages the estate. His family have worked for my family for generations. Therese cooks and cleans. She comes from Romania and she's been with me for six months now."

"How did she end up here?" Phil enquired.

"I placed an ad with an agency and she was by far the best candidate. She comes from Bran in Transylvania and moved to Glasgow a couple of years ago. She'd been working in a hotel before I employed her."

"Bran? Isn't that where Dracula comes from?" In an attempt to show off the limited knowledge of geography he had, Phil blurted out the first thing which came to mind and the words were out of his mouth before he had time to think about what he was saying.

"Hardly, young man. Bran castle was the home of Vlad of Wallachia, who became popularised as Vlad the Impaler. He may have been brutal but he was a great hero to his people, leading them in battle against the Ottomans and succeeding against all odds. True, he did have the patronym of Dracula. But by contrast, the Dracula of whom you speak is a fictional character written by an Irishman and set in Whitby in England and in Transylvania. He may have stolen the name and taken some inspiration from Vlad's brutal reputation, but it's hardly the same thing. I certainly would caution you against making comments like that within Therese's hearing. Who knows, she might bite you," he added with a laugh. Daniel's speech was slightly laboured and slurred but he was perfectly coherent and he seemed to be enjoying the lecturing role he had taken on.

"Can you tell us when you last saw Hector?" Sandra enquired.

"I spoke to him on the telephone yesterday afternoon, but I'd not seen him for a couple of days prior to that." Once again, Daniel answered Sandra's question looking at Phil.

"Do you have a problem speaking to me?" she asked, unable to hold back her irritation any longer.

He was still looking towards Phil as he replied, "As a matter of fact, I do. I've been at the forefront of business in this country since before you were born. I'm used to mixing with the top figures in government and in society. I've been to dinners with the Home Secretary, the First Minister and various Chief Constables on several occasions. There's been a serious incident which happened on my premises and who do the police send round to visit me? Some wee lassie barely out of nappies, that's who. Yes, I do have a problem speaking to you."

Sandra was seething. She found it difficult to put into words what she wanted to say. She took a deep breath before replying slowly, in a low menacing tone, a technique which she'd learned from Alex.

"I'll have you know, Sir, I am hardly a 'wee lassie, barely out of nappies.' I'm an honours graduate and I've now served in the police force for six years. I was selected as a detective because of my skills, training and ability and I've since been promoted to Sergeant. You are correct that we're investigating what we consider to be a very serious incident. Detective Chief Inspector Warren is the senior officer on this case and he's been called back to head office to deal with unrelated matters. He has sent me here as the next in charge. If you feel your position justifies that you can only speak to him, then I will arrange it. I will have a squad car pick you up in five minutes time and drive you into Glasgow and there you can wait until he's available to see you. In fact, I'll arrange for that now." Sandra lifted her mobile from her pocket and flipped it open.

Phil had seen Sandra in action before and was all too familiar with how assertive she could be. She was not one to be crossed and he knew she wasn't bluffing. He struggled to keep a straight face.

"No, that will not be necessary," Daniel replied. "I will answer your questions." His tone was short but for the first time he was looking straight at her to give his response.

"Can you tell me why Hector called you?"

"It was a business issue, confidential company matters."

"Was it to do with the potential sale of the distillery?"

Daniel looked up, surprised.

"Perhaps regarding his planned meeting with Chuck Holbein?" Sandra pressed home the advantage.

Daniel examined her with a new respect. "Why yes, how on earth did you know about that?"

"How did you feel about the meeting?"

"It was a total waste of time and I told him so. He didn't have the authority to have such discussions. He needed my approval to take any negotiations forward and he knew I wouldn't give it."

"I was told that since your illness, your children had taken over control of your shares and that you can no longer legally act on your own behalf."

"It wasn't an illness, it was a stroke. I was temporarily incapacitated. They had to be able to manage the business in my absence, but I'm back now. I am well enough to resume control."

"Is that how they see it?"

Daniel paused for a second. "They won't go against me," he stated in little over a whisper. "They know I could take it to court and I'd win. I won't take it lying down. They'll do what I want."

"Is this what you were discussing with Hector?"

"I suppose, to some extent."

"Did you have similar discussions with Georgina, Quentin and Stanley?"

"No, I didn't need to. And what's all this got to do with Hector's death, anyway?"

"We're just trying to get a full picture of all the relationships."

"Well, don't waste my time with tittle-tattle."

"We're hardly doing that, Sir. Hector is dead. We don't have the medical reports yet but we're fairly certain he's been murdered. He was the managing director of the distillery business and he was taking part in takeover negotiations which could have been either unknown or hostile to some of the other shareholders. It could also have upset other people within the company or within the industry. It's not 'tittle-tattle,' it's our job to investigate unusual goings-on to identify who could have an interest in seeing Hector dead or indeed a motive."

"If you're trawling for everyone with a motive and everyone who'd have been happy to see the back of Hector then you'd better have a big net. In fact, to paraphrase Brody from 'Jaws,' 'You're gonna need a bigger boat.'" Daniel started laughing at his own joke and he only stopped when his guffaws turned into a coughing fit.

"That may be the case, but we have to start somewhere and this is where we've chosen to start. It would help and save us all time and effort if you would just answer the questions. Were you aware of the details of what Hector was discussing?"

"No, he didn't want to give me the details because he knew I'd oppose him whatever was being offered and he didn't want to give me any ammunition. He was right, I suppose."

"Did you discuss the deal with Georgina, Quentin and Stanley?"

"Not really. I've had talks with Quentin. Georgina's not had a lot to say and, other than board meetings, I don't see too much of Stanley. He doesn't have any real interest in what goes on in the business. Just give him a bit of solitude, a paintbrush and canvas and he's happy."

"How about your grandchildren?"

"Sam follows his father's guidance and the other three haven't much clue what's going on. They're young, give them another five years and they'll all look on it very differently."

"Patrick Gillespie must know what's going on."

"I'm sure he does and I'm sure he'll be in complete agreement with me. And before you ask, I reckon Callum McPherson and the other managers and staff will all feel the same way too, if they know anything about it."

"None of the others should know what's going on though."

"You're right, they shouldn't, but there will always be rumours. Hector could have a bit of a loose tongue, especially when he's had a drink and this is a small community. It's not very easy to keep hold of a secret for long."

"We understand that there was more than one company showing interest in buying Benlochy."

"Yes, I suppose that's true. We have a very good and profitable company. It has a name with worldwide recognition so any of the major players would love to get their hands on it. Hector started off speaking to Hanser and they are an obvious player and one of the biggest. They operate producing a whole range of drinks in Europe and the States and they are known to be on the acquisition trail. They raised a lot of cash on the stock market last year and it's burning a hole in their pocket. They have publicly stated their growth aims and they need to make purchases soon or their shareholders will get restless.

"If I had been looking to sell, then they'd have been the first ones that I'd have approached so I suppose it was a smart move by Hector, if only we'd actually been for sale.

"Anyway, somehow word got out that they'd been talking and there've now been a number of other would-be purchasers sniffing about. It could start a bidding war. All the main companies are interested as well as a few smaller ones. There's one Japanese outfit that's been very keen to get in to talk to us. They're not all that big but they are ambitious. They manufacture their own version of Scotch whisky in Japan and it's had good reviews. They've won a lot of awards."

"So has Hector been speaking to many of them?"

"I don't think so. As far as I know, he's only met face to face with Holbein from Hanser."

"And he was scheduled to meet him yesterday?"

"He was scheduled to meet *her* yesterday. The CEO of Hanser is Chuck Holbein and she's a woman. Chuck stands for Charlene. It's still largely considered a man's industry, so she's happy to adopt what's normally considered a man's name. She has a reputation in the industry as a real go-getter, quite a power house. She's been in charge of the company for fifteen years now and it's grown from strength to strength. She's one lady who it doesn't pay to underestimate."

"I've met a few of those," Phil piped up. He looked as if he may have said more but didn't proceed after receiving a frosty stare from Sandra. "Point made," he whispered inwardly.

"I'll keep that in mind when I go to see her. Do you know how long she's staying in Glasgow and where she'll be?"

"According to Hector, she was going to be around for a few days and wanted to see the whole board. I told him that wasn't on, so your guess is as good as mine whether or not she'd still have stayed. As for location, Hanser owns a villa in Pollockshields, just off St Andrews Drive. They use it for their execs, when they move them around, and sometimes also for corporate entertainment. Chuck may be staying there or if she wanted the city centre she'd be in the Hilton."

"Thanks, I'll check it out. Now, I'd like to ask you about the tunnel?"

"The tunnel?" Daniel paled slightly.

"Yes, we've learned that Hector was in the habit of turning up in his office at night without going through the security gate. The most logical explanation is that he used the tunnel."

"Well, that could be an explanation. It's probably the sort of thing he would do."

"How did he find out about the tunnel? I thought it was meant to be secret."

"I couldn't say," Daniel answered curtly.

"You didn't tell him about it?"

"Not me, maybe Georgina said something."

"Not according to her or Quentin. Did he ever talk to you about it?"

"He may have done. I can't remember. No wait, I seem to recollect we had a discussion about it years ago. He was asking about its early history and about how safe it was."

"How safe is it?"

"It ought to be very safe. Most of it was formed through extending a natural cave that was already there. The front of the cave was originally used to house a still back in the old days before it became a legal business. When that happened, the new distillery building was constructed in front, replacing the old bothy. I take it you already know the background; the tunnel was made years ago and it was used as an escape route and for smuggling. Over the years, it was reinforced with timbers and brick and it's really quite solid. My children used to play there when they were young, and I would never have allowed them if I wasn't sure it was safe."

"When were you last there yourself?"

"It was quite a while back."

"Where is the entrance?"

"The front used to open to a doorway into the cask room and the other side came out in an old stone building on the other side of the hill, an old but an' ben."

"Is this on your land?"

"Yes, that's right. If you follow the farm path just before the entrance to my driveway, it's about half a mile down the track."

"Thank you. One of my colleagues is already checking it out. One last question, it's just a matter of routine. Can you tell me where you were last night?"

"I've not been out the house since yesterday morning."

"Do you have anyone who can verify that?"

"Well, both Travers and Therese live in this house as well. Travers was at home, you can get him to confirm it. It was Therese's day off and she was away visiting friends of her family; she only came back at breakfast time today."

"Thank you for your assistance. Hopefully, that will be all and we won't need to disturb you again, but we'd like a word with both Travers and Therese before we leave."

"Fine, I'll call them in," Daniel stood up and shuffled towards the door. Before leaving he added, "I hope you get this sorted out quickly and we can get back to some sort of normality."

"Thank you. We hope so too and, by the way, we're sorry for your loss."

Sandra felt battle weary, as if she'd just gone ten rounds in a boxing ring, but she was content that she'd given at least as good as she'd got.

Chapter 8

Sandra and Phil returned to Quentin's office and met up with Sanjay and Mary.

After briefing them on her interview with Daniel, Sandra enquired about their progress and Sanjay was enthusiastic with his reply.

"After we left you, we drove down the farm track and came to the old stone building. The 'but an' ben,' as Daniel described it to you. The track was made of gravel, and it was pretty well maintained considering it ended at the shack. It wasn't overgrown and the path looked as if it had been frequently used. The property looked unoccupied and fairly derelict from the outside. The windows were boarded up. I tried the door and it opened without resistance; the hinges didn't even creak. Inside were two medium-sized rooms; they were empty of any furniture. It was dark, because the windows were covered over, but I saw a light switch just inside the door. I didn't expect there to be any power but I flicked the switch and it worked. I went back outside to look for power cables or a generator but I couldn't see any trace."

"Could the wiring have been underground?" Phil suggested.

"I don't think so, not for a single remote building, and one so small, it would have cost a fortune.

"Anyway, I went back in and checked the place out. There was a stone floor but no dust to speak of and it was clean. Someone has been taking care of it.

"The inside walls were stone covered in plaster and they were painted white. The second room was fitted out as a kitchen, although fairly basic. There were units along one wall and the side wall had a large cupboard door. I opened the door and the inside was wood panelled. I thought that a bit strange as there was no wood panelling anywhere else in the house. I tapped it and it sounded hollow. I found a couple of recessed handles and I pulled them and the whole of the backboard pulled away revealing a narrow corridor, and at the end, there were stairs leading downwards. Again there was a light-switch and I turned it on. I could see a tunnel at the bottom of the stairs. I went down for a better look. I had to duck because it was only about five feet high but it looked very solid. Most of the walls and ceiling were natural stone but in places it had supports. I could see a line of trunking going off into the distance, and I'm guessing the electricity both for the tunnel and for the building was coming through from whatever was on the far side of the tunnel. I came back out and called Anne Dixon to bring her team across for a look. The timing was good because she was just about finished with Hector's office. You might be better hearing the rest of the story from her directly, if she's still about."

Sandra sent Mary to find Anne and they returned within a few minutes.

"We've not finished all our checks yet and we've taken a number of samples which need to be tested in the lab. We've also lifted a lot of paperwork that needs to be looked through. But even with that disclaimer, I have a number of items of interest and I can give you a quick run through what we have so far."

"Yes, please do," Sandra replied. "We'd be happy for any leads you can give us."

"I don't know about leads. There's a number of things we've found which raise questions. If you can get answers to the questions, then you might have leads."

"I'll settle for that. We can't expect to begin with answers, but knowing the right questions to ask is certainly a good start. So what have you got for us?"

"We started with the body, and you may know this already as I've already told the Chief, but our first impression is that the cause of death was him being hit on the head with a blunt instrument. There's a small circular depression to the left temple between the eye and ear and slightly above eye level. It looks like a single impact but with quite some force. From the angle and position of the wound, it's most likely to have been caused by an assailant standing in front of him which suggests the assailant would have been right-handed and about the same height, maybe slightly taller than the victim. If it helps, he'd most probably but not conclusively be male. The assumed time of death is some time after midnight, a window of perhaps two hours. There were fine glass particles found close to the wound and some similar ones on the floor. There was also broken bottle glass on the floor but that was very different. There was a whisky spill, a damaged rack and a broken keg in the area. I believe the bottle and keg might have been damaged to divert attention from the other fragments. We don't yet recognise that glass but we'll try to find out more.

"The doorway to the adjoining shop had been left open overnight, which was out of the ordinary. There was no indication of forced entry, and we think it was opened with a key or maybe it wasn't locked in the first place. The shop itself was untidy and there was missing stock, which again was out of the ordinary. I've questioned the staff and they've advised that it had been cleaned and all the stock replenished last night at about eight. If that's true, then something happened between eight and midnight to change things. We've taken prints, but I don't expect them to lead us anywhere.

"Next, Hector's office looked a bit of a mess but from what we've been told that was its natural state. There was no sign of any skirmish, and we don't believe anything untoward happened there. We've gathered up papers off the desk and from drawers to have them checked over, but I don't have any information to give you on them yet. There was something else in one of the drawers, a large box of condoms."

"Was that a large box of condoms or a box of large condoms," Phil quipped.

Anne's expression didn't need words to convey her disdain to the interruption. Without looking in Phil's direction she continued, "When I say a large box, I mean a distribution pack used by retailers, not the sort of box that would have been sold over the counter, or under it for that matter. Also, it's not a normal brand for the UK. It's American I think, a specialist one, not what you'd be able to buy in Boots or out of a vending machine. He's most likely to have purchased it while abroad or else over the internet.

"The outer box says it contains two hundred condoms, but it had been opened and nineteen had been removed."

"Why would he keep them in his office desk?" Sanjay speculated, and then replying to his own question added, "Maybe he didn't want to leave them at home so his wife wouldn't find them."

"I doubt if that would have bothered either of them too much," Sandra replied. "Was there anything else in the office?"

"Not yet, I'll let you know if there's anything in the papers. He had a private phone line and it had a phone with a memory bank attached. Here's a list of the numbers of the last ten calls made and another list of all the numbers on speed-dial with a note of when they were last used. There was also a digital recording device attached to the phone, so he must have been taping some of his calls for some reason. Any calls taped have been deleted, but normally that only means the access links are removed and the messages remain on the core memory. We might still be able to access and decode to see what's on it."

"That's curious. Why on earth would he be taping his calls?" Sandra asked.

"It is strange. These things are normally used by marketing companies to keep tabs on what their sales staff are saying to customers and to be able to confirm details of orders taken. For Hector to be using it on a private line suggests he was trying to keep exact records of specific conversations or else he was trying to trap someone," Sanjay suggested.

"We'll know more if and when we have the transcripts," Anne concluded.

"After all of that, we went to check out the tunnel. As you can judge, we've had quite a day of it."

"And we really appreciate your help," Sandra commented.

Anne smiled benignly and continued, "The first thing we looked at was the approach road. It looked as though there had been a lot of vehicles using it and quite a mixture too, cars, motorbikes and cycles, but there was nothing specific for us to pinpoint. There was a parking area sitting behind the cottage, big enough for three vehicles, and Hector's Jaguar was sitting there. It hadn't been locked so we were able to check over the contents. There was no evidence to suggest anyone other than Hector had been in the vehicle recently. Next we went into the cottage to look for the tunnel."

"We didn't have a search warrant. Could that create any problems?" Phil enquired.

"There are no absolutes but I wouldn't think so," replied Sandra. "We asked Quentin and we were given his permission to check out the tunnel from both ends."

"But the cottage is on Daniel's land?"

"Yes, that's true and hopefully it won't be a problem. Quentin, together with his brother and sister, still have a power of attorney so we did have authority, but for any evidence uncovered it could be a moot point. The fiscal will need to consider it carefully and we'll flag that up to him," Anne replied.

"Which suggests that you've found some evidence?" Sandra asked.

"Yes, we've found quite a lot. So far we don't know what it all means and how relevant it might be to the murder, but yes, we've found some evidence."

"Go on," Sandra prodded.

"Okay, to start with, the cottage. The place was clean and it had recently been swept out, but it hadn't been mopped and there was still some evidence of footprints on the floor. In the main, they've been caused by dust carried up from the tunnel or wet footwear coming in from the outside. Notably, it was very wet last night. We've recorded the markings and there were a lot of them. We need to eliminate Hector, Sanjay and Mary, then see what we have left. There was evidence of a smaller shoe size, quite possibly a woman's, and a lot of scuff marks as well. It's as if something small was being dragged across the floor.

"We looked carefully at the light switch and at the removable wallboard but couldn't detect any prints, only smudge marks. Whoever's touched them was probably wearing gloves.

"Next, the tunnel itself. The floor was mainly stone or rock and I'm sure that's what's given rise to the dusty footprints. Once again, a lot of footprints in the tunnel and scuff marks. We also confirmed the trunking was carrying electricity from the distillery along the tunnel. Although not a lot, we found some tiny paw prints and droppings which are consistent with vermin."

"Well, remember the old adage that we're never more than six feet away from a rat," Phil offered.

Sanjay shuddered and looked rather uneasy.

"I'm not so certain about six feet away from a rat, but from what we've been told, we've got our own six-foot rat lying in the mortuary," Sandra added, breaking the tension.

"Back to business," Anne continued. "We thought it was hardly surprising to find rodent traces in a tunnel, so no real impact on the investigation. But moving on, it was what we found further along that was most interesting."

"Now you have me intrigued," Phil looked up and gazed directly at Anne.

"At various points along the tunnel, there were boxes of whisky and some individual bottles. A few were quite old and special vintages, but we also found others that were fairly new and some standard bottles, if you can describe bottles of fifteen and seventeen year old, single malt whisky as standard, and you know what that means?"

They all looked up expectantly waiting for the answer. "It means that someone, either as an individual or a group, was continuing to smuggle whisky out of the distillery."

"But who? And why?" Mary expressed what they were all thinking.

"The who, we can make an educated guess at. The why could be multi-fold. Firstly, to make personal gain without it going through the books and then, because it wasn't going through the books, to defraud the excise man and the Inland Revenue."

"Can you explain?" Phil asked

"If it wasn't going through the books, it's unlikely that duty was declared and that would defraud the excise man. Also the company profits would then be understated so the tax man would be cheated."

"Should we report this to HMRC? The customs boys would surely want to have a close look."

"First, wait until you hear what else I have to tell you, but in answer to your question, yes, we should, but we'll probably want to hold off for a bit. We're dealing with a murder enquiry and that takes top priority. If we bring in the tax people right away, then we won't have space to breath, let alone think, so I believe we hold off telling other government departments for the time being, at least until we've exhausted our on-site enquiries."

"Okay, that makes sense," Sandra replied, appreciating Anne's advice.

"That was only the tip of the iceberg. About three-quarters of the way along the tunnel we found a bend leading off towards another cave. It was blocked by a heavy timber door. We managed to pick the lock and found a veritable treasure chest."

"A what?" Mary enquired.

"I was just speaking figuratively," Anne replied. "There were barrels and bottles and bottling equipment. Someone had created a secret store for keeping and maturing whisky and then for bottling the product. It was quite a little manufacturing set up too."

"How on earth did it work?" Sandra asked.

"As a first step, they must have diverted some of the whisky that came out of the still into extra barrels which were routed down there instead of to the cask room."

"Wouldn't someone have noticed? Wouldn't the records have shown shortages?" Sanjay probed.

"In theory, yes, but it would depend on who controlled the records. Someone senior enough could have falsified documents to cover up. It wouldn't have been too difficult."

"Don't they have to keep records for Customs to check? Isn't it all automated now?"

"I couldn't tell you what the regulations say and, as for automation, I don't know what they do now, but a lot of the barrels stretch back for many years. Remember you need to keep whisky in the keg to mature it. I've not yet checked the details on what's in there but I'm having an inventory prepared. I can't say at the moment whether there are any recent barrels, but I'll be able to tell you soon.

"This has been a big scale operation. Our fraud specialists will want in on it and HMRC too, but as I say, let's get our investigations more advanced before we risk losing control of the site."

"So for how long has this been going on?" Sandra asked.

"The youngest barrel I can remember seeing was about eight years old and there were some more than three times that age. This has been going on for years, and for all I know, it could date back generations. There was a long tradition in the whisky trade of trying to beat the excise man. I thought it was all in the past, but from what I've seen today, it appears the tradition lives on, at least in some places."

"Well, it's safe to say that Hector wasn't responsible for starting it," Phil stated.

"Maybe so, but that doesn't mean he's not had his finger in the pie," Sandra replied.

"Yes, but if he only took over as M.D. three years ago and if there are no newer barrels in there, then maybe he wasn't involved at all," Sanjay added.

"There may still be new barrels in there which I didn't spot," Anne replied. "Also, even if there aren't any new ones, it could be they've stopped because of new controls, it doesn't mean it's because of a change of manager."

"The other thing is Hector was in charge of the office before he became M.D. He was the one in charge of the paperwork. Even if he was a bit of a plonker, as Sandy suggested, it would have been hard for anyone else to be operating a fiddle as big as this without Hector getting wind of it," Phil continued.

It was becoming a brainstorming session with each of them developing ideas on the back of another's comments.

"There were quite a few mutterings we heard which suggested that Hector had some kind of hold over Daniel. Maybe Daniel was behind all of this and Hector found out and confronted or even blackmailed him." Sandra's summation brought an end to their conjectures. They all looked at each other and nodded grimly, thinking they now had a working hypothesis.

"I've not finished yet," Anne resumed. "We walked to the end of the tunnel. There was a heavy wooden door with draw-bolts and a lock. We managed to get it open. There was a small space and then we were faced by a lightweight pine door. We pulled that open and found that it formed the backboard to the inside of a cupboard. The cupboard was more or less empty, but it too was locked. We opened it and found ourselves in a narrow corridor which separates the ladies' from the gents' toilets at the back of the shop, next to the cask room."

"Well, that solves the mystery of where the tunnel starts from," Phil offered.

"It was very well disguised. Nobody would have guessed it was there. Not that anyone would have been looking, but even if they were, there was nothing to give away that it was anything other than a cupboard.

"Obviously we checked all around it and in the toilets and the shop, looking for anything suspicious or any evidence of who'd been there recently. Again, we'll still have to wait for test results, but no obvious clues. Well, just one actually."

"What's that?"

"Immediately after you come out of the cupboard, where the corridor opens out into the shop, we found a torn bit of a wrapper from a condom packet. The same brand which Hector keeps in his desk."

Chapter 9

The earlier brightness waned and a deep grey pervaded, much more typical of the season. Alex had his headlights on full beam, not only to illuminate his pathway, but more significantly so as to be visible from a distance as he sped along the country road, retracing his path from earlier in the day. Traffic was quiet and he was able to turn his attention and plan for what lay ahead as he made progress towards the city.

He already had an appointment arranged to see Simon Anderson, a deputy fiscal, to discuss some pending court cases, but he knew from Sandra's briefing, the Abdallah case was likely to dominate their conversation.

Alex stopped his car on the double yellow lines outside his office at Pitt Street. It took him less than five minutes to rush up the stairs and collect the papers he needed, but by the time he returned, there was already a traffic warden eyeing his vehicle and preparing to record his registration. The look of disappointment on his face was unmistakable as Alex flashed his warrant card and slid back behind the wheel, trying to suppress a smile.

He restarted the engine and flipped on the wipers to clear the screen from the first drops of rain which were now starting to fall. No sooner had he manoeuvred the car round the one-way system towards St Vincent Street and the slip road to the Kingston Bridge, than the whole sky was illuminated by a flash of lightning which was almost immediately followed by the resounding rumble of thunder. The car vibrated under its force. A heavy storm was breaking and it felt as though it was immediately overhead as further flashes came. To begin with, large splodges landed on the screen then the rain intensified. Before long it was as if a power hose had been pointed at the screen, and even with the wipers at full speed, Alex's visibility was very limited. He pulled the car into a bus lane at the side of the road just ahead of the on ramp and switched on his hazard warning lights. Although he knew the rain could continue for some considerable time, he was aware the intensity couldn't be sustained and he decided to wait for the worst to blow over. The motorway was only a short distance away and Alex shook his head in amazement watching the blurred shapes of speeding vehicles blindly following the taillights of the one in front and travelling at a velocity which allowed no room for error. Gradually, the rain lessened but was quickly replaced by hard balls of ice. Hailstones the size of marbles startled to fall with a ferocity which Alex feared could dent his car's bodywork. While most bounced off the paintwork, some of them were softer and exploded onto the windscreen, emulating the impact of a snowball. On the motorway, overhead, gantry warnings guided motorists to reduce their speed to twenty miles per hour, but Alex could see the signs were being ignored as most drivers were still trying to maintain or exceed the urban motorway limit of fifty. It lasted less than five minutes, but in that time, all sorts of catastrophes were being risked. The precipitation eased to a steady drizzle and Alex rejoined the traffic and set off over the bridge.

His meeting was to be held in the building of the Crown Office and Procurator Fiscal Service in Ballater Street, only yards away from Glasgow Sheriff Court and close to the southern bank of the River Clyde.

Having used the motorway to cross the river by the Kingston Bridge, Alex took the first exit then turned left to follow the riverside. A right turn into Bridge Street followed by a left along Oxford Street brought him to the Court Building. He left his vehicle in the official car park then braved the weather to cross to his meeting venue.

Alex presented his identification at the reception and was shown into a meeting room. It was modern, small and comfortable with four armchairs set out around a low coffee table. There was another small table in the corner of the room which had an already bubbling coffee filter set on it, alongside sat a tray of coffee mugs and a bowl with milk and sugar sachets. A rich nutty aroma filled the room. Alex half filled a cup with the dark liquid and relaxed into a chair, thinking about the contrast to the interview rooms in Pitt Street. It was the first time he had stopped all day.

His rest was short-lived, however, as the door flew open and Simon Anderson sailed in. Alike many of his legal associates who have the right to present cases at the High Court, Simon was flamboyant. He was six feet tall and, although reasonably plump, you would never have guessed as his perfectly tailored, three-piece, chequered suit provided an ideal camouflage. The suit was complemented by a starched, white shirt and a colourful cravat. Alex knew him to be fifty, but to look at his impression was ageless, with his shock of sandy coloured hair extending into bushy sideburns which came down to the level of his lips. He wouldn't have looked out of place as a character in a Dickens' novel.

"Good afternoon, Alex. I'm glad you could make it. I wasn't certain that you would. I've heard you've had a spot of bother relating to a distillery?"

"You're very well informed."

"All part of the job."

"I've heard you've had your own bit of bother?"

"Oh yes, the Abdallah case, that could to be very problematic."

"Do you want to deal with it first?"

"No let's keep it until the end. Why spoil what will otherwise be a good day until we have to?"

There was a buzzing and Alex felt a vibration in his pocket signifying another text. He lifted his mobile while mouthing an apology. "Sorry, I'd meant to switch it off," he added.

'Dad, need to talk to you about a problem, something important. Will you have time tonight?' Alex read.

He was a little bit unnerved. What sort of problem might Andrew have? He was always the level-headed one. Might it be personal to him or a family issue, he conjectured?

"A difficulty?" Simon enquired.

"I hope not," Alex replied, "But I can't be certain yet." His fingers flew across the keypad, saying, 'Don't worry I'll make time,' then he switched the phone to silent and again apologised.

Simon and Alex ran through a number of outstanding issues and allocated action points for each of them to progress.

"Just before we move onto Abdallah," Simon added, "You know the Forbes case coming up next month. Word is that he'll put in a diminished responsibility plea, maybe volunteer to be sectioned. He'll do anything to avoid a standard prison sentence. A former senior police officer doesn't want to be banged up alongside some of the villains he'd helped to put away. One other thing, he's asked if you'll visit him in Bar-L."

"Who me?"

"Yes, he says you have history and he wants to ask for your help."

"Well after what he put me through, I'm the last one he can expect to help him."

"Entirely up to you, I'm just passing along the request. Don't shoot the messenger."

"Okay, now about Abdallah, how serious is the problem?"

"I can't be certain, but possibly fatal."

"You have to be joking? I thought we had him bang to rights."

"It did look that way, but now it's all changed."

"What? Just because some idiot said something stupid to him?"

"That's only a small part. Your boy Fulton..."

"Stop right there. Fulton's not one of my boys. You can't pin this one on me. He wasn't even a proper police officer."

"Okay, okay, don't get so touchy. Fulton called him an Afghani, and he's complaining about racism. Worse still he's calling it institutional racism and stating he was only arrested because he was considered to be Asian. To cap that, he's not even from Afghanistan. He is a Moslem but he's a Yemenite. Admittedly, he has travelled to Afghanistan, but that hardly helps."

"But we caught them with the weapon and the money."

"If you remember the details, we have three suspects in custody and they all live in the same building in Allison Street. Mohammed and Faisal are cousins living in the apartment where we found the evidence and Abdallah has his own flat across the landing. Then we had two witnesses who picked out Abdallah at the crime scene."

"Right, so what's the problem?"

"Our witnesses are not so sure about the identification now and say that, while it was definitely someone who looked like him and with Asian complexion, they can't be certain it was him."

"Oh Christ, not the 'all blacks look the same to me' argument?"

"Not exactly, but not too far removed."

"Do you think someone's got to them?"

"It could be, but we could never prove it."

"Our next problem is that Abdallah's from a different country from the other two, and Fulton sticking his foot in it certainly makes it worse. Then to cap it all, Mohammed and Faisal are Shi'ite Moslems. That's fairly unusual for Afghanistan but not that rare. Abdallah is a Sunni and they traditionally hate one another. There's nothing to say they didn't act together and, personally, I'm pretty certain they did, but if we take this to court it could turn out to be a hornet's nest."

"What about the other two?"

"No problem there, but I think we're going to have to release Abdallah. We can't afford to give him a platform to preach about racial hatred and police brutality. If we had a strong prospect of a conviction, it would be worth it, but the case is disappearing before our eyes."

"Oh Shit!"

"No Shi'ite, I already explained," Anderson retorted. "On a lighter note, I heard a story from my cousin which might amuse you."

"Go on."

'He'd been on holiday in France where he has a second home in the Dordogne. He's a bit of a couch potato normally and, experiencing dry weather for the first time in months, he overdid it a bit playing petanque and jiggered his shoulder. He practiced his best French before going to see a local doctor, only to find the doctor spoke better English than he did. The doc took one look and prescribed him a heat rub and some painkillers. It worked fine but on his return home, he thought he'd better report to his own G.P. to make sure it was on his medical record. He went to see Doctor Singh. Singh had been his doctor for the last twenty years and they'd become friends, quite often socialising together. Singh sneered and asked what the 'French' doctor had given him, showing great disdain. My cousin showed him the prescriptions and Singh hummed and hawed, saying, 'I suppose it's okay and won't do you too much damage.'

"My cousin challenged him saying, 'Christ, man, you're a bloody Indian, you're not even British. What have you got against the French? How can you look down on French doctors?' He answered, 'Well I've got my degree from Edinburgh University. Who's ever heard of the Sorbonne?'"

Alex laughed as he stood to leave. "The whole world is prejudiced. Whether it's race, nationality, religion, gender, wealth or education, there's always an excuse for snobbishness. It's a natural phenomenon, people are different and the mere recognition that the difference exists is technically a prejudice. It's not wrong unless it's used to hurt or disadvantage someone. But the law has gone overboard with multiculturalism."

"Thanks for coming in, Alex. It's always good to see you." The two men shook hands before Alex made for the door.

Chapter 10

It was already dark when Alex emerged from the office. He checked his watch and to his surprise saw it wasn't five o'clock yet. Ordinarily he'd have returned to his office to put in another hour or three of work, but he was due to take the boys swimming tonight and he sensed urgency in Andrew's request and didn't want to let him down by being late.

He knew someone would call him if he was needed, so he decided to make it a very rare early finish. It had been a long and arduous day and Alex was apprehensive about Andrew's problem. It was so unlike the boy. He always took everything in his stride, so for him to be seeking help on 'a problem, something important' indicated something serious.

After leaving the Court car-park, Alex drove back to his flat in Shawlands and was there inside fifteen minutes. He didn't like to eat anything substantial before swimming so he lifted a tub of his home-made vegetable soup from the freezer and placed it in the microwave. While it was being converted from ice cold to piping hot, he cut and buttered a couple of slices of crusty bread to help mop it up. Alex relaxed and savoured his food, then collected his swimming shorts, goggles, a towel and shampoo and slung it all in a sports bag. By the time he had scanned through his emails to delete the spam and check there was nothing urgent, it was already time to leave.

Alex's marriage to Helen had broken down some three years before, but amidst the considerable acrimony of that time, he had consented to her retaining the family home, a three bedroom bungalow in Clarkston, to minimise the ill effects on the boys. He retained his relationship with his two sons and he took every opportunity to utilise his limited custody rights. He had now rebuilt an acceptable working relationship with his ex-wife and their dialogue had re-established a cordial tone, verging on friendliness at times.

Although Alex's natural disposition was to be punctual, over the years the pressures and obligations of his job frequently required him to attend to emergencies and change his personal plans at the last minute, often resulting in him missing or being late for domestic arrangements. This placed a great strain on his marriage and was certainly a contributory factor to its ultimate demise. Now being in the more senior position of Chief Inspector, Alex had a little bit more control of his schedule and, being more sensitive to his past failings, he went to great efforts to avoid the boys seeing him as unreliable.

The earlier rain had abated and, as the traffic was unusually light for the time of day, it took little time for the journey from his Shawlands flat across to the family home. Alex glanced at the clock on his dashboard and noted with satisfaction it showed only six-forty as he mounted the pavement to park in front of the house.

Heralding his arrival, Alex's heavy footsteps crunched on the pathway and he heard Jake, barking a welcome.

A few seconds later, the door flew open and the dog bounded out, bouncing all around him trying to land a lick in the region of his face. Alex caught the mutt in mid-air and hugged him close, struggling to carry his squirming three stone bulk through the doorway, while Jake was endeavouring to slaver over his ears. Alex stumbled into the house and deposited the dog on the floor. Andrew looked on, clearly amused by Jake's antics.

In the few days since he'd last seen his son, Alex was certain he'd grown and his face looked thinner. Andrew could never have been described as fat but he was muscular and well built with a rounded, healthy look and he had a full face. Today Alex felt the boy appeared rangier.

"You look as if you're taking a stretch."

Andrew was pleased. "Yes, I'll soon be catching up on Craig and then he won't be able to boss me around as much."

"Where is your brother? I was hoping you'd both be ready so we could go straight out."

"It's okay, he has his kit ready but he disappeared up to his room about half an hour ago. I think he's on his iPhone talking to his pals or else he'll be on Facebook. I don't know, maybe he's talking to his girl-friend," Andrew added, grinning, showing he was giving away what was meant to be a secret

"Oh, what's all this about?"

"You don't know about Craig's girlfriend?"

Alex said nothing but looked questioningly.

"Her name is Jenny and they've been out to the cinema together. I saw them kissing and Craig's been telling me about things ... you know?"

"I don't know if you should be telling me about this. Is it right for you to be telling tales about your brother?"

"It's not telling tales. You're a policeman. I thought you relied on informants to let you know what goes on." Andrew couldn't suppress a wide grin.

"That's all very well for work, and yes, I want to know what's going on. I want to know if a crime's taking place and I want to know if anything dangerous is happening so I can do something about it. But that's different to talking about people's private lives. If Craig wants me to know about something then he'll tell me himself. And if he's got a question then he'll ask it." Alex was caught between natural curiosity, wanting to hear the gossip and trying to advocate an acceptable code of behaviour.

Andrew looked crestfallen. "I thought I was doing good."

"I'm sure your intentions were good and we'll say no more about it. Now, I take it that's what you were anxious to talk to me about?"

"No, Dad. There's something else and it's a lot more serious, but I wanted to speak to you alone and it could take a while. Can we do it after the swimming because Craig might walk in?"

"Yes, of course." Alex was both concerned and intrigued. "But can't you give me a clue?"

"It's to do with a teacher at school." The words were hardly out of his mouth before Alex heard the thundering footsteps of Craig racing down the stairs from his attic bedroom.

"Hi, Dad. I thought I heard you come in." Alex looked up and saw the tall gangly form of his son walking towards him. It struck Alex how the boys were growing up. Craig was not far off becoming a man already and was starting to look the part. Although thin to the point where his bones were evident, he was tall with broad shoulders and there were distinct signs of facial hair. Being blonde he'd get away with it for a bit longer, but a requirement for regular shaving wasn't too far away.

"Yep, are we all set, 'cause the time's going in."

Both boys lifted their bags and headed for the door,

"We've changed into our swimmies already, so it will take less time to get ready when we get there," Craig said.

"That was good thinking. Is your mum at home? I didn't see her."

"She's out with Colin, they said they'd be home sometime after eight so she should be home when we get back if you want to have a word."

"That's okay, just make sure you lock up properly because nobody's home."

"Jake's there," Andrew replied.

"Lock up anyway."

They settled into the car and clicked their seatbelts. Craig being the senior claimed the front seat next to his father.

"I thought we might try Barrhead Baths this week. The last time we went to Eastwood, of an evening, it was very busy."

"Okay, let's give it a try," the boys echoed in unison.

Alex turned the ignition and started to accelerate.

"Hey, I was just talking to my Jenny on the phone. She told me 'Chippie' the maths teacher's been suspended. There's been some funny business that's being hushed up," Craig informed them enthusiastically.

"Oh no. It's awful. That's what I wanted to talk to you about, Dad. It's so unfair."

"You'd better tell me all about it."

"I wanted to talk to you in private, to see if there was anything you could do. But if Jenny knows about it and told Craig, I suppose the story's already out so there's no point trying to keep it secret."

"So, what's the problem?"

"Mr Carpenter is my maths teacher. He's great, probably the best teacher in the school. He put my class forward for the national maths challenge and I won an award, you remember? He's meant to be taking four of us through to Paisley next week for the prize-giving."

"Well, there's this boy in our year, his name's Sean Connelly and he's a complete troublemaker. He's a bully and he goes around threatening other kids. He's always disrupting classes and causing bother. He's had loads of warnings but he doesn't seem to care."

"You've never mentioned this to me before. Has he been giving you trouble?"

"No, not me. He's not in any of my classes, well not normally. Well, anyway, today Mrs Simpson was off and there weren't any spare teachers so her class was split and half of them joined my class, with Mr Carpenter."

Alex's attention was divided between his driving and taking in what Andrew was telling him. He rounded Clarkston Toll and, when the road straightened out, he took a moment to glance in his mirror. He could see Andrew was quite animated and looked upset, not far from tears.

"After the lesson started, Sean began to make a fuss, shouting and screaming. None of us could concentrate on our work. Mr Carpenter told him to be quiet, but Sean took no notice. Instead he climbed up onto his desk and threw books and pencils and things all around the class. It wasn't just the disruption, he was hurting people. Mr Carpenter shouted at him to get down and go and sit in the corner and still Sean ignored him. Then Mr Carpenter went over and lifted him off the desk and took him by the arm and dragged him out the door. He called to us that he was going to the Rector's office and would be back in a minute and we should continue with our work.

"Well, he did come back about ten minutes later, without Sean and everything seemed normal. But later in the day, Sean was in the playground and he was telling stories. He said he'd got his parents to make a formal complaint that Mr Carpenter had assaulted him and that he'd touched him where he shouldn't. From what I heard, Mr Carpenter was called out of class and sent home."

"Well if he is a perv, we don't want him in our school," Craig interrupted.

"He's not a perv. He's a great teacher and a really good person. It's Sean Connelly who's an evil little shit. He thinks by making an accusation against Mr Carpenter that it'll get himself out of trouble," Andrew countered.

"I'm afraid when an accusation of that type is made then it has to be taken seriously and properly investigated. When it's a teacher who's been accused, it's even more serious because of the school's responsibility," Alex replied.

"But it's so unfair," Andrew cut in. "He's done nothing wrong. I thought you were meant to be presumed innocent, unless proven guilty, but this is the other way around."

"I can't argue with you, Andrew. But like I just said, when an allegation of this type is made, it has to be investigated. In my experience, even when an accused proves their innocence, they are still damaged. Mud sticks and there are always people who choose to believe the worst. I'm sorry but that's the truth."

"Is there nothing you can do to help him?"

"I can't promise anything, but I'll see what I can find out. I'll call Brian Phelps, the deputy head. I've known him for years. We were at

University together and we were quite good friends. I'll see if there's anything he can tell me and if there's anything I can help with."

"Thanks, Dad, I knew you'd be able to do something."

"Don't get your hopes up too much. I said I'd look into it but the chances are I won't be able to do anything. I will try though."

The miles had passed as they'd been talking and they were already in Barrhead. Alex turned the car into the sports centre car-park and squeezed into the only available space. They opened the doors, being careful not to scratch the adjacent vehicles, walked through the doorway and up to the reception desk. They each lifted out and showed their East Renfrewshire 'All Access' discount cards. Alex handed over a ten pound note and asked for one adult and two juvenile tickets.

"You know it's a fun night?" the receptionist replied, her low seat almost hiding her behind the counter.

"We're here for a swim, so yes, we were hoping for a fun night," Alex replied.

"No, I mean from six till eight it's a fun time in the pool. The big inflatable slide and toys are put in to play with so there's not much room for swimming. Go take a look and see what I mean."

Alex, Craig and Andrew walked through the cafe to the large window overlooking the pool. They could see what the girl meant. A massive inflatable platform with a tall built-in chute took up half the swimming area. Children were jumping about and screaming. They were climbing up and sliding down the chute or trying to swim closeby, but there was very little available water to swim in and what area there was had a high concentration of people sharing it.

"This is no use," Alex said. "Let's go back and try to get into Eastwood instead."

With a curt wave of thanks to the receptionist, he jogged back out to their car, followed by the boys.

As they sped past the recently built housing estates, Alex was aware of the diabolical state of the road surface, no doubt exacerbated by the construction traffic and the deep frost of recent months. He manoeuvred past the potholes and trenches and was relieved to turn into

Darnley Road which was considerably wider although still quite badly chewed up.

It took only a few minutes to arrive at the Eastwood complex but almost as long to find a parking space. They arrived at reception at seven-twenty.

Alex asked for the tickets and was told that the pool was only available until seven forty-five. He glanced at his watch and considered for a few seconds while he did the calculations. If they were quick, by the time they had changed and showered they would still be able to swim for close to twenty minutes.

"Go on then," he replied. "We'll just have to make the most of the time we have," he added, turning to the boys.

The boys rushed to the changing rooms, found lockers, and quickly stripped down to their swimwear. Alex followed, needing slightly longer as he required a cubicle to change.

Craig and Andrew were already in the pool by the time Alex reached the showers and he was dismayed to see that the bottom third of the pool had been roped off and was being used by a water aerobics class. The upper two thirds of the pool was crammed with four times as many people as the exercise class. "Shit," he muttered under his breath, thinking this evening was not working at all as planned.

Alex joined the boys in the water and they decided it would be easier to swim breadths rather than partial lengths under the circumstances. It wasn't easy to conduct any conversation because of the loud dance music which reverberated through the entire area. They spent a frustrating few minutes trying to chalk up a series of laps while their attempts were frequently disturbed having to detour round other bathers who were either swimming up and down the pool or just frolicking about in the water.

They detected the swimming area becoming quieter as they progressively had more space to exercise and then realised the pond attendant was signalling, indicating it was time to leave the pool. Alex glanced up at the wall clock and saw it was just after seven thirty-five. He had been in the pool for barely more than ten minutes. He didn't know whether to be more relieved that the torture was being brought to an end or angry that he and the boys weren't getting the amount of time they'd expected.

Alex climbed out of the water and approached the attendant. "This is bloody ridiculous. We didn't arrive until seven-twenty. We've only had ten minutes of swimming time. Admittedly, we were told the pool would close at seven forty-five, but that's another ten minutes away. We weren't told we'd only have half the pool available and the whole thing's been a complete waste of time and money." When Alex looked round, he saw the aerobics class was still in full swing. "And what about them?" he added. "Why have we been asked to leave but they're still here?"

The attendant was a young lad, barely out of his teens. He was short, very puny and had pale, acne scarred skin and ginger coloured hair giving him the appearance of a giant lollipop. Seeing Alex's powerful frame lumbering towards him and hearing his voice booming to be heard over the dance music, he started to shake uncontrollably. "I'm really sorry, Sir," he apologized. "You should have been told at the cash desk when you came in. If you tell them and show your tickets on the way out, you can get your money back. We have to clear the pool early because it's a ladies' only session from eight o'clock onwards and we have to have the changing area emptied before then. There are only female attendants on duty then as well. The aerobics class is allowed to stay on a bit later because they're all women."

Alex felt sorry for the lad but he was still annoyed and didn't want to let him off too easily. "So what night is the men's only session?"

"There isn't one."

"Well, that doesn't sound very fair. In fact, it sounds like prejudice to have special times for women only and not to have the same for men."

"I think it's something to do with religion. With some faiths, women aren't allowed to be in swimming when there are men around. There are also a lot of women who don't like the idea of being in their swimsuits or of getting changed when there are strange men around," the attendant answered wanting to appear knowledgeable.

"Are you calling me strange?" Alex quipped. "But seriously, I don't see how you can make special provisions and not make the same for men. It's prejudice," Alex couldn't help thinking about his conversations earlier in the day.

"I don't know, Sir. You'd need to take it up with my bosses."

"No, I think I'll take it up with the European Court for Human Rights instead," Alex challenged. The attendant just looked confused.

Unable to resist, Alex added, "It's no wonder the country has such obesity problems when the local authority make it so difficult for a working man to get some exercise in community facilities." By this time, Alex was starting to feel a bit chilled from standing, near naked, in the cold air. He turned and walked towards the shower area to join his sons who were standing sniggering, listening to the exchange. The attendant just stood open-mouthed, unable to think of any response.

Only a short while later, they were dried and changed and in the car. The boys were laughing and talking about his comments, but having had time to think, Alex was contrite. "Take no notice of anything I said back there. I was wrong. I shouldn't have taken it out on that poor lad, it wasn't his fault. In truth, I was to blame. I should have checked the timings and facilities before we went. In hindsight, we should have stayed at Barrhead, either that or gone another time."

Before there was time for any further discussion, a loud ringing interrupted them. Alex glanced at the Parrot screen and saw it was Sandra calling. He pressed a button on the hands free unit to accept the call and immediately spoke to alert her he was not alone, to ensure she was guarded in what she said.

"Hi, Sandra, I'm just driving the boys back from the swimming. Have you any good news for me?"

"That would explain it. I've tried you a couple of times, so you'll see the missed calls. I don't know if you'd call it good news but we have made some progress and I just wanted to bring you up to speed. Remember, I won't be in tomorrow morning, so could you give me a bell when you're free?"

"Will do, maybe half an hour to an hour's time, okay?"

He clicked off and a few minutes later drew the car to a halt outside the house.

"Are you coming in, Dad? I forgot that I wanted to show you my invite to the Maths Challenge prize-giving."

"Yes, of course, but I can't stay too long. I've some work to catch up on."

"Yes, we heard," Craig replied tonelessly.

Chapter 11

Craig opened the door with his key and Alex received another enthusiastic welcome from Jake, although not quite as boisterous as the previous one.

Craig went off to his room and Andrew disappeared upstairs to find his letter. Alex saw that Helen and Colin were sitting in the lounge. Seeing him entering the house, they called him in and offered him a seat. Their welcome appeared sincere and they switched off the television.

"Have you eaten yet?" Helen asked. "I know you often take the boys out straight from work."

"I got home early. I had a bowl of soup."

"You must be starving. Let me get you a sandwich."

Before he had any opportunity to protest, Helen had gone and he could hear her rattling around in the kitchen. She returned after a couple of minutes with a ciabatta roll stuffed with sliced roast beef covered in mustard. To wash it down, she'd also brought a glass of Irn Bru.

Alex was surprised. This was better and more attentive treatment then he could remember receiving when they'd been married, he thought, although he wasn't brave enough to comment. In his experience, Helen was not renowned for her gratuitous hospitality and he suspected there was a cost to pay. He expected Helen wanted a favour or else she was anxious to talk to him about something."

"This is terrific, just what I needed. Thanks very much."

Andrew came back with his letter and Alex, Helen and Colin all voiced enthusiasm for his achievement.

"But what's going to happen about getting there now Mr Carpenter's gone?"

"I'm certain the school will arrange something else, but if they don't, then I'll find a way to get time off," Alex replied.

"What's all this about?" Helen asked. "What's happened to Carpenter?"

Andrew told her, giving the same impassioned pleas as he had earlier.

"I've heard about this Connelly family," Colin advised. "One of my friends is into property letting and he told me the story. A guy he knows from the Landlord Association is a professional landlord with about forty properties. He's very experienced but rents to anyone, private, students and DSS, sometimes to people fresh out of prison. He does his own assessment of the prospective tenants, but he takes some risks which nearly always pay off. However, he made a real blunder with the Connellys. They came to see a two bedroom flat he had in Busby. They said they wanted it and had cash for the deposit and the first month's rent. They had letters of reference which looked good and when the guy phoned up it all seemed to check out. That was eight months ago and he's not received a penny of rent since."

"How can that happen?" Helen asked.

"Quite easily, apparently, Connelly doesn't work and neither does his wife. The paperwork and references were all false, they'd been forged. When the guy checked the phone numbers, it was one of Connelly's mates. When he checked the credit rating, he got a good result because it was for someone else with the same name. Identity fraud, I suppose," he said looking at Alex, who nodded.

"Connelly should be entitled to housing benefit, but the landlord can't get it unless Connelly makes the claim and, even if he did, there might be arrears which he owes the Council which would be taken off first. The landlord is distraught. He's been trying for months to get them out, without success. Whenever he goes near to the flat, or even if he parks next door, where hes got another flat, Mr Connelly phones the police and claims he's being harassed. The landlord's served a notice to quit, but they've ignored it and he's still waiting for a court date so he can get an order to have them removed. Even once he gets the court order, they might not move and then he'll need to employ Sheriff's Officers to get them out. It's cost him a fortune and God only knows what state the flat will be in when he eventually recovers it."

"It's true, there's so much law to protect tenants and precious little which helps landlords," Alex commented.

"One of the most ridiculous things is that Shelter is advising the Connellys how to avoid or delay being evicted. They're meant to be a charity to help the homeless and they've a really good and important job to do, but they're helping useless cretins like the Connellys who are not deserving cases and whose only purpose is to beat the system. All that's going to do is alienate good landlords and make them more reluctant to take a chance housing genuine homeless people.

"Anyway, the whole Connelly family are a bad lot. Both parents and the older boy have been caught stealing and the younger one is a really nasty piece of work. They know the system inside out and this whole charade is probably a scheme to stop Sean from being excluded from school and maybe to help stop them being evicted."

"I told you Mr Carpenter won't have done anything wrong," Andrew exclaimed.

"Well as I said before, I'll see what I can do, but no promises." Alex added.

Andrew excused himself to go up to his room and prepare for school.

"Good night, Son. I'll let you know if I can do anything and I'll see you at the weekend anyway."

Helen turned to Alex, "There's something else I wanted to discuss with you."

I knew something was coming, he thought, but what? "Okay, shoot?"

"It's about Craig. He's got a girlfriend."

"Yes, I heard."

"What, did he tell you?"

"No, not a word. Andrew said though."

"I'm worried about him. I think it's getting quite serious."

"He's not fifteen for another month. How do you mean serious?"

"The girl's name is Jenny and she's nearly a year older than Craig."

"So?"

"Well it's unusual. At that age, girls normally mature a lot earlier than boys. What could she want from him?"

"What sort of question is that for a mother to ask? He's smart and he's a good looking young lad. He's decent and he may not be wealthy, but he's not short of cash either."

"She's a pretty girl and she goes to his school. I'm worried she might be too experienced for him."

"I'm sorry, and how is that a problem?"

"You know. Craig's young and inexperienced. She could take advantage of him."

"He should be so lucky."

"No, I'm serious. Have you ever spoken to him? You know, the father and son conversation."

"At his age, I reckon there won't be too much he won't know. I had the 'birds and bees' talk with him when he was at primary school and I did the same with Andrew. They weren't learning very much new because they'd already had sex awareness and education classes in school. They were telling me as much as I was telling them," Alex quipped.

"But he's too young to be getting involved."

"Maybe so, but you're not going to stop him by telling him not to do something, quite the opposite, most likely. Yes, we can talk to him about relationships and responsibility and being careful to avoid health risks, but that's about the limit. We can even talk about the age of consent."

"Will you do that?"

"Me?"

"Well yes, you are his father. I can't and he wouldn't take it from Colin."

"Okay, I can have a chat with him and make sure he knows all the things he should know, but that's as far as it goes. I can't regulate his behaviour and I'm not sure I would want to."

"Okay then," Helen sat with pursed lips and a stubborn expression. "What, you mean now?"

"Is there a better time?" Through all of this, Colin sat next to Helen, perhaps providing her with moral support, but he took no part in the conversation. His face was flushed and he looked embarrassed.

Alex climbed the stairs and knocked on Craig's bedroom door, turned the handle and opened it an inch. "Can I come in?"

"Yes, sure," the boy replied.

Alex opened the door fully and walked in. Craig was in an office chair sitting in front of a desk with his desktop computer illuminated in front of him. He quickly flicked a few keys and the screen changed to an open word document with what appeared to be a geography project in progress. Alex pulled up a chair beside him but spotted icons at the bottom of the screen which showed internet sites depicting naked bodies.

"Hi, Dad. I didn't realise you were still here."

"Yeah, I thought I'd come up for a chat before leaving. What are you working on there?"

"It's a project on deserts."

"Very hot?"

"Yes?"

"Is that why nobody's wearing clothes in the other photos you have open?"

Craig's face went bright scarlet and he was flustered trying to think what he could say. "I'm not a kid anymore," he started defensively.

"I'm not suggesting you are. I just thought there was an adult filter on your internet connection."

"It's easy enough to get round," Craig replied sheepishly. "Besides, these pictures are all quite innocent compared to some the boys at school can get on their phones."

"Don't panic. I'm a crime detective, not the morality police. I'm not here to give you a hard time."

"Why are you here?"

"Your mum thought I should maybe have a little chat with you," Alex started in cowardly fashion. "She cares and she's worried about you."

Craig rolled his eyes. "What's her problem now?"

"That's not fair," Alex admonished. "She only wants what's best for you. We both do."

"Okay, what's this all about? As if I couldn't guess."

"You've got a new girlfriend and she, no we," Alex quickly corrected himself, "are concerned that you're getting too involved and too serious."

"How can I be too serious? We've only been going out for three weeks. We've been to the cinema twice and we've met at the cafe a couple of times."

"Have you brought her round to the house?"

"God no. I'm not stupid. Mum would give her the third degree."

"Have you been to her house?"

"Not yet, but I've been asked round for tea this weekend."

Alex raised his eyebrows and Craig correctly interpreted the question. "We won't be alone. Jenny's mum will be there. She's the one who invited me."

"You've already met her?"

"Yes, she picked us up after the cinema last week, she seems really nice."

"And she didn't give you the third degree?"

"Well, that's different."

Alex shrugged, "It's the same the world over, parents want to know what their children are doing and they want to know about who they're with so they know they're safe."

"I suppose."

"Well if it goes well this weekend, maybe you'll bring Jenny back here so your mum can meet her, then she won't worry either."

"I'll think about it."

Alex knew it was the best answer he could hope for. "Well, how serious is this becoming?"

"We're not having sex if that's what you're asking."

"I only want to know that you're safe and you're being responsible."

Again Craig rolled his eyes, but this time he had a half smile on his face. "Yes, Dad, I've been to all the classes, I know all about safe sex and I've got a drawer full of condoms that we were given at the classes. You've got nothing to worry about."

"Well that's fine. I'll leave you to get on with your homework. And I mean your desert project not the other sites," he said grinning.

"Yeah, and you've still to phone your girlfriend back. You said you'd call within an hour and it's already much later than that."

"She's not my girlfriend, she's the police sergeant working under me on an investigation," Alex replied defensively, if a little unconvincingly.

"Come on, Dad, I heard the change in the tone of your voice when you answered the phone. And I remember her from when she came to visit you in hospital after you were stabbed last year. Anyway, what do you mean by working under you?" Craig replied with a broad grin.

"We'll have less of your cheek young man. I'm not having this conversation," Alex replied, but was unable to hide his smile. He didn't know whether to be more angry or proud at his son's perceptiveness. He was also acutely aware that he and Helen were maybe being a bit presumptuous seeking to lecture Craig about relationships after the mess they'd made of their own.

Alex returned downstairs and imparted the good news, telling Helen not to worry and preparing her to meet a possible guest in a week or two's time.

Chapter 12

Alex settled back into the car, turned the ignition, slowly drove around the corner, then pulled into the kerb and called Sandra's number.

"I'm sorry, I'm a lot later than planned, but I've had the latest domestic crisis to sort out."

"What's the problem?"

"You really don't want to know, other than Craig has worked out that we're an item. He could have a future in the force."

"Are we an item?"

"Well that depends on your definition, what would you call it?"

"How about coming over and we can see if we can work it out? My parents are away, visiting my aunt in Aberdeen, and they won't be back until tomorrow."

"I'd really love to, but I'm totally knackered. I need to get some sleep because tomorrow's likely to be a heavy day as well."

"That's a pity. But if I'm not seeing you, I'd better let you know what's been happening." Sandra proceeded to pass to Alex all the information which had so far been gleaned.

"I'm going to the agent to sign up the flat first thing tomorrow and then I'll be moving some of my stuff in. All being well, I should be back on the job before midday. We've arranged an appointment to see Chuck Holbein at the Pollockshields house. We've made it for ten-thirty. Sanjay could lead it if you're unavailable or if you'd rather be at the distillery. But you know what it's like with American business people and status and she is a big time player, so you may want to do that one yourself, maybe with Phil. You could meet in the office first. That way Sanjay could go straight out to Benlochy and keep an eye on things and I could join him as soon as I'm free."

"Yes, that would be best. I've still to drive home and it's getting late to call. Could you send them a text to set it up? And tell Phil to dress appropriately."

"No probs. I took a drive past my new flat about half an hour ago. I could see all the lights were on in the flat above and I could hear the thud, thud of dance music from out in the street. Maybe I've been a bit ambitious in what I've taken on. What if I can't sort out the troublemakers?"

"I don't think you've anything to worry about. You'll have it sorted in no time whatsoever and, let's face it, on a worst case scenario, you can just give back the keys. You wouldn't even lose the deposit."

"You're right, it's just nerves. I'm getting jittery. It will all go fine."

"Right, I'll need to love you and leave you; I need to get home now. Good luck tomorrow"

"Did I just hear a four letter word?" Sandra enquired, teasing.

"Take it any way you like," Alex replied and clicked off.

* * *

Alex had a restless night, waking frequently from troubled dreams. In between, and no doubt affecting his slumbers, he kept thinking about the various relationships currently affecting him. On a work basis, he considered the dysfunctional Burns family, with all the interweaving of hatreds and dislikes and criminal activity and what it all might mean. He thought about Andrew's poor teacher whose life might be in ruins because of the manufactured accusations by the Connellys. He thought about Craig and his girlfriend on the threshold of adulthood, but most of all he considered his own personal situation, his failed marriage and his current relationship with Sandra. Where was it going and how involved might it become? They'd been having fun and they enjoyed each others' company, but it was becoming time to carefully consider the implications. If Craig could work out their relationship, then it could hardly be a secret and people at work must suspect too. He'd need to have a serious talk with Sandra.

He was normally an early riser, but on this occasion Alex had to scramble back to consciousness as he reached out to mute his radio alarm. Nirvana's "Smells Like Teen Spirit" was playing and at seven in the morning, it just didn't feel right. His head was muggy and he felt even more tired than when he'd gone to bed. He now regretted not accepting Sandra's invitation. He wouldn't have been any less tired but he'd have been a lot happier.

Alex plodded into the shower and set the jet to high and cold. After a couple of minutes, he felt awake and moderated the temperature to a more acceptable lukewarm.

He allowed himself a leisurely shower and, after rinsing off the shampoo and shower gel, he shaved carefully and went to his wardrobe. Although he refused to spend a lot of money on his clothes, Alex took pride in his appearance and liked to always convey a professional image. He had a choice of suits which he'd purchased from Slaters Menswear. The family owned business had now developed into a sizable chain with internet retailing and branches throughout the country, but Alex still enjoyed the shopping experience of their original city centre Glasgow store, which claimed the distinction of being the world's largest menswear shop. Knowing he would be interviewing the CEO of a major international company, Alex was determined to look his best. He recognised this was still a murder enquiry and Holbein would get no better treatment than anyone else, but Alex considered his own position. He was also acting as an ambassador for the police force and the country when meeting high profile individuals.

He selected a dark, pinstripe, Pierre Cardin suit which he'd only worn a couple of times since he'd purchased it off a clearance rack in the Slaters' sale. He chose a white, Peter England shirt, a self-coloured, blue, silk tie and Loake shoes to complete the correct image. He looked in his full-length wardrobe mirror and felt quite satisfied.

The morning was dry, if somewhat overcast and grey, and the temperature was mild. After depositing his vehicle in the car-park, Alex walked at a sprightly pace towards his office building. On the way, he spotted the same traffic warden he'd seen the previous afternoon. Believing in cooperation amongst public servants, Alex gave a cheerful wave and called, "Hello."

The warden reflexively reciprocated. Being in a job where his presence is seldom, if ever, welcomed, however, it slowly dawned on him where he'd seen Alex before and his smile changed to a grimace as he walked by.

Although still tired, Alex had a spring in his step and he bounded up the stairs to his office. Phil was already at his desk and Alex was pleased to note that he looked clean and tidy. This was not unusual for Phil, but there had been the odd occasion when his dress sense, if not his detective skills, had approximated to Colombo's. Gladly, today was not one of those days. He came through to discuss developments in the case and the strategy going forward. Once this was done, Alex tasked Phil to contact Stanley Burns to arrange for them to interview him later in the day. He then told Phil about the problem with Andrew's teacher and asked him to make some background enquiries about Carpenter and also about the Connellys.

Alex had a few minutes to spare so he consulted his phone book then called Andrew's school and asked to speak to Brian Phelps.

"Hello, Brian, Alex Warren here. How are you?"

"I'm doing really well, Alex. It's good to hear from you, but I'm afraid I only have a moment because I'm due in class and it wouldn't do to be late. You never know what the little buggers will get up to."

"That's okay but I was calling to ask a favour, I'm looking for some information and it's all off the record. Are you free this evening? Could I meet you for a pint?"

"I'm afraid I've got something on this evening, but I could maybe meet up for half an hour. Say about six. I'm still in Muirend so could we maybe meet at the Bank? The pub just down the road from Sainsburys."

"That's a deal, I'll see you at six."

Alex returned his attention to the Hector Mathewson case. The provisional Medical Examiner' report was now in and it confirmed there was no doubt about it being murder. Alex pored over all the transcripts of yesterday's interviews and the notes taken. His head was starting to throb when Phil knocked on his door to alert him, advising it was time to go.

The journey time was only a few minutes by taking the motorway then along Haggs Road and St Andrew's Drive.

Alex parked on the roadside and they both alighted from the car. The building was large and detached, constructed of blonde sandstone with a slate roof and was built in the late nineteenth century. They walked along a broad, mono-block paved driveway to approach the front door, climbed the first two of the three large, semi-circular, polished marble steps and pressed the door bell.

"I wouldn't want to be racing up these on an icy day. Beautiful looking but a bit treacherous," Phil remarked.

Within seconds the door was answered by a tall, thin, young man dressed in a morning suit. "Can I help you gentlemen?" he enquired.

Phil just stared at him but Alex showed his identification and replied, "I'm DCI Warren and this is DC Morrison. We've an appointment to see Ms Holbein."

"Yes, she's expecting you, please come in," he said, depriving Phil the opportunity to repeat his joke from the previous day.

As the man turned to lead the way, Phil looked at Alex and mouthed the words, "They've actually got a butler."

They were shown into a large lounge. The room was tall, almost ten feet in height, and had elaborate plaster moulding on the cornicing and the ceiling. Very large windows overlooked the garden and driveway and they were framed by rich velvet drapes held in tie-backs. The flooring was covered in a deep pile, Axminster, tartan carpet. The room was comfortable, lavishly furnished and decorated, but with a complete lack of style. For furniture, one of the long walls was covered in floor to ceiling high book shelves which were overflowing with a profusion of leather bound texts. There was a mis-matching of sizes, genres and colours. Volumes of classics were interspersed with modern fiction and antiquarian text books. The only common feature was that they were all books and they all had leather bindings. The shelves were lined with them, but in some cases stacks of books sat in front and on the floor. The overall effect was most disjointed and untidy.

At the centre of the opposite wall was a large open fireplace. It was stacked high with burning logs and every few seconds they heard a crackle or spit from it. Despite its cavernous size, the room was hot and had a homely feel. Three large, deep-buttoned couches separated by matching style, but more upright, armchairs standing in the corners, completed a square shape around the fire, and this continued the leather theme set by the library. At its centre was a colourful Chinese carpet which clashed with the tartan beneath it. A heavy, wooden sideboard sat against the remaining full wall. On top were advertising leaflets stacked beside a display of bottles exhibiting some of the many brands distributed by the Hanser Group. The range was extensive and included several Bourbons, Scotch, Irish and Japanese whiskeys together with a range of rums and vodkas and a number of specialist liqueurs. Alex noticed that a bottle of twenty five year old Benlochy sat amongst them. A bit presumptuous, he thought.

Being keenly interested in art, Alex recognised the works in the room and he considered they looked totally incongruous to everything else. On the wall above the drinks display were two, large, framed paintings. One was by Jack Vettriano and looked like an oversized picture postcard. Alongside it sat one of Peter Howson's industrial style portraits. Alex considered the juxtaposition almost painful to the eye. Not quite as bad, but nevertheless unpleasant, the wall with the fireplace had one picture on each side of the chimney breast. To the left was a Hornel landscape and to the right was a Holbein portrait which Alex was certain had to be a print. Originals of Hornel, Vettriano and Howson were not cheap but they could be afforded. A Holbein was something else. Alex found it difficult to imagine four artists whose styles would have clashed more. Phil did not have anything like the same interest but nevertheless looked around open-mouthed.

Their musings were disturbed by the approaching sound of heavy and laboured footsteps.

"Gentlemen, please take a seat." They heard the voice before she entered. It was a strong and confident voice with only the slightest American intonations.

Alex and Phil turned to see the source. The look matched the voice. The lady appeared to be in her early forties and was of medium height, but there was nothing else average about her. Her deeply tanned face accentuated her sparkling, deep blue eyes. She had a pretty face with a button nose and high cheek bones and not the slightest indication of cosmetic enhancement. Her hair was short and curly. Her slim physique was shapely and shown off to best effect by a perfectly tailored dark blue trouser suit. However, the overall impression was slightly spoiled by a plaster-cast which covered her ankle and halfway up the calf of her left leg. She limped into the room aided by an aluminium crutch which clipped around her arm with a support just under her armpit.

"I'm Chuck Holbein," she added extending her arm in greeting.

"Pleased to meet you, we're very grateful you could make time to see us." Alex returned her firm handshake and then passed across his business card.

"Skating accident," Chuck said, anticipating their curiosity. "My own stupid fault. I used to be quite competent in my younger days and hadn't recognised the years that have passed. I went over on my ankle, strained it and chipped a bone."

"Did it happen here?"

"Yes, just a few days ago, last Sunday. I took my daughter to East Kilbride and thought I'd show her there's life in the old gal yet. Mistake." She laughed aloud and it had an ironic tone. "There was I, wanting to impress her and look cool and what happens? She's mortified, embarrassed at being seen with me as I get dragged off in an ambulance while a group of her contemporaries looked on and applauded."

"What age is she?" Alex enquired

"She turned fourteen last month, but as with all teenagers she thinks she knows it all and she's hypersensitive, particularly when she's in sight of other teenagers."

"Yes, they can be rather touchy, I know that only too well," Alex replied, wondering if Craig may have been one of the onlookers as he and his chums often congregated at the ice rink on Sundays.

"Now please sit down," she invited.

Alex and Phil sat on the couch to the side of the fire, hoping to avoid the fierceness of its heat. Chuck slipped into the upright chair facing them and dropped her crutch to the floor.

Alex appreciated Chuck's skill in welcoming her guests and putting them at their ease. He was only marginally disturbed by their seating arrangements. He knew from training and experience the psychological advantage of having someone you are questioning having to physically look up to you. Chuck had achieved the reverse with the obvious excuse of her damaged leg.

"You're no doubt a bit curious about the artwork?" Chuck asked, seeing Alex was unable to keep his eyes off the pictures.

"Yes, I am, it's not the most likely combination."

"No, I'm afraid not. It was my father's choice. When he ran the business, he bought this house so it could be used for visits and for business meetings. He was always proud of his Scottish roots; his maternal grandparents came from Stirling. Because of his heritage he, wanted to buy Scottish art to decorate it. He knew nothing about art and asked a dealer to buy pieces that he thought would be a good investment. I'm not certain he got it right though."

"What about the Holbein?" Alex asked. "Not Scottish, is there a family connection?" he added smiling.

"We wish. There's no connection that we're aware of. We're not even certain that there are German roots. But because we have the same surname, he thought it would be a good idea."

"Not an original though?"

"Again, we wish. The original of this one's in the Louvre and it's worth millions, but it's not a bad copy, well print actually."

"Yes, I recognise it. The others are worth a few bob too. The Hornel's a good one; I've seen others similar in the City Chambers. The Vettriano has been used for posters and postcards, so I hope you're entitled to the copyright royalties, and the Howson's one of his early ones, before he was 'discovered' and started churning them out."

"You know about them, I'm impressed. My father bought the Howson after he heard Madonna had one, and you're right, it's one of his earlier works. I didn't expect art appreciation to be part of police training."

"It's not. Much as I'd enjoy talking about that with you, we've come regarding a much more serious issue."

"Yes, how can I help you?"

"We understand that you've been having discussions with Hector Mathewson about taking over the Benlochy Distillery."

"Any discussion about a takeover is commercially sensitive information."

"We understand that, but Hector was found dead yesterday morning and we believe he's been murdered. We have to investigate all information about his recent activities, business and recreational."

"Oh my God. I met him for dinner the previous evening."

"That confirms the information we were given."

"But what happened?" Chuck Holbein had a stunned expression.

"We're still trying to piece together the whole picture."

"I saw on the Scottish news, yesterday, that there had been a death reported at Benlochy and that visits to the distillery were temporarily being curtailed. I would never have guessed it was Hector. I tried calling him when I heard the news but the receptionist said he wasn't available. Now that's a euphemism if I ever heard one. I tried his cell but it just went to voicemail. I never suspected it might have been him."

"You said you had dinner the night before he died. Can you please give us all the details and the background?"

"Okay, I can understand your need to know. It's public knowledge that Hanser is on the acquisition trail. We raised cash on the money markets a few months ago and we're looking to grow. We're not far off making the Fortune 500 and we're planning to get there before the end of the year. So far that's all in the open.

"I've known Hector for a number of years. We met at industry conferences and trade events, things like that. Hector called me about a month ago and asked if I'd be interested in buying Benlochy. I thought he was joking at first because it's one of the big names amongst the independents. It has worldwide recognition. Premier league, I think is how you express it in Britain. Our Scotch labels are also-rans. Don't get me wrong, we do very well with them, the blends in particular, but if we had Benlochy in our portfolio, then we'd be challenging for the top slot in the industry. Of course I was interested. I asked Hector to prepare the key facts for my board to look at and we signed a confidentiality agreement, so I'm a bit cagey on what I can say."

"I think you'll find a criminal investigation for murder trumps a commercial agreement, but check with your lawyers by all means."

"No, you're right, I don't need a lawyer to tell me. Besides, with Hector dead, the agreement is void. It probably wasn't going anywhere anyhow."

"Why wasn't it going anywhere?"

"I'd rather not say."

"I think you may have to, but for the time being let's just hear about what happened between you and Hector."

"Hector emailed me the data I asked for. He presented it as a formal Information Memorandum and it was just as I suspected; they had the throughput and the market penetration we were looking for. Their figures were even better actually, except for the net profit. That didn't bother us too much as they're a family business so we'd expect a lot of unusual costs. They'd all be cleared out after a purchase. It's the underlying profit that interests us most, not what's declared in their accounts and, of course, even more so, we wanted to evaluate the potential we could exploit. Our combined strength would give us access to some markets that neither of us could penetrate individually. The whole being greater than the sum of the parts.

"There's no rocket science in any of it, it's standard evaluation tactics in a takeover or merger.

"Anyway, I met Hector the night before last so we could see where we were taking it. This was the first real meeting and we didn't want it to be too heavy so it was just the two of us. We needed a neutral venue so we met at the Rogano for dinner. Hector brought me a gift of a vintage bottle. That's it over there on the sideboard."

"I noticed it earlier. I wondered what it was doing amongst your brands."

"You don't miss a lot, do you, Inspector?"

"Chief Inspector, actually," Phil cut in, the first words he'd spoken aloud since being shown into the house.

"My apologies, I'm not familiar with the structure the police have in this country."

"No problem," Alex replied. "Did you talk business over dinner?"

"A little, although it was mostly talking over old times and about how the business has been changing over the years."

"Was your relationship with Hector only ever business?"

Chuck's face flushed. She chewed on her lip and looked downward, unable to meet Alex's appraising gaze. For the first time, she lost her confident air, but only for a few seconds. In the short space of time, she seemed to be considering how to react; should she be affronted, angry, honest or what? She decided on her course of action and her head lifted and she stared straight back at him.

"A few years ago, we had a fling. I was between husbands at the time and quite lonely. We were at a marketing event in London and we spent some time together. There was nothing else to it. We were both consenting adults and we had a few days with no strings attached. We parted as friends which was why he felt he could call me."

"And what about Wednesday night?"

"Nothing happened then. True, Hector suggested we could pick up where we left off, but I wasn't interested."

"How did all this come about?"

"Over coffee, we were discussing the business and he suggested taking me out to see the operation, there and then. He placed his hand on my knee, the uninjured one, and it was more than a friendly gesture. I'm not a vain woman. I knew from that moment exactly what he was suggesting. He said he'd take me out and show me the distillery and it would be our secret as nobody would know. He said if I was up for a bit of adventure, we could have some dirty sex on the premises. I think he came out with an expression along the lines that, if I wanted him to let me screw him on a deal, then the least I could do was let him fuck me first. I declined his offer."

Seeing Alex's deadpan expression, Chuck continued, "You don't seem shocked, or even surprised?"

"Not really, we've already heard about some of his exploits. Now, you've said that the distillery visit would have been a secret, did he explain how it could be kept secret?"

"Not exactly. He did say he could get us in without anyone knowing, but he didn't say how and I didn't want him to think I was interested in his invitation so I didn't ask."

"He made no mention of a tunnel?"

"A tunnel? No, and just as well as I hate small spaces. That would have really put me off."

"Not that you needed putting off anyway," Phil interceded with one of his few remarks.

"No, young man, I didn't," she shot back.

"How far did the business discussions go?" Alex asked.

"We discussed the figures and I asked why he was looking to sell. He told me he was wanting out and wished to maximise his cash. He said there was no-one else in the company able to take over. Daniel was too old and ill, Georgina hadn't been involved for years, Stanley wasn't interested and he didn't rate Quentin and said he couldn't carry the support of the others anyway."

"I don't think Quentin sees it that way."

"That's what I said too. I've known Quentin for years as well, our fathers' friendships went back even longer, but I was never close to Quentin."

"Not the way you were with Hector?" Phil enquired.

"No," she replied frostily. "I asked him how the family felt about the sale and he just soft soaped the answer. When I pressed, he said there would be some resistance but he was convinced he could pull it off. He said he'd want us to be a bit creative in the package though, with either retained employment or generous payoffs for those family employed by the company. I told him I wasn't going to waste time and expense pursuing a valuation and an offer until I knew it would be properly considered. I asked him to provide me with a board statement approving a sale or at least consideration of a sale."

Chuck paused for a few seconds, her eyes scanned around the room. She appeared uncertain whether to continue. "There's something else, I don't know if I should be telling you."

"Let me be the judge of that, if you please. Any information could be relevant and important."

"Hector told me there was a second business, run on the side. He said all the Benlochy turnover didn't go through the accounts and that he had a special operation which provided a very useful cash stream, the emphasis being on 'cash.' I asked if it was legitimate and he didn't answer, he just raised his eyebrows and said he didn't believe in paying tax and duty that he didn't have to. I was curious and asked him how he sold it and he told me he had special contacts. I stopped him and told him not to go on. I said, in no uncertain terms, that Hanser was a big company and totally above board. Yes, we use accountants and lawyers to ensure we present figures the right way and to ensure the structure and residencies are optimised to reduce tax, but we won't break the law. We have major ambitions and we have a Wall Street listing. We're not going to prejudice our position by becoming involved in anything dodgy and we certainly aren't going to get involved with criminal distribution channels."

"I think we already know what that's all about so you needn't worry about betraying confidences," Alex advised her reassuringly and she seemed to visibly relax.

"I think that's all I have to ask for the time being, but we may want to speak again. How long are you staying in Glasgow?"

"I'm flying back to New York on Monday. Melissa needs to be back for school. You can always get hold of me though. Here's my card, it has my private cell and my email. Please excuse me if I don't get up to show you out but I'll get Jeeves to do it."

"Jeeves?" Alex and Phil questioned in perfect harmony.

"His real name is Hartley, but it's our little joke."

Chapter 13

Once back in the car, Alex turned to Phil. "If Mathewson was supplying underworld contacts with illegal whisky, then he must have been mixing with some very dangerous people. That industry is controlled by organised crime syndicates and the gang lords involved are not ones you'd want to mess with. If he'd welched on a deal or let someone down or if he'd let them get wind that he was pulling out of the business, then they'd have thought nothing of squashing him. This whole business is taking on an even nastier taste."

Before switching on the engine, both Alex and Phil checked their phones, recovering them from silent mode. Alex saw he had two missed calls from Sandra as well as a voice message. He pressed and held down the '1' key.

"Hi, Alex, I'm in the flat and it's great. I'm planning to go up and confront the neighbours soon and thought I'd just check in the unlikely event that you could be available." Alex checked the detail and saw the recording was made only three minutes before. He called back, and while it was ringing, he quickly got out and stood beside the car.

"It's great, Alex, it's just perfect."

"I can't chat just now, I'm outside Holbein's house and I've got Phil in the car. Hold on there for twenty minutes and I'll join you so you don't have to go upstairs alone. I'll go now, see you soon."

Without waiting for a reply, Alex clicked off then climbed back in the car and switched on the ignition, made a U-turn and retraced his earlier route.

Phil started, "I've had some feedback from the enquiries this morning. First, Stanley Burns is at home and will be in all afternoon so we could go there now if you want as we're already on the South Side."

"I'm afraid I've something to attend to first. I'll drop you back at the office and pick you up half an hour to an hour later, okay?"

"Sure thing. You're the boss. I'll grab a bite of lunch in between."

"You said 'firstly,' what else have you got?"

"Sorry, I nearly forgot. It's just a bit of feedback on the enquiries you asked me to make. Carpenter came up clean. No criminal record, not even a parking ticket. He's married with two children, both at primary school. He graduated with a 2/2 honours from St Andrews and then went to Jordanhill teacher training college. Eastfarm is his second teaching job and everything sounds kosher. He met his wife at TTC and she taught primary until their sprogs came along and then she packed it in. Her record is clean too. He plays badminton and table tennis at county standard and he's a keen chess player and helps coach in these activities at school."

"That's good, anything on the Connellys?"

"Oh yes, but they're not so squeaky clean."

"Tell me more."

"Paul Connelly's the father. He has half a dozen convictions ranging from car theft to aggravated assault. He's also under enquiry for making fraudulent benefit claims. He's served a bit of time, but that was several years ago for one of the assaults. Since then he only has sentences of community service. He's aged thirty-seven and never held down a proper job in his life. His wife, well, partner really because they've never been married, is Margaret Doherty. She's been done for shoplifting several times and on one occasion she made a claim of sexual assault against some guy who was interviewing her for a job. She didn't get the job, or any job as far as the records show. She applied for Legal Aid and found a lawyer to represent her, but the case was dropped before it came to court and there was suspicion that, on this and maybe other occasions, it was a scam. She makes some spurious claim against some poor sod and gets a payout not to drag him through the gutter."

"That sounds really helpful. It could be they're varying the formula and using the boy for the same scam. Did you get anything on their children?"

"Not a lot, because a lot of the records are inaccessible but there are two boys. Dean is aged thirteen and Sean is twelve. There are stories about both of them extorting money with threats of menace from other school kids. The reports date back from their previous school in Barrhead as well as Eastfarm. As far as I could tell, the young one, Sean, is the really evil one and the older one just follows his example. Another thing, there's a court case pending to have them evicted from their flat. Apparently they've never paid any rent and there are several other claims on them for bad debts. Did I do good or did I do good?"

"I couldn't have asked for more, well done."

The heavy clouds had cleared and blue could be seen in the sky. It was illuminated by a bright, if watery, winter sun. Alex dropped Phil outside Pitt Street and considered his best route to the West End to meet with Sandra. Although further in distance, he chose to take the Clydeside Expressway so as to avoid the heavy traffic on Dumbarton Road. This enabled him to travel most of the route at a steady fifty miles per hour instead of five. On the way he was able to appraise the advancing construction for the new Hydro Arena, the latest addition to the Scottish Exhibition and Conference Centre complex. Alex had read an article showing the new national arena would hold 12,000 fully seated and would be the largest entertainments venue in Scotland. In progress it looked like any other building site but with a structure comprising of large steel bones sticking out of the ground at strange angles. resembling a dinosaur skeleton.

Alex passed the main West End exit, instead coming off at Whiteinch and doubling back towards the city. In all it took less than ten minutes before he reached the flat and saw Sandra looking out for his arrival. He exited the car and approached the front entrance. He heard the buzz from Sandra remotely releasing the security entry system before he reached the door and was through it and up the stairs to meet her in a few seconds.

"I'd like to show you round but I know you're in a hurry so it can keep until later. Let's go up now. You know what I've got in mind."

Alex looked at Sandra approvingly, she was so clean and fresh and wholesome. He could smell soap and shampoo. She was slender and lithe, wearing skin tight jeans and a sweater which clung to her shape accentuating her curves. Alex said nothing: he just nodded and gave her hand a reassuring squeeze before she climbed the steps to the next floor. Alex followed, admiring her swift, sleek movements, then he took up his position to the side of the entrance. The door didn't look substantial. It appeared to be more the style of an internal, panelled door with a rough surface which had been badly painted in a light colour. This only fully masked the green underneath in places, but the whole surface was blotchy. The door frame itself was still a bottle green colour except where natural wood showed through with rough splinters. Alex reckoned that it must have been forced open, probably with a crowbar, on some previous occasion and white paint had been used in a futile attempt to cover up the worst of the effect. There wasn't a doorbell and instead a brass knocker was pinned to the middle.

Alex observed as Sandra loudly chapped the knocker. There was no response at first so she waited a few seconds then tried again. A dog yelped, then there was a muffled shuffling sound and what sounded like an exaggerated yawn, followed by a metallic click. A glimmer of light escaped through a small gap as the door was prised slightly open.

"Who are you and what do you want?"

"Good morning, my name's Sandra Mackinnon and I'm your new neighbour. I'm just moving in downstairs and I thought I'd come and introduce myself," she called enthusiastically.

There was a creak as the door was pulled fully open, revealing a man, aged in his early twenties and dressed only in boxer shorts. He was small of stature and slim, with sweaty, sandy coloured hair stuck to his brow and two or three days' growth of facial hair. He smelled stale. On seeing Sandra, his face lit up in a broad smile, but some of his front teeth were missing and those that remained were dirty and nicotine stained.

"I'm Mark, pleased to meet you, come on in. Sorry I'm not dressed yet, I've just woken up. I had a late night with a few friends round. We quite often have parties; maybe you'd like to join us?"

"Thanks for the invite," Alex called out and both he and Sandra pushed forward through the hallway and into a filthy and cluttered living area with discarded clothes covering a couch, the only designated seating in the room. A small but morbidly obese Jack Russell terrier was seated amongst the clothes looking up. The young man followed then craned his neck to look up at Alex fearfully. "I didn't see you there."

Alex left Sandra to do the talking.

"Yes, as I said I'm your new neighbour and this is my friend, Alex Warren, Detective Chief Inspector Alex Warren to you. I'm Detective Sergeant Sandra Mackinnon and yes, we are both in the police force. As you can imagine, we work very hard and we work long hours so we want to be able to get complete rest when we get home. Thank you for your kind invitation to your parties but we will not be accepting. We will also be expecting not to suffer any nuisance from any guests you might entertain or we'll hold you responsible. Do you understand?"

Mark just nodded, his mouth was open and his eyes were wide and terror stricken.

"There are a couple of other matters I want to mention while I'm here. First, there's a distinct smell of cannabis in this room and, unless I'm mistaken, that's what you've got in the bag on the table. I don't want to see it, I'm not in the drug squad and I'm not too interested in what damage individuals want to do to themselves, but if I have any trouble whatsoever from you, then I'll ensure some of my friends pay you a visit and keep a very close eye on you. The other matter is that I checked the back court this morning and it's full of dog poo. Now, I'm a dog lover as much as anyone else, but I'm not going to tolerate you allowing your pooch to mess up what's part of the common area. I'll give you until Sunday morning to have the area cleaned up and, if it's not or if you let your dog mess anywhere again without cleaning it up, then you're going to have some serious problems. Is that all abundantly clear?"

"But some of it wasn't my dog."

"Which means a lot of it was. I've given you my instructions."

Mark gave a kind of a nod. He was trembling and his knees were shaking. It wasn't from the cold.

"I didn't hear you. Is that all abundantly clear?"

"Yes," Mark replied mournfully.

Alex and Sandra left and went back down to her flat. She unlocked the door, "I don't know how I did that. Now, it's done I'm shaking like a leaf."

"Nowhere near as much as he is. You handled it perfectly."

"Will you come in?"

"I'd love to but I must get back. I'll catch up with you later."

"Thank you so much for coming, it gave me strength." Sandra threw her arms around Alex's neck and hugged closely, rubbing her cheek against his and nuzzling his ear.

"Alex enjoyed feeling the warmth of her body close to him. He lingered in the embrace for a few seconds then affectionately pinched her buttock as he moved back. "Just hold the mood until tonight. How's about I come over after work with a nice bottle of wine to christen the flat?"

"Sounds good to me, I'm not much of a cook, but I'll put something together so we can eat in."

"I can bring dessert as well."

"I'm relying on it," Sandra replied lewdly in a husky voice.

Alex shook his head as he skipped down to the car and jumped in. The suggestion of food made him realise he hadn't eaten anything yet and he foresaw a long afternoon's work stretching ahead. Sandra had never cooked for him before and he wasn't too sure what to expect. Maybe she was at gourmet level and kept it a secret and she had just been modest. On the other hand, he'd never before heard her talk about food. She may have been telling the truth and instant 'Pot Noodle' with toast would have been a challenge. He decided not to take too big a chance and he called ahead to Phil.

"Are you ready? I'm on my way back and it should take only ten or fifteen minutes. If you can, will you pick me up a sandwich?"

"No problem, Boss. Just tell me your order. I could go to the new bagel place round the corner. Oh, and something new. Anne Dixon called and suggested we'd want to speak to her and Connors, they have the ME's results from the PM and other tests they've done and thought we'd want to know right away."

"Ask Dixon if she and Connors can see us now. I'll be there in a few minutes then we can head over to see Stanley Burns. If you could get me a tuna melt, a Danish and a packet of cheese and onion crisps, I'll settle with you when I get back."

Alex clicked off and didn't pay too much heed to the speed limit as he raced back to his office.

On arrival, his guests had arrived for his meeting, his food was sitting on a plate and next to it was Styrofoam cup half-filled with steaming coffee.

He shook hands with Connor and Dixon. "Sorry about the rush but I'm on my way out to another interview. Have you offered our guests coffees, Phil?"

"He has, but we're not desperate enough to drink stuff from that machine," Connors replied. "After all, who'd be left to carry out the forensic tests on our remains?"

"Fair point," Alex replied. "Please excuse me eating but I haven't much time." He lifted a half bagel and bit through the squelchy cheese and tuna topping.

"No problem for us, although you might not feel like eating while we're discussing stomach contents," Connor continued with a flicker of a smile. "I'll let Anne give you the details as she was managing the department while I was away."

"Okay," Anne started, "to begin with we've tied down time of death to between midnight and one a.m. This is confirmed by body temperature together with digestion of stomach contents based on the time we understand he had his dinner. He had expensive taste. Unless we're mistaken, he started with smoked salmon then went on to have lobster thermidor and there was some fairly undigested clootie dumpling, at least that's what I've been told it's called. It was washed down with an ample amount of white wine, a Sancerre might have gone nicely, I'd speculate."

"All very enthralling but I don't think it takes us any further forward," Alex replied.

"No, but you may be happier with this. Mathewson was involved in sexual activity only a short while before his death."

Alex looked up at her, clearly now a lot more interested. "Can you tell us any more?"

"Yes, we detected a number of pubic hairs. His partner was female, white, blonde and likely to have been between the ages of eighteen and sixty."

"Can you be any more specific?"

"Would it help if I told you she was twenty-two, her hair was bleached platinum, green eyes, five foot six in height with a mole two inches above her left nipple and that she has a bunion on her right big toe."

Alex looked at her in amazement. "You have to be joking?"

"Yes, I have to be joking," Anne replied. "Forensics has advanced considerably over the last few years but we're not magicians. We can test pubic hairs and tell sex, race, true hair colour and stage of development – that is child, adult or elderly but not much more, unless you have the fictional equipment you see on CSI."

"Is there anything else?"

"Well yes, he'd been wearing a condom and the lubricant was consistent with the packets we found in his desk."

"So he practiced safe sex. That's about the only thing we've ascertained in his favour. What about the condom?"

"Well that's the strange thing. We didn't find one."

"That's a bit odd. Where did you look?"

"Everywhere that seemed realistic. It wasn't anywhere near the body. It wasn't left in any bins or cupboards. We checked the waste containers as well and no luck. We don't think it could have been flushed down the loo. It's not impossible but it's unlikely, we checked the plumbing and no sign of it."

"Well, maybe he had sex before coming back to the distillery?"

"That's possible. If it did happen on site then it raises the questions who with and how did they get in? Did he bring them in? Could they have killed him and then exited the same way they entered?

"On the other hand, did he have sex before coming on site? If so, he would have had to have taken the condom with him, which is quite possible because he may have been hoping to hitch up with Holbein. If that didn't happen, he wouldn't have had much time, which raises the questions of where, when and who with? Or could the person have followed him then killed him? In any event, the partner has to be a suspect. If the sex was on site, is it likely the partner would have removed the condom and taken it away? And if so, why? Unless they carried out the killing and wanted to remove evidence that they'd been there?"

"So it's a major priority to discover who he slept with?" Alex asked.

"Or didn't 'sleep' with to be more to the point," Phil added.

Ignoring the quip, Alex continued, "So that's given us something to go on. Is there anything else?"

"The usual routine tests and checks," Anne replied. "It'll all be in the formal report and you'll get that tomorrow. We thought you needed the information about the sex and the condom sooner rather than later."

"You're right, thank you very much. I can see why my good friend Connor, here, was so quick to hire you."

"Yeah, but I'm not so sure now it was a good decision. She said she wanted the job to learn from me. She's only been here for a few weeks and already she's close to overtaking me. I think she's going to be after my job next," Connor interjected.

"You've got no worries. It'll be a long time before that happens," Anne replied.

Chapter 14

Phil called ahead to let Stanley Burns know they were on their way and then Alex and Phil made for his car. He'd left it parked on a yellow lined space on Pitt Street outside Glasgow High School, thinking he'd only be a couple of minutes. In any event, their session had lasted a bit longer, and as Alex approached his vehicle he could see a green coloured piece of paper in a plastic wrapper pinned under his windscreen wiper.

"Bastard," he uttered, condemning his own laziness and stupidity in not taking time to park properly, rather than addressing anyone in particular. Phil looked over, a little bit concerned thinking he had done something to invoke Alex's wrath and fearful he may, for some reason, be made to take the brunt of his anger.

"It's okay," Alex uttered. "My own stupid fault." He couldn't help wondering if it was the same warden he had encountered the previous day and then again this morning, who'd finally been able to exact his revenge. He was annoyed to have to write off the sixty pounds fine for the sake of saving a few minutes. Even though he had been on police business, he knew he couldn't recharge the cost as the police could not be seen to condone his misdemeanour, even if it was incurred for their benefit. Alex lifted the plastic envelope and stuffed it in his pocket.

A short while later they arrived at Stanley's house in Newton Mearns. It was similar in age, size and shape to Alex's family home in Clarkston, only three or four miles away.

They made their way up the driveway and Alex pressed the bell. The door was answered by an Adonis-like creature. Only slightly smaller than Alex, he was broad shouldered with deeply bronzed skin. He had tightly-cropped, spiky blonde hair and a face which wouldn't have been out of place in an advert for razor blades or gents' toiletries. His muscles rippled as he moved and his tight fitting vest did nothing to hide his six pack physique.

"We've an appointment to see Stanley Burns," Alex offered, not certain who he was speaking to.

"Come in and grab a seat in there," came the reply, while pointing to an open door to their right.

Alex and Phil followed the direction then looked around at the minimalist and fastidiously clean room. The walls were even and cream coloured, complimenting the beech laminate flooring and the furniture was a simple red coloured, three-piece suite surrounding a low, beech coffee table. The only decoration was a large crystal vase sitting on the table, overflowing with dozens of daffodils which were all in full bloom. The heating was set at high and the room felt airless and claustrophobic.

They heard a voice from outside, "Stanley love, that's your guests arrived," then in an undertone loud enough for them to clearly hear, he added, "and they both look very dishy, even if they're not in uniform, especially the tall one." Returning back to a normal volume he continued, "Do you want me to hang around in case I'm needed, or should I head off for the gym?"

Alex didn't hear the response but the same voice went on, "Okay then, just so long as you're sure. I'll take the Harley and then you can drive down and join me when you're free." The door slammed and they heard footsteps outside the window and then the distinctive tone of a motor bike being started and revved before the engine noise faded into the distance.

No sooner had the last echo disappeared than a new figure appeared in the doorway.

"I'm Stanley Burns, I'm so sorry to have kept you, but I was getting changed so I was ready for the gym. I've sent Barry on ahead so we'll be free to talk, but can you tell me how long this will take because I've told him I'll meet him at Parkview as soon as we're finished." Stanley had the same initial appearance as his brother and the other male members of the Burns family, sharing the same facial shape and pronounced ears. However, that's where the resemblance stopped as his figure was wiry and muscular, no doubt maintained by his regular gym training sessions. He was also very camp and was dressed in loose fitting, turquoise-coloured track suit-shaped clothing. The fabric was shiny but didn't appear to be a cheap synthetic. It had a Chinese look about it with colourful embroidery around the cuffs and neck and it could possibly have been silk. "I have my gym gear underneath so I can change quickly," he explained. He raised his arm in greeting and his handshake was soft and moist, barely making contact.

Alex and Phil strained to stop themselves staring at his flamboyance as he sleekly glided across the room to approach a chair opposite them.

"Can I get you some fruit juice? I have some freshly squeezed orange if you'd like or there're other choices from a carton. I can't offer you any tea or coffee because I don't keep it in the house. I just can't stand caffeine, I think it's evil."

"And what do you think of whisky?" Alex enquired.

"I can't speak against it, it provides me with my standard of living, but I never touch it myself, I'm more into gin when I drink spirits."

"Thanks, but we're okay, besides we don't want to hold you back any more than we have to." Without waiting for Phil to react, Alex answered for them both.

As he spoke, Alex noticed movement near the floor and, as he looked down, he saw a beautiful, Siamese cat strolling arrogantly towards him. It was elegant, slim and stylish with a well muscled body and triangular head. Its colouration was seal point, its eyes almond-shaped and light blue, and it had large wide-based ears positioned more towards the side of its head. Alex was familiar with the expression of dogs frequently looking like their owners; in this case, he thought it could also apply to cats. Maybe, he pondered, it was more a case of pet owners choosing a breed with similar characteristics to themselves.

The cat stopped a few inches away, appraising the visitors encroaching on its territory and then, seeming to grant approval, it sidled first against the couch and then rubbed its side against Alex's leg.

Although fond of animals, Alex had never formed any close attachments to felines. He felt cats were too independent and were never truly domesticated. Dismissing having a cat as a pet, Alex felt that it was the cat which fostered its human associates and not the other way around. The human was trained to attend and care for the cat, but any returned show of affection was rare and could never be relied upon. A dog, by contrast, might not be as intelligent but was considerably more likely to be loyal and loving.

Phil lifted a tissue from his pocket and dabbed at his eyes which were watering profusely. "I'm sorry, Mr Burns, but I'm allergic to cats, could you possibly ask it to leave."

Burns looked at Phil as if he'd just stepped from another planet but then relented and picked up his beloved pet. "Come on, Sheba, I'll take you next door," he said while stroking its back and placing tiny kisses to the rear of its head.

Alex resumed the conversation, "I take it you'll already have heard about your brother-in-law?"

"Well, sort of. I heard he was found dead in the distillery, but that's as much as I know. Georgina called to tell me."

"We don't know too much more ourselves, yet. We're still trying to piece together who's who and what might have happened. I'd like you to help us by telling us what you know."

"I'm happy to give you any help that I can."

"Well, let's start by asking when you last saw Hector?"

"I'm not sure, it must be over a week now. Yes, that's right, it was at a board meeting last Wednesday."

"Where was that?"

"It was in the board room, in Benlochy. The meeting lasted until about one in the afternoon, then we had lunch, then I went home."

"Where did you go for lunch?"

"We didn't go anywhere. It was served in the board room. We bring in outside caterers. They're very good. I can give you their number if you'd like, I can even tell you their menu."

"Thank you, but I don't think that will be necessary. Have you seen any other members of the family since the meeting?"

Stanley paused for a moment's thought. "No I haven't. Georgina came to a gallery I was exhibiting at, but that was the previous Sunday."

"So do you keep in close contact?"

"With Georgina? I suppose so. I was the baby of the family. Georgie's six years older and Quentin eight. Georgie always looked out for me."

"What about your parents?"

"I was very close to my mother but she first took ill when I was still in my teens. She had a chronic heart condition and it eventually killed her about ten years ago." Stanley's eyes looked sad and watery. "My father, by contrast, was unemotional and uncompromising. It was always his way or no way. Mother protected me when I was young, but after she became ill, it took all her strength to look after herself. Georgie helped a bit."

"And what about Quentin?"

Stanley's face went stiff. "Quentin and I don't get along."

"What do you mean?"

"Quentin was always cruel, even worse than father. It started when I was young. I think he knew I was gay even before I did. He teased me mercilessly and he made a fool of me at every opportunity. He belittled me in front of Mother and Father and Father let him get away with it, he even encouraged him."

"Does he still bully you?"

"He doesn't get a chance any more. Mostly I stay out of his way, but added to that, he's afraid of Barry. Barry and I have been together for a few years now. When we first met, he was a Tae Kwon Do champion and it scared the shit out of Quentin. He doesn't keep it up now as he injured his knee but Quentin still keeps a distance."

"Is it because of Quentin that you don't take an active part in the business?"

"It's the main reason, I don't even like being in his company. He still taunts me. I'm an adult but he still has a way of making me feel small and inadequate."

"But you attend the board meetings?"

"Yes, I'm fairly good at understanding what's going on and I do participate in decisions. I've a right to be there as I'm a shareholder and a trustee for the family trust. What's more, I like to be there because I know it annoys Quentin. He can't stand the fact that his faggot baby brother has a vote that carries the same weight as his."

"I can see how that might work. How did you get along with Hector?"

"We tolerated each other. I never liked the way he treated Georgie and I told him so on more than one occasion, but other than that he was okay with me. He made sure I received my salary and dividends."

"Can you tell me where you were on Wednesday night through until Thursday morning?"

"Barry and I went out for a meal and then onto the theatre in Glasgow. After that we went home and stayed in. We got back about eleven o'clock, maybe a little bit later."

"Where did you go to eat?" Alex enquired, wondering if his path could have crossed Hector and Chuck.

"We went to the Barolo Grill in Mitchell Lane. Why?"

"Did you know Hector was in town? He was dining at the Rogano. It's in Exchange Place; it can't be more than a hundred yards from the Barola."

"No, I didn't know. Does it make a difference?"

"It might, he was dining with Chuck Holbein."

"What? Holbein from Hanser? Why?"

"I don't think you need me to answer that."

"There's been some talk that Hector was looking to sell us out, but I thought it was all gossip. Did my father know about this?"

"As for your father knowing, you'd be best to speak to him yourself. From your reaction, it's apparent that you weren't aware of any sales discussions. Is that right?"

"I knew nothing about it."

"We were led to believe it was discussed at your board meetings. Maybe we should check the minutes."

"No, I was never told, but maybe it wouldn't be such a bad thing," Stanley mused. "But where does this leave the deal, with Hector dead?"

"As far as I'm aware there hasn't been a deal."

"I'll maybe give Georgie a call and see what she knows."

"Yes, maybe do that. She might appreciate your help arranging the funeral as well."

Alex's sarcasm was lost on Stanley.

"Yes, I'd better call her and see what I can do," Stanley replied.

Alex felt they had exhausted their enquiries, for the time being at least. He thanked Stanley for his cooperation and left with Phil to return to the car. By the time they were seated, Phil's nose was streaming and his eyes were red and blotchy. "I wish I'd known beforehand, I'd have taken some anti-histamine."

Chapter 15

Although it was a cold day, they completed the drive from Newton Mearns to Glasgow city centre with the windows open and the ventilation fan on full so Phil could inhale fresh air, or as close as they could get to some with the abundance of petrol and diesel fumes. At any rate, the combination seemed to help and by the time they'd returned to Pitt Street, Phil was breathing normally again and his eyes and nose had stopped streaming.

They returned to their office, on the way discussing the stage they'd reached in the investigation.

"There could be organised crime involvement here. Should we bring in the specialist teams?" Phil enquired.

"You're right about there being involvement with illegal whisky distribution and yes we need to keep our people in the loop, but I'm certain the godfathers weren't responsible for killing Mathewson. If they thought Mathewson was at it, then they wouldn't have taken care of him in such a simple fashion. They'd have wanted a more spectacular killing so as to make a public statement. That way everyone would be warned not to mess with them. A single blow to the head is not their style."

"So where do we go from here?"

"I don't know about you but I've got a load of paperwork to catch up on. What's more I'm leaving at the back of five. I've an appointment out on the South Side at six. In the meantime, I need you to check anything new that's come in and ensure all the admin has been correctly completed. Look over all the interview data, ensure it's been correctly transcribed, signed off and filed. Check records on the evidence collected so far, make sure it's tagged and transportation has been recorded to show there's no chance of cross contamination. That should keep you busy for a while."

Alex was feeling totally exhausted. He closed his office door and sat down at his desk. He folded his arms and lay his head down for a moment's rest. Thinking a short catnap would re-energise him, he closed his eyes. The ringtone from Alex's mobile startled him back to life in what he imagined was only an instant later. He didn't immediately recognise the caller's ID and he inhaled deeply, wanting to ensure he didn't sound too drowsy. Spotting the clock on the screen, Alex was stunned to see that he must have been unconscious for approaching half an hour. In frustration, he shook his head while pressing the receive button.

"Warren."

"Hello, Alex. It's Simon here. This is just a courtesy call to let you know that we're releasing Abdallah. We don't have enough to ensure a successful prosecution and we don't want the bad press we'd get from a failed one. Everyone would be after us. The Asian groups and leftists would criticise us for racism and all the Daily Mail readers would have a go at us for incompetence in not putting him away."

"I can't say I'm happy but at least I was prepared for it after our talk yesterday. I'm certain he was involved and not just involved, I think he led it. I guess our only chance is if the others throw him in it and I can't see that happening."

"In that case, we will just have to wait until you can pin something else on him, and I wish you luck."

Alex spent the little time he had left filing reports and catching up on his emails. He wanted to ensure he didn't arrive late, so he gave himself plenty of time to travel to his meeting. He arrived on Clarkston Road with ten minutes to spare. There were about a dozen parking bays in the small cul-de-sac at the side of the pub but every one of them was taken. Clarkston Road on this side had double yellow lines and parking was restricted at peak times on the opposite side. Alex wasn't prepared to risk another parking ticket by leaving his car where it could be booked so instead he drove on to Sainsburys', which was only a hundred yards beyond, and found a space in their car park. As a customer, he'd be allowed up to two hours of free parking and it was his intention to be a customer after his meeting.

Alex crossed to the Bank and checked first to ensure Brian hadn't already arrived. The pub was aptly named, having previously served the local community as a savings bank. Following mergers, it was closed and had lain empty for several years before being extended and refurbished then re-opening as a pub/restaurant. The outside had an ornately carved stone frontage befitting its former status and the inside had been modernised, modifying its former austerity into a fashionable meeting place. Alex approached the bar and ordered a pint of soda water with lime. He found a vacant barstool and tried to relax, sipping the refreshing drink. Ten minutes later Brian arrived. They greeted each other warmly and shook hands enthusiastically.

"What'll you have to drink?" Alex offered.

"A Guinness for me, thanks."

"Guinness? I thought you were always a lager man."

"Times change, and besides, you know the old saying, 'If the bottom's falling out of your world and you want to reverse it, then drink Guinness.' "

"I've not heard that one. I've heard the ad that 'Guinness is good for you,' but not that it's life changing. Don't tell me they've proven it has beneficial medicinal effects?"

"Not at all, what I'm talking about is a play on words. Instead of the bottom falling out of your world, the world falls... Well, you know? It works even better if you have a curry as well."

"Too much information. I hope that's not the sort of thing you're teaching the kids. Anyway, I should have seen it coming. I'm a bit slow today."

"That's not like you Alex."

"I suppose, I've just got a lot on my mind. I'm supervising three ongoing cases, one's a big one that's just started, as well as a dozen or so closed cases waiting to go to court and one of them's just gone pear shaped."

"Tell me more?"

"I'd love to, but if I did I'd have to shoot you."

"What do you mean, I thought you were CID, not Special Branch or MI5, or is it MI6?"

"Take your pick, but yes I'm just CID. I still can't talk about an open investigation, though."

"I'm pretty knackered myself, after another week looking after all these brats."

"Before you drop yourself in any deeper, I think you need to remember that two of these brats are my sons."

"Well that being the case, I shouldn't need to explain anything to you. Fair enough, they mostly are good kids but even the best of them have their moments. Okay, what did you want to see me about?"

"Let's get a table it will be a bit more private."

For early on a Friday evening, the pub was unusually quiet. Normally the bar would be teaming with commuters dropping in for a drink or two at the end of the week before returning home. There was also normally a steady stream of customers looking for reasonably priced snacks and meals as an alternative to slaving over a hot stove.

Brian looked around him and spotted a couple of empty tables which he suggested to Alex.

"No, let's go upstairs. This place is bound to fill up soon."

Brian drained his glass. "Time for another quick one if you're game?"

"No, I'm still fine. I have the car with me so I'm on soft drinks at the moment. I'm planning to make up for it later."

"Your choice," Brian replied and ordered a refill to his drink before following Alex up to the mezzanine area and settling into a table overlooking the main bar area. The upper floor was warm and stuffy so they both removed their jackets and hung them from the backs of their chairs.

"This is serious. You want to see me at short notice, you want privacy and you're not drinking alcohol."

"Hey, I'm meant to be the detective here. It sounds like you've gone back to reading Conan-Doyle."

"I can't go back to what I never stopped," Brian replied, a broad grin splitting his face.

"The only reason I'm not drinking is that I've got the car, like I said before. I suspect you can guess what this is about," Alex continued. "I'm aware there's an alleged problem with one of your staff."

"Forget the alleged, there's a problem with most of my staff."

"Carpenter?"

"Ah. Now that's no joking matter." Brian demeanour changed, the ever-present smile left his face. "What's your interest?"

"I told you this would be off the record. It's a private matter for me. Carpenter's Andrew's teacher and he sees him as being on a pedestal like some kind of god."

"And you want to know what he's really like and if Andrew's been at any risk?"

"No, that's not it. I know Andrew well enough and I can trust his judgement. He's upset about what's happened and I'm looking to find out more and see if there's any way I can help. Of course, I want to ask about the arrangements for attending the Maths Challenge prize-giving as well, but that's just a practical issue."

"The prize-giving is the easy one. There are four kids involved and Mrs Rankine will take them through to Paisley. As for Jimmy Carpenter, you're right, Andrew does have sound judgement. Jimmy's a very good teacher and one of the nicest guys I know. His wife and my Trisha are quite close friends too. 'God-like' might be carrying it a bit far, but I'd say he's one of the best loved and most valued teachers we have. He's good at his job, he gets excellent results and he can cope well with the mischief makers. Well, he could up until now. There's never been the slightest hint of any issues with his behaviour, and if you'd asked me to name teachers we could have allegations made against, I reckon he'd be about the last one to add to the list."

"That's pretty much the feedback I've had from my own people. What about the complainant?"

"Ah, now that's a whole different ball park. Sean Connelly is bad news all round. A complete little toe rag – no, worse than that, he's an evil little bastard." Brian looked around him to check he was out of earshot of anyone else. "The whole story, as far as I know it, is that he joined the school last summer. He'd been at Barrhead before, but because he moved into the area he was given a placement. He's been nothing but trouble since he arrived. He disrupts classes and he bullies other kids. He's known to be involved in thefts and extortion but we've never had any evidence that would stick. The other kids involved have been too scared of him to make a formal statement. Even some of the teachers are scared of him."

"Can't you do anything about it?"

"Not without hard evidence, I hardly need to explain to you. He's had countless warnings, particularly for the lesser problems, and in the good old days, he'd have been expelled long before now, but you know what the system is like. He needs to be caught red handed for something pretty serious before we can even give a temporary exclusion.

"The worst part is that now he's made this allegation, he's made himself almost bomb proof. While the enquiry is ongoing, he can just about get away with murder. If we're seen to take any action against him, then it could be interpreted that we're picking on him because he's made a complaint, so we'll have to treat him with kid gloves, if you'll excuse the pun."

"Shit, that's the last thing I wanted to hear."

"Let me assure you, Alex, it's the last thing we want too. As I understand it, he's made a formal, criminal complaint. That means your people are involved, but I'd be amazed if it went anywhere. However, the education department enquiry is something else. Poor Jimmy's been suspended, and while that goes on, the wee bastard turns up for school every day to rub our noses in it. To any outsider looking in, it appears as if Jimmy must be guilty because of the way it's being handled.

"There's a rumour going round that the Connelly's are at risk of being evicted from their flat and this whole charade is a concoction to fight against it. They think they can argue to the court that it would be too unfair and upsetting for the boy's life to be disrupted when he's already gone through the trauma of being sexually assaulted. Do you reckon that could work?"

"In theory, there should be no chance. Provided there are grounds for eviction, there's a legal contract and the papers have been properly served, then the outcome should be automatic, but there's a lot of 'ifs' in there and you know what it's like when you get a smart lawyer and an indecisive Sheriff. It shouldn't affect the outcome but it might stretch the timescales."

"Even if he does get evicted, then he has to go somewhere. The family would be unlikely to get replacement accommodation close by. But even if they're moved a distance away, the wee swine could apply for an out of area placement so he can keep going to the same school. His family aren't likely to put themselves out, but I can just imagine the Council paying for taxis to bring him in."

"It's not the news I was hoping for, but I can't say I'm too surprised."

"The saddest part is he's a really intelligent child and he's full of energy. If it could only be channelled in the right direction, he could do really well. We've tried and tried but he's not interested in bettering himself, well, not by legitimate means."

"So it won't be a 'Good Will Hunting' story with a happy ending?"

"Christ, no. More like 'City of God.'"

"It's such a pity, if only kids like that had some order, some discipline, then maybe they could turn out okay. Maybe bringing back National Service would help?"

"Yeah, brilliant idea, Alex. The evil little bastards aren't bad enough already, you want to teach them how to fight and use weapons?"

"Okay, fair point, but it could work for a lot of them."

"Sure, and the ones it didn't work for would kill us in our beds. Still, it would be good for business for you."

Brian caught sight of his watch and jumped to his feet.

"Oh bugger, I'm running late. I'll need to get going. We ought to get together more often. It's good to catch up and have a natter. We still can't put the world to right any more than we could when we were at Uni, but we can have a bloody good moan. I'll call you if I hear anything new," and with that he grabbed his jacket and fled down the stairs and out the door.

Alex sat for a couple of minutes longer reassembling his thoughts and wondering what he could possibly say to Andrew which wasn't as jaundiced as he was currently feeling about the system. He remembered he was now off duty and was planning to take a lot of the weekend off. There was some work he'd planned for Saturday morning, but he had tickets to take Craig and Andrew to a football game in the afternoon and keep them with him overnight. Sunday was as yet unplanned and might depend on the progress of the Mathewson case. To start his weekend, Alex was invited to spend the evening with Sandra in her new flat.

He wanted to buy her a flat warming present but didn't know what she might need or want, so he deferred that decision until he had carried out the research and had more time. For this evening, he had promised to bring wine and dessert and he dashed across to Sainsburys thinking he would find what he was looking for there.

First he located a bottle of Moet, believing champagne was the best start for the celebration. While he was in the wine section, he spotted a familiar label, it was 'Longue Dog', a rich fruity red from the Languedoc region. Alex remembered Sandra talking about her parents owning a second home in the region and her raving about the excellent quality of food and wine when she'd visited them there. He added this to the basket and went in search of something sweet. Maintaining the French theme, he located a delicious looking Tarte au Citron, and to complement it, he added a tub of fresh blueberries and a carton of double cream. He quickly spun round to the aisle which held stationary, and after a few minutes searching, he located a tasteful greetings card with the message 'Welcome to Your New Home.' He then moved back to the doorway and chose a bunch of a dozen red roses. Satisfied with his selection, he walked towards the checkouts. It was a small supermarket and being a quiet time of day there was only one checkout operator on duty and a queue of three people waiting to be attended. Realising he only had seven items and seeing there were four self-service automatic checkout locations, of which two were empty, Alex went directly there to save time. He scanned the barcodes and found himself so irritated by the recorded instructions telling him what to do that he started talking back to the machine. Only when he had completed his transaction and loaded his bags did he realise the champagne had a security tag on it. He watched the queue of people he'd avoided all complete their purchases and leave the store while he marked the minutes going by, standing, having had to call and wait for an assistant to come and remove the tag so he didn't trigger the shoplifter alarms when he exited the shop.

Alex raced the couple of miles back to his flat and was lucky to find a vacant parking space immediately outside the entranceway. He lifted his bag of goodies and ran up and opened the door. In keeping with what he'd told Brian, he was anticipating imbibing in alcoholic refreshment and, not wanting to be burdened by his vehicle, he phoned for a taxi asking to be picked up from his address in twenty minutes time. He discarded his clothes, leaving them where they fell and dived under the shower. He then had a very quick shave and cleaned his teeth before locating a fresh, casual shirt, sweater and chinos. He just had time to gather his work clothes into a laundry basket before his mobile rang announcing the taxi's arrival. Lifting his wallet and his jacket, he dashed out, and was halfway down the stairs before he remembered the 'goody' bag. He raced back to collect it and at the same time picked up a pen so he could write a message on the card while travelling.

Chapter 16

Alex checked his watch and saw it was approaching eight-fifteen as the taxi pulled up outside Sandra's flat. He had hoped to make it by eight but, all in all, he felt he'd done quite well.

He pressed the button on the entry system and was about to announce his arrival, but there was a buzz and the door opened almost immediately.

He resisted his first inclination to bound up the stairs, instead taking them at a steady pace and preserving more of his strength.

Sandra's front door was already open before he reached the first floor and she was standing just inside. Alex caught his breath at the vision. She was wearing a fine velvet evening gown. It was azure blue in colour which perfectly matched her eyes. It hung from one shoulder and clung to her slender, athletic figure as if it was a second skin. In length it came far below her knee but had a slit along the side rising to halfway up her thigh and, from the angle Alex was approaching, he was treated to the sight of her shapely leg. Sandra's rich dark hair was shining, having been freshly washed, and although she was wearing hardly any make up, Alex detected the slight waft of Angel perfume. He recollected the fragrance as Helen had purchased it once, but it hadn't suited her, whether because of her natural body oils or her character, but the delicate flowery sweetness just didn't seem right. On Sandra, however, it was perfect. She was wearing high heels and Alex could see her toenails had been varnished and he could tell she wasn't wearing tights or stockings. Alex's eyes opened wide and he consciously had to stop his jaw from dropping. He'd never seen Sandra clothed in anything other than either casual or work-wear before and he was completely captivated by her appearance. He stopped, frozen, a couple of steps from the landing and just gazed at her in admiration.

Sandra, thinking he was play acting, laughed at his reaction. "Cat got your tongue?" she enquired while reaching down for Alex's hand to guide him inwards to the flat. "Mind you, from what I've heard, cat's already had some impact on Phil, maybe not his tongue, just his eyes and nose."

Alex partially recovered his senses. "I'm sorry, you caught me unaware. I've never seen you in a dress before."

"I can take it off if it makes you feel more comfortable."

"I'm not joking, you are stunningly beautiful, and as you know I don't give complements lightly."

Sandra's smile in response was beaming. "Well, thank you, kind sir," she leaned over and gently brushed her lips across his. Although it wasn't a passionate kiss, it was comfortable and right for the moment, betraying their true closeness. "Now, come on in and I'll show you round."

The flat was warm and comfortable and Alex slipped off his jacket and hung it on a hook in the hallway, also depositing his bag before progressing.

Sandra led Alex through the lounge, kitchen and bathroom pointing out how excellently appointed and decorated the flat was. Their tour continued as she swung open the door to the bedroom. The dark drapes were already drawn over shutting out the darkness. Within, the room was brightly, if plainly, decorated and it had built-in, teak coloured wardrobes and a free standing dressing table. Alex's suspicions were confirmed when he looked on this and saw amongst an assemblage of cosmetics there was a bottle of Angel. Against the opposite wall was a king-size bed already made up with pillows and a duvet. The pillow cases, duvet cover and sheets were all black satin and looked soft, comfortable and alluring.

Remembering his bag, Alex stated, "I've brought some things."

"Oh, your overnight clothes, just hang them in a cupboard."

"No, I brought some wine and stuff. I didn't bring an overnight bag. I wasn't expecting…" the missing words hung in the air.

"I didn't know if you would, but in case you decide to, I bought some disposable razors, foam and a spare toothbrush you can keep here. Extra hard, okay?" Sandra winked and reached over to stroke the side of Alex's face. She brought her face closer and this time their embrace lacked no intensity. Their bodies collided in a lustful hug and their lips attached then they used their teeth and tongues to explore each other's faces, necks and ears. Their shapes moulded together as their arms encircled each other with hands roaming over backs and limbs. They could feel the warmth emanating from each other's bodies and Alex could feel Sandra's firm breasts pressed against his chest. From the sensation, he was certain she wasn't wearing a bra. Squeezing her back and pulling her even closer to him, he was left in no doubt and he luxuriated in the heat from the closeness of their skins.

It was several seconds before Sandra came up for air, enquiring in a mimicked child-like voice, "What have you brought me?"

Alex recovered his bag from the hall, first presenting the flowers. "Here's a card to welcome you to your new home and some flowers to brighten the place, not that they're needed." Digging deeper, he extracted the dessert.

"Mmm, that looks yummy," Sandra acknowledged.

"And now so you can celebrate," Alex lifted the champagne then said, "or if you'd like to have this with dinner?" The bottle of red wine followed.

"My, my, Mr Policeman. I think you might be trying to get me drunk."

"No, no," Alex replied defensively. "I didn't mean you had to drink them all at once."

"Well, we'll see. You open the bubbly and I'll find us some glasses." Alex followed Sandra into the kitchen, tearing off the foil wrapper and detaching the wire cover as he walked.

Sandra produced two 'ballons' and stated, "These will have to do, I don't have champagne flutes."

"I'm sure they'll be absolutely fine," Alex prized the cork upwards until, with a loud pop it, exploded suddenly from the bottle, bounced off the ceiling and the kitchen units then fell spinning a couple of times before coming to rest on the floor. As Alex watched the cork's movements, frothy liquid flowed out and cascaded down the side of the bottle.

"Damn, I didn't have time to chill it properly," he cursed as he reached across to fill the glasses, hoping to minimise the loss from liquid escaping. The green tinged, bubbly liquid frothed out and quickly filled the glass.

Sandra laughed gleefully as Alex filled the second glass. She lifted one, clinked it off the other and called, "Here's to us," before swallowing a mouthful. The effervescence bubbled in her mouth and throat and she coughed a couple of times while simultaneously laughing.

Alex raised his glass in the air and toasted, "Here's wishing you everything you want for yourself and good luck in your new home," before swallowing a mouthful and following Sandra's example.

As Alex lifted the bottle to refill their glasses, they heard a bang followed by a loud scuffing noise from the flat above. They both looked upwards as if they expected to use X-ray vision to see through to what was happening.

"I'd better check it out while I'm still sober enough," Alex volunteered.

"I'll come with," Sandra replied.

"No, you wait, I'll handle this, just listen out at the door."

Alex's appearance had become slightly dishevelled from their intimate embrace and he straightened his clothes as he walked.

By the time he reached the upper floor, he was happier that he looked sufficiently sombre and threatening. He was about to hammer on the door when he realised it was slightly ajar so instead pushed it open another few inches. In the hallway, he could see three black bin sacks overflowing with clothes, bedding, DVD's and other unrecognisable paraphernalia, and beside them sat a microwave oven and a ghetto-blaster style music centre. Alex clipped the knocker and his voice boomed out, "Hey, anyone in there? What's going on?" Judging from the size and shape of the hallway, the flat was the same as Sandra's apartment below. Unlike Sandra's it was dark and dingy and unwelcoming.

A head popped out from what Alex judged to be a bedroom door. "Yeah, what is it?" It was the same young man he'd seen earlier in the day. He had a worried look on his face. He stepped into the hall and was followed by two others. One of them was holding a knife.

"We heard a lot of noise from downstairs, what's going on?"

"Nothing for you to worry about, we're just packing up and moving out."

Alex kept his gaze on the lad with the knife, carefully monitoring his movements.

"I think you should put that down, Son, before someone gets hurt."

The boy said nothing but withdrew back into the bedroom.

"Where are you going?"

"I'm just moving in with my mates for the time being."

"You'd better leave me your forwarding address. Your landlord might need to contact you."

"What's it to you? I'll be seeing the agent," he replied unconvincingly.

Alex said nothing. He just raised his eyebrows and remained where he was, looking menacing.

"It's just along the road in Scotstoun, Larchfield Avenue."

"Number?"

"67, opposite the Kingsway flats."

"That's okay then. Make sure you don't take anything that doesn't belong to you and keep the noise down. How are you getting there?"

"We've got the wee, blue van downstairs."

"Did you clean up the mess out back yet?"

"I'm moving out, I don't need to."

"That's where you're wrong. Sergeant Mackinnon gave you until Sunday to clean it up so you have all day tomorrow before we come looking for you. Do I make myself understood?"

The boy nodded miserably.

Alex took careful note of the appearance of the three lads and then went downstairs and out the front of the building to write down the van's description and registration before returning satisfied, to find Sandra standing in her doorway.

"That was a good job done. It took you less than twelve hours to get rid of him and now you have your perfect flat and at an enormous discount. The only problem I see is that upstairs will likely need a bit of renovation so there could be a bit of noise and to'ing and fro'ing while that goes on, but hopefully you'll get some decent neighbours as a result."

They listened and watched for the next few minutes as the boys loaded up the van and then drove off.

"I put a stopper in the bottle. Hopefully it won't have lost too much fizz."

Alex tried to judge if he should interpret her words literally of whether she was alluding to the lost spontaneity of their evening, after the interruption. He needn't have worried, for as he turned to reopen the bottle and refill the glasses, he felt her hands on his shoulders and the ever so gentle embrace of Sandra's lips on the back of his neck.

He slowly moved to return the caress. "Maybe we should leave the wine for later."

Sandra eased slightly away, "No, we have the whole evening, go ahead and pour and I'll get us some food. I'm famished. There's a few business matters we need to discuss as well, so maybe we should get that all out of the way first then we'll be able to sit and relax."

"I don't like the sound of that, but you're right, we should deal with anything we have to first and then our time will be our own. While we're dealing with serious matters, there's some important things we need to discuss."

The smile disappeared from Sandra's face. "Should I be worried?" she asked.

"No way, but I'd like us to discuss where we're going. Maybe this is the worst time to bring this up. We're meant to be having a celebration."

"We'll still be having our celebration, don't you worry, but you've started something and there's no putting the genie back in the bottle. Now pour us some more bubbly and I'll get our starters out of the fridge."

Alex did as he was asked and sat at the table as Sandra placed a plate in front of each of them along with cutlery. She then sat a salad bowl between them, stacked with mixed green leaves, cherry tomatoes and thinly sliced pieces of red pepper. A slab of pâté was then produced along with a jar of epicurean onion marmalade and a plate of rough oatcakes. The table was completed when she added bottles of balsamic vinegar, virgin olive oil and matching battery operated mills to freshly grind sea salt and black pepper.

"Would you like butter or Flora with it?"

"No, I'm fine with it just as it is. This looks really good."

"And easy too. I knew I wouldn't have a lot of time so I just popped into Morrisons on the way home." Realising the meaning of her own words, Sandra smiled then added, "And it is my home now. It feels right".

Alex smiled back, genuinely pleased to see her so content. He looked closely at the crockery and cutlery and saw they were good quality, Denby and Viners respectively. "I wanted to buy you a housewarming present but I'll need to be inventive, you seem to have everything you need."

"Yes, you have to remember I had a flat years ago, with my then partner. I bought or was gifted everything I needed back then. When the relationship broke up, I packed all my stuff away in my parents' basement so it was all ready for me when I needed it. There's nothing I need so don't bother thinking about a gift. You've already brought the champers and the flowers."

Alex cut a slice of pâté and lifted it onto his plate then added the accompaniments.

"The pâté's a Forestiere with wild mushrooms, I think you'll like it."

Alex thickly spread one cracker then he bit into it. The oatcake broke apart in his hand and he clumsily managed to cram the crumbling pieces into his mouth. "Yes, it's delicious," he managed to splutter with his mouth half full.

Sandra lifted some food to her own plate. "Okay, out with it. What's on your mind?"

Alex swallowed another mouthful of wine to give him courage.

"You know I really care about you."

"Oh Christ, where's this going? Is this the big push off?"

"No, no, certainly not. I care for you and I want to be with you. I want to take you out, to date you, but the way things are, we can't do that."

"What are you saying?"

"We're both police and that isn't an issue, but we work in the same department and on the same cases and you work under me and that's not acceptable."

"Would you rather I worked on top of you? No sorry, I shouldn't be joking."

Alex tried to ignore the comment but his face was creased, unable to hide his amusement.

"If the top brass find out, then we'll both be in trouble, particularly me as I'll be seen to be taking advantage of a subordinate. It's not right that we should be working together if we have an intimate personal relationship. You know the rules, the risk of collusion and all that tosh."

"Well, what can we do?"

"There's no easy answer. We both love our jobs, we're both ambitious and neither of us would want it to change."

"Can't we go on as we are?"

"I don't think that would work either. People are bound to suspect. I'm sure they already do suspect. Even Craig was asking me questions about you being my girlfriend. We can't keep it a secret much longer, and besides, I don't think it's fair to you, to either of us. We should be able to go out and about together, to mix with other couples, and if things work out I'd like you to meet the boys properly and not be hiding from them. I'd like to meet your family too."

"You might think differently if you do. So what's the answer?"

"There's not a simple one. Maybe if one of us was to get a transfer."

"But I enjoy working with you and the rest of the team. Mind you, if I'm to get my promotion to Inspector, I'll most likely have to move anyway. I've already turned down an opportunity to move back to uniform because I don't want to leave CID. I could maybe move to a different unit."

"I don't want you to move either, but it might be the only solution and it may be the best thing for your career as well. There could be some new opportunities coming up with the Forces unification."

"How do you mean?"

"You're already only too well aware of the havoc that's going on. From next April, Scotland will have one police force, merging the eight constabularies. You can see all the bitching and backstabbing that's going on in the top corridors as they're jostling for position. Strathclyde and Lothian each think they're entitled to rule the roost but who's to say what might happen and where the new top man will come from. There's a fair chance someone totally new could be foisted over the top."

"Do you think it will be an improvement?"

"In the long term, yes, it has to make sense and be more efficient to have one set of systems over the whole country and it will allow for more specialisation. In the short term though, I can see difficulties because each area has its own systems and methods and they need to be made able to talk to each other. There's the other problem of personal egos and individuals wanting to keep control of their own petty kingdoms. That's why I think there might be opportunities, there has to be some slimming down at the top, but there needs to be a lot of people working on the consolidation and anyone involved in that will have more opportunity to get seen and known. Look out for any positions being advertised in that area. I don't know where they might be based though."

"I don't want to move away, I've only just found this flat. Besides, if I moved away, how would we be able to be together?"

"Let's just take this slowly and carefully."

While talking, they'd devoured the rest of the food on the table and finished the champagne.

Alex leaned across and put his hand over Sandra's and gently squeezed. In response, she intertwined her fingers. "We have tonight with no restrictions and nobody to look out for. We don't even have to worry about disturbing the neighbours," she chuckled. "Now, you've brought another bottle so I'll get you a corkscrew to open it and I've slices of Country Pork Pie to put out as well. Would you like it hot or cold?"

"Cold is good for me and don't bother with the corkscrew because it's a metal screw cap. Only the best."

"Okay, most bottles are screw tops or synthetic corks now. When I've holidayed with my folks in France, we would go along to the wine shop or cooperative with our own containers and they would fill them up with locally produced wine out of a barrel, at prices starting at not much more than a euro a litre. Most people use three or five litre plastic tanks. The wine tastes really good too, although it doesn't travel well or keep very long. It doesn't get a chance to anyway. There's so much stupid snobbery with wine and you get some people claiming that it should always have a real cork. I remember reading that as many as a third of the bottles sealed with cork are infected and the wine tainted."

"Yeah, I've read that too. Listen, you said you'd something to discuss about the case. Let's get all the business out of the way and then we can enjoy ourselves."

"Sounds good to me. There have been a few developments since you left this afternoon. Nothing too earth-shattering, but you never know where it might lead to.

"First of all, we're meeting in the office tomorrow at ten to compare notes, brainstorm what we have and identify who does what next.

"Now, the new things we have. Donny has been working in Pitt Street and carrying out some background research. He has Mathewson's mobile and he's been going through the address book and linking the names and he's also been checking the activity on the phone log."

"Okay, standard checks, what's he come up with?"

"Everything and everyone you'd expect, various members of the family and managers, some employees and various other business contacts from the industry and the local community. Chuck Holbein was in it and the dates and times tied in with what we might have expected from what she'd told us. However, he found there was also a number of calls both received and made to another number. It turned out to be a Mister Yakimoto, or should that be Yakimoto san, I've never been too knowledgeable on Japanese titles."

"You don't need to be, Mister will do, and if he doesn't like it then too bad. Who is he?"

"He's the International Commercial Director of Teiko, they're a large, fast growing Japanese-owned drinks company. Donny checked into them and it's an old established business which used to produce sake, but only in the last thirty years they started making whisky in Japan. They've been very successful and won a shed-load of awards in the international markets. Over the last ten years, they've grown enormously and they've made a number of acquisitions of European and North American companies. I reckon Mathewson's being talking to them as well about selling Benlochy. Donny said there were a couple of angry sounding voice messages left yesterday morning asking why Mathewson didn't turn up for a planned meeting."

"Very interesting. Has Donny contacted him yet?"

"No, he wanted to check with you first."

"Okay, when we have the team meeting in the morning we can sort out who'll take it forward. Anything else?"

"Yes, Mathewson's two children are due back from holiday tonight. They're on the last B.A. shuttle so they're probably at Heathrow as we speak waiting to board. I've arranged we can go out to their house to speak to them in the morning. Georgina knows to expect us. Also,

Callum McPherson's due back tonight as well. You remember he's the Materials Controller, the other senior manager. He went away on Wednesday night because he had meetings up north to see a number of suppliers. We've spoken to him on the phone and there was little point in dragging him back early. He ought to be home by now and we've arranged to see him in the morning as well."

"Is that the lot?"

"I reckon it's enough. For the meeting tomorrow, I've arranged Sanjay, Phil, Donny and Mary will all be there. Are you available for it?"

"Yes, I was intending to come in for part of the morning and I reckon it would be worth being in on it."

While they'd been talking, Sandra had served the pie on a plate along with some vegetables she'd heated in the microwave. Alex had opened and poured the red wine and they'd already quaffed their way down most of the bottle. They were both feeling comfortable and mellow and a little intoxicated.

"I have some cheese and biscuits if you'd like or we can go straight to the dessert." Sandra offered.

"I'm really quite full up. I'm happy to skip the cheese and I don't know if I could manage dessert either. I really enjoyed that, good food, good wine and best of all good company."

Sandra felt her cheeks burning but didn't know if it was from embarrassment or intoxication. "You are very kind but the meal was just thrown together from items I picked up at the supermarket. One day, when I have more time to prepare, I'll cook for you ploppelly," she replied stumbling over her consonants.

"You cook too? What other hidden talents might you have?" Alex asked in a slightly leering tone.

She went to the cupboard and lifted out two snifters with a bottle of Remy Martin and walked back and placed them on the table. She stood next to Alex and stroked his face before lowering her own towards him and grazing his lips with hers. "I've been saving this for a special occasion. I think it's a lovely way to end a meal and we could take our glasses through next door."

"I'm sorry but I'm going to pass on the brandy too. We both need to be up and driving tomorrow morning and you know how paranoid I am about drink driving. I've had about as much drink as I can take for me to be totally sober to drive tomorrow. Let's keep the brandy for another time but I can think of better ways to celebrate." Alex stood and pulled Sandra against him, he framed her face between both his hands then gently kissed her eyes and nose before their mouths came together. After a few seconds, Sandra withdrew a pace and held Alex's hand in hers as they walked from the kitchen towards the bedroom.

Chapter 17

The room was still dark as Alex's eyes fluttered open. The curtains hadn't been properly closed and the yellow glow of a streetlight reflected through the crack. When he turned his head, he could just make out the clock radio on the far cabinet showing a few minutes before seven a.m. The air was warm and only a sheet covered his naked body. Sandra was still asleep beside him, her arm stretched loosely over his chest. He could feel her warmth and hear her steady rhythmic breathing. He took a moment to admire her shapely outline, her slim muscular limbs which had so recently been intertwined with his own. He carefully lifted her arm to enable him to escape, slipping from under the sheet. As he collected his clothes and reached the door, he looked back at the bed and fought the temptation to slip back in to resume their physical union. Alex walked into the bathroom and turned the shower to cold, deciding it best to cool his ardour if he was hoping to get any work done. His head was still a bit muggy from the combined effect of his exertions, lack of sleep and the after-effects of the wine. A few minutes standing under the ice cold jets and he felt more ready to face the day.

Alex tore the wrappings off the new toothbrush Sandra had provided and discovered it hadn't only been a joke when she said she'd purchased extra hard. He cleaned his teeth but found the tough bristles tearing at his gums and he made a mental note to replace the brush with something softer. The disposable razor allowed him to clean his face but not as effectively as his own razor, and again he thought he'd need to supply a more appropriate replacement. Sandra had done well in providing for him at all and he was grateful. He hoped staying over could become a regular occurrence but didn't want to seem too presumptuous bringing his own gear.

Alex threw on his clothes and stepped out of the bathroom, only to see Sandra walking towards him. She looked sleepy and her hair was tousled. She was wearing a dressing gown over her shoulders but the front hadn't been tied, leaving her exposed. The effect of the cold shower was instantly lost as he found this appearance was more sexy and more alluring than if she'd stayed naked.

"You're up bright and early."

"Yes, I need to get back to Shawlands to collect my car and papers. I was just about to call a taxi."

"No need for that, just give me ten minutes to come to and I'll drive you over."

Sandra followed the direction of Alex's gaze. She smiled, and shrugging the gown from her shoulders, it fell on a heap at her feet. "I'm going for a shower, care to join me?" Sandra reached for his hand.

"I've already had one, a cold one, but I think the effect's worn off."

"All the more reason for another." Sandra met no resistance when she led Alex back into the bathroom and assisted him in disrobing. She turned on the shower and stepped under the jet, but only for a split second. "Bloody Hell, you were serious about having it cold." She adjusted the thermostat and then more cautiously stepped back under the flowing water, reaching out to draw Alex in with her. They took turns in lathering one another using soap-covered hands and fingers to explore each other's form, pausing over lumps and bumps, creases and crevices. Their lips came together and their tongues wrestled as, amidst laboured breathing, they vied to bring comfort and pleasure to one another.

It was over an hour, instead of the ten minutes suggested, before they left the flat for Sandra to drive Alex home. In that time, they'd exhausted their sexual appetite, at least for the time being, having showered as well as being fed and watered.

Sandra turned on the ignition, and as the engine fired into life, so did the car radio.

'We're caught in a trap
And I can't walk out
Because I love you too much baby'

Roland Gift's unmistakable intonations greeted them singing the Fine Young Cannibals cover of 'Suspicious Minds.' Albeit with a different intended meaning, so much of the lyrics represented Alex's and Sandra's current relationship and their discussion of the previous evening. Simultaneously, they looked at each other, laughed ironically, and their hands met as they both reached to switch off the radio.

* * *

Alex raced up to his flat, collected his briefcase and car keys and returned before Sandra had time to complete turning her car around. They both headed back into Glasgow to find suitable parking and made their way back to their office. Alex arrived within a couple of minutes of Sandra and he noted that the rest of the team were already at their desks. He wasn't certain if it was just his imagination or whether he detected covert glances and smiles being exchanged as they looked between him and Sandra.

"Is this your weekend clothes?" Phil enquired, eyeing his casual wear. Alex realised, with time being short, he hadn't thought to change into his normal working attire. 'Maybe I'm becoming paranoid and that's all they were looking at,' he pondered.

"I'm only here for an hour or two then I'm taking my boys out. I'll stay for the meeting, of course, but I won't be taking part in any interviews. Since everyone is now here, why don't we kick off early?"

Alex pulled the team together and they all sat in a circle. "Let's go over what we have. Sandra, you start and everyone else cut in whenever you think of anything."

"Right, Boss. We've got loads of questions and not too many answers. The answers we do have just lead us to even more questions, so we really need to find something to give us a breakthrough. We know Mathewson died sometime on Wednesday night, probably between the hours of midnight and one a.m. He was hit by a single blow to the head and died almost instantly.

"We haven't found the weapon nor can we be certain what it might have been. The wound was small and circular and caused by some force so it could have been something like the head of a hammer or another thing that could be wielded. Maybe even a pole like a spear."

"Could it have been something fired, like a pellet from a gun or a slingshot?" Mary suggested.

"I don't think so but we can't rule it out. There's also the charade with the broken racks and bottles and the mystery about the glass. What was it and where has it come from? It could be a red herring but it might also be an important clue if we could only work it out.

"For motives, we have too many options. Mathewson has upset a lot of people over the years. As always, family have to be considered as prime suspects. Mathewson's fought with many of his. His marriage is a sham and he has issues with his brother-in-law and father-in-law. We don't know yet about his children. He's had at least one failed business in the past, so he's certain to have made enemies there. He's been trying to sell Benlochy, which could have upset a lot of people, and we know he's been involved in supplying illegal booze, therefore it's most likely he's been involved with organised crime to do it. As if that's not all been enough, he's a serial womaniser. It would probably be easier to identify anyone who didn't have a motive to kill him than those who did.

"Now for opportunity, that's pretty tricky. The body was found in the cask room and he wasn't recorded as being in the distillery. We're fairly confident he used the tunnel but we've got no evidence to prove it.

"Was the murder premeditated or was it a spur of the moment thing? We still can't be certain. Who would have known where to find him? And of those, who was either already on the premises or else knew how to get in without being noticed? Whoever it was knew how to cover up. They didn't leave any evidence and they removed the weapon. That suggests premeditation, either that or whoever it was must have been really smart and able to improvise."

"Or very lucky," Phil added.

"Yes, possibly."

"If it wasn't someone already in Benlochy, could Mathewson have brought them in through the tunnel?" Sanjay asked.

"That's distinctly possible, otherwise they knew about it themselves and let themselves in. When I mentioned being able to cover up, that applied to the tunnel and the shack and not just the distillery, so whoever it was is really well organised and knows enough about investigative procedure to know how to hide."

"Do you think it's specialist knowledge or just picked up from watching T.V. or reading novels?" Mary enquired.

"Who's to say? I don't believe it's specialist, but that's only a guess because it's been good enough not to give anything away.

"Let's run through potential suspects and alibis."

Donny kicked off. "There's all the family for starters. His wife Georgina claims to have been home alone and doesn't have an alibi. His two kids we've still to speak to later today, but we already know that at the time of the murder, they were on holiday at Klosters, and we've confirmed with the hotel that they were on the slopes on both Wednesday and Thursday, so it rules them out."

"I don't disagree, but we don't have confirmed statements to completely close them out yet," Sanjay added.

Sandra continued, "Next there's the father-in-law, Daniel Burns, and we know they have a history and more recent disputes about the company sale. But Daniel has limited mobility since his stroke, and in any event, he was given an alibi by his servant, Travers. So that would take collusion.

"Then we have Quentin. He and Mathewson detested each other, so no shortage of motive, but why now? His wife Fiona gives him an alibi and they confirmed their son Frank was home too. Samuel wasn't home until very late, and we've still to corroborate where he said he'd been."

"That's number one on the 'to do' list," Sanjay noted.

Resuming her summary, Sandra followed on, "The other brother, Stanley, seemed to get on okay with Mathewson. Arguably he'd be disadvantaged by his death, but we can't be certain he saw it that way, particularly with the talk of selling out. He was at home and his partner, Barry gives him an alibi."

"What about outwith the family?" Mary asked.

"To start with, there's his sexual partner on the night of his death. We've still to track down who that is."

"Maybe it's like a black widow spider; she has sex with men and then kills them," Donny suggested.

"I don't know, for someone really special, I might be prepared to take the risk. Only one lick of the honey pot and then dead. What do you say Sandra?" Donny leered.

"You can forget about the sex, but I might just have to kill you anyway. Go on with your summary."

"For other possibilities, there are the other managers at the distillery," Donny continued. "Patrick Gillespie's about ages with Daniel Burns and doesn't look like he has the strength to strike a match, never mind a killing blow. His statement shows he was at home, alone, at the time of death. Gillespie's nephew, Callum McPherson, is a more likely prospect. If he knew about the sale talks, he wouldn't have been too happy, not with his strong Nationalist views. He's been away and we're due to talk to him today."

"When did he leave?" Sanjay asked.

"That's what we need to find out. His first meeting was in Inverness at ten a.m. on Thursday. He was meant to drive up Wednesday afternoon or evening which would rule him out. The company has its own flat so there aren't any hotel records for us to check. He could have been around for the evil deed and still have had time to get away, then be up in good time for his meeting."

"We can find out more when we speak to him. Surely he must have credit card usage or receipts which could evidence where he was and when. Certainly if he went up on Wednesday, he's bound to have bought a meal or a coffee or something, quite possibly a petrol receipt. Having said that, be careful if he's too quick in offering that type of corroboration because it's fairly easy to fake," Sandra suggested.

"Yeah, yeah, we know. Trust nothing and nobody, the standard rules," Donny mumbled dismissively, then continued with his appraisal. "There are loads more employees at Benlochy, and it's sure as shit that Mathewson will have pissed off most of them at some time, but no obvious contenders for the starring role. If we look outside the distillery, it's the same story, a near infinite number of folk he's screwed or screwed with but no obvious prime suspect. With all the talk of a takeover, that brings in a whole new raft of possibilities and there's some important names involved. Chuck Holbein's known to have been in negotiations. She's already been interviewed, and this Teiko character could be seen today. God knows who else is lurking in the background, as if we don't have enough problems without importing them. No offence, Sanjay."

Donny's lame attempt at racist humour was received with stony glares from the rest of the team.

"On top of all of that, we know he's been involved in selling counterfeit whisky or maybe it was real product but sold under the counter. He'll have been dealing with some really unsavoury characters. It looks as if that was going on for a long time, going back before Mathewson was in charge, so I reckon Daniel Burns might be due another little visit as well."

"That's where we're up to. Where do we go now?" Sandra prompted.

Phil was first to answer, "If I'm not stating the obvious, we need to talk to the Teiko guy today. Maybe Sandra and I could see him. We could go on to Daniel Burns afterwards. Mathewson's sons also need to be checked, so maybe Sanjay could do them along with Mary to give continuity because she's already been to their house with the boss. Then there's Callum McPherson, if they could see him as well. Scene of crime are still trying to research the glass. Donny's been doing a great job on the research and coordination, so perhaps he could check Samuel's alibi then continue following up on the drink sales links, his gambling debts and anything else on the business scene."

"Sounds like a plan," Sandra concluded.

"You've been very quiet, Boss," Phil continued.

"It's the sign of good management when you have a team you feel confident in delegating to, and I am happy enough with how it's being handled. I'd have been quick to say if I saw anything being missed. Now let's get to it."

Sandra told Phil to call Yakimoto and set up their meeting, and while he was doing so, she went to the ladies room to freshen up. She was standing checking her appearance in the mirror when Mary walked in.

"How are you settling in, Mary?"

"Really great and I'm so lucky to be on a big case so soon. It's a great team. Donny's a bit of an old grouch, but everyone else has been so welcoming, and as for the DCI, he's a real hunk. I've been hearing he's single as well."

"He's divorced, but he has two sons and he's devoted to them. That's where he's heading off to now."

"It sounds as if you're trying to put me off. I can see you're both very close. Maybe you want him all to yourself. I hope you don't mind another woman in the team, or will I be cramping your style?"

Sandra's first inclination was to snap back telling Mary to show her some respect and to mind her own business, but she stopped herself. In truth, she did want Alex all to herself, but she also knew Mary's words were just idle chat, girl talk, and reacting aggressively would be the worst thing she could do. It would be guaranteed to oil the rumour machine. She'd be best to play along with the banter.

"No problem, I don't mind a bit of competition, besides the DCI and I are good friends..." Sandra didn't have time to finish her sentence but regretted her starting words the moment she'd said them.

"Ahhh, just good friends, nod, nod, wink, wink, we know what that means."

"No, actually I meant it literally. We've worked together for a few years now, and last November, we were on a case where he claims I saved his life. Well, you know the old Japanese custom, at least in the movies, if you save someone's life, then you're responsible for them forevermore," Sandra replied, showing a big grin which she hardly felt. She remembered her conversation with Alex the previous night and knew he had been right; they'd have to make some difficult decisions.

"I heard about that case. An assistant chief was arrested, Forbes wasn't it? And one of the arresting officers was slashed. Was that the DCI and you?"

"Yes, it was, but it goes for nothing now. You're only as good as the case you're working on." Sandra was relieved to have changed the subject and had brought it back to their current investigation. "Oh, and by the way, you're right about Donny; he's old school and he's due for retirement fairly soon. He's a good copper but he's got his prejudices. He doesn't like women, certainly not when they're in superior positions, and he's a WASP."

"A WASP? What do you mean?"

"White Anglo-Saxon Protestant, he's not too tolerant of anyone else, so watch your back."

"Thanks for the heads up."

* * *

Alex had only just stepped back into his office when his mobile rang. The caller display showed it was Brian Phelps.

"Hey, Brian, we've not talked so often since we were back at Uni. What can I do for you?"

"Hi, Alex, I hope I've not caught you at a bad time. It's bad news I'm afraid." There was a pause. "It's about Carpenter, he attempted suicide last night. I told you before his wife knows Trish well, and she called her this morning to say what had happened."

"You said 'attempted.' How is he? And what actually happened?"

"He's been taken to the Southern General and had his stomach pumped. He swallowed a bottle of pain killers and washed it down with vodka. Fortunately, he's not much of a drinker and he threw up, but there's no telling how many pills were in the bottle or how many he might have ingested. That's why they pumped him to get out everything they could. They have confirmed there's not enough left to kill him or cause critical damage, but he may have done some harm to his stomach lining. He's going to feel pretty awful for a while too, but it's his state of mind that's most worrying."

"Poor bugger, he'd been under a lot of pressure."

"He's been really depressed with the enquiry going on, but it was something that happened last night which made him snap."

"Go on."

"Some thugs, we know now it was Connelly and his crew, went round to his house with spray cans. They painted the word 'pervert' across his door and windows and all over his car."

"Little bastards."

"He saw them doing it, apparently, and phoned the police. He even managed to take photographs of them. He handed his camera over and made a statement. He seemed okay at the time. His real problem came later when he saw how upset his kids were. His wife tried talking to him but he just seemed to draw into himself. She thought he'd just need time to come to terms with it, but she was wrong. In the middle of the night, he got up and raided the medicine cabinet, locked himself in the loo, then took the pills with the vodka. She heard him being sick and forced the door, then phoned for an ambulance. She's acted quickly enough to save him, but it'll be a while before we know how he really is.

"The only silver lining is that we won't need to see Connelly back at the school. After what's happened, we won't have to take him back. We can cite it as being for his own protection."

After closing the phone, Alex sat staring at his empty desk. His earlier contented demeanour was overtaken by shock and sadness. Although he didn't know Carpenter personally, he had an overwhelming feeling of sympathy for what he and his family had been put through, and he knew their lives would never be the same again. It would be some considerable time, if ever, before he'd be permitted to return to teaching, and his wife and children would also suffer as a result.

Alex knew he'd have to tell Andrew what had happened. The boy had expected or at least hoped his father might have been able to do something, but Alex felt helpless. He wasn't looking forward to being the bearer of bad news, but he knew it was necessary.

Alex picked up his internal phone and made a couple of calls. By the end, he had confirmed that Sean Connelly and his father had been charged, as well as two of Sean's former school friends from Barrhead. The photos taken by Carpenter were damning enough, but there was plenty of supporting evidence. Connelly and his troupe all had paint residue on their skins and there were a couple of canisters in the boot of the father's car. There was clear evidence they'd been at Carpenter's house and had given no justification of why they might even have been in the vicinity.

Chapter 18

With Mary navigating, she and Sanjay arrived at the Mathewson house by mid-morning. They'd already made arrangements to see McPherson at his office afterwards.

It was only after the allocated spread of duties had been agreed that Mary thought to prepare Sanjay by telling him about the Rottweilers. She normally liked dogs but was uncomfortable about their size and strength. She knew Sanjay wasn't happy with any dogs and even shied away from Yorkshire Terriers. It was, therefore, with some trepidation that he approached the entrance, perspiration shining from his brow, and this was exacerbated by the deep reverberations of barking. Their concerns, however, were unfounded, as due to their visit being expected, the dogs had already been shut into one of the back rooms. Agnes opened the door and showed them into the same lounge where they'd previously been. The lid of the piano was open and sheet music was stacked on it, indicating it had been recently played, but otherwise Mary considered the room looked the same as before. She ventured a quick glance at the music and saw it was mostly ragtime style, confirming her expectation that it wasn't consistent with mourning.

After a few moments, Georgina entered the room. She acknowledged Mary and held out her hand in introduction to Sanjay.

"Grant and Henry will be here in a moment." Georgina stood in the doorway and introduced her sons as they arrived. They all went to take a seat, but Sanjay asked Georgina to leave them so he could speak to the boys alone. She seemed a little uncertain at first but accepted his request.

They noted the formal details then exchanged pleasantries, Sanjay and Mary seeking to put the boys at their ease.

"You only came back last night?"

Grant took the lead. "Yes, we were invited to stay with a friend who was having a party but thought it best to get home quicker. We flew from Zurich into London yesterday evening and then took the last shuttle up. We arrived home late last night."

"How long have you been away?"

"We left ten days ago, on the eighth. We met up in London with my cousin and then went over for a week's skiing."

"Your cousin you say?"

"Yes, well second or third cousin to be more precise. Tabatha's mother and Mum are first cousins. We stayed with her for a couple of days and then flew out on the eleventh. I've still got the tickets if you want to check. We flew British Airways; I think I still have the boarding cards as well."

"Who else was there?"

"There were eight of us in total, ourselves, Tabatha and five others. We've been friends for years and it's an annual event when we all get together."

"Can you give me names and addresses for everyone in your party?"

"Yes, I can, no problem, but surely we're not suspects?"

"No, don't worry. It's just routine so we can tick all the boxes and show that we've proven who was where and when. It's like police-work by numbers. You know, like in the Sherlock Homes quote, 'When you eliminate the impossible, then whatever is left, however improbable, has to be the explanation.'" Sanjay smiled lamely.

Grant nodded slowly. "So, was Dad definitely murdered?"

"Yes, we're now certain of that."

"Have you any idea who did it?"

"The investigation is ongoing and we are still collecting evidence. Please tell us anything you know which may be even remotely relevant. Have you heard your father arguing with anybody or did he say anything about having any problems or being afraid of anyone?"

Grant and Henry exchanged knowing glances but said nothing.

"Have you something to tell us?" Sanjay goaded.

Grant remained silent but Henry spoke out for the first time. "There hasn't been anything unusual. Dad was always having little squabbles with people. We never really took much notice."

"Who were the squabbles with?"

There was another exchange of glances and Grant gave an almost imperceptible nod. "Dad and Mum didn't always get along. When we were younger, they would argue all the time. More recently, they seemed to get along better."

"Did they fight physically or was it just arguing?"

"No, it was never more than shouting."

"Go on."

"Dad sometimes fought with Grandpa and with Uncle Quentin."

"And when you say 'fought'?"

"No, again it was words, although I remember once, about a year or two ago, Quentin got really angry and threw a punch. Dad caught it in his hand and pushed Quentin away and then just laughed at him."

"There was nothing more recent?"

"Not that I'm aware of."

"What about anyone else?"

"He might have mentioned names, but nothing that meant anything to me."

"Okay, thank you for your help."

Sanjay and Mary were happy to escape to their car before the dogs were set loose again.

"Is that what they call the privileged classes?" Sanjay asked.

"Yes, they just go swanning off around the globe and never do a day's work in their lives," Mary replied.

"It doesn't seem to do them very much good, they might have an easy life but they don't seem too happy with it."

"I guess the more you have, the harder it is to find something to please you. It's a problem that I wouldn't mind having to deal with," Mary answered.

"Let's move on, we've still to go and see Callum."

A few minutes later, they were waved through the security gates into Benlochy and found Callum in his office working his way through correspondence delivered while he was away.

Both Sanjay and Mary did a double take when they saw him. He was completely bald, but apart from that difference, he was a younger version of Daniel Burns. Neither of them had actually seen Daniel in the flesh, but they could tell enough from seeing his photograph, and there was a distinct similarity to Quentin as well.

Anticipating their question, he offered, "No, I'm not related to the Burns family, at least I'm not considered to be related to the Burns family. My uncle is Patrick Gillespie. He grew up with Daniel and they were best friends. My mother was Patrick's young sister and she died when I was ten years old. The only memories I have of her are that she was very sick. She and my father were engaged when I was born and it doesn't take a genius to work out that my natural father was Daniel. Nobody's ever told me officially, but I don't need a DNA test to prove it. My father brought me up all by himself and I love him dearly. I'd never do anything to hurt him."

The words seemed to flow out of Callum in one long release without requiring any prompting. "When I left school, I went to college, and after I got my qualifications, Uncle Patrick got me a job here. I started at the bottom working in the stores on minimum wage and I then worked in production before I tried out in other departments. At the same time, I did more studies using evening classes and correspondence courses. I got a BA degree and then I worked for my MBA. I worked my way up in the company by sheer hard graft. Nobody did me any favours, I wasn't given any time off for studies and I had to pay for it all myself. I worked hard and I earned my promotions. It took me years to make it to junior management and even longer to where I am now. I'm really doing a director's job, but I'm still not recognised at the top table and I don't get near to the salary paid to Samuel or Stanley for doing bugger all."

Callum paused for a moment and then continued, "I'm really sorry, I don't know what you must think of me. I don't normally go around speaking to strangers about the company or the Burns family that way. No, I've never said these sorts of things in the past whether to strangers or anyone else. I guess I'm still a bit in shock with what's happened. I just started talking and it all came out. I'm sorry, here I am sounding off and that's not what you came here for."

"Is everything you've said true?" Sanjay asked.

"Yes, I suppose it is. I've probably thought about it but I've never voiced those thoughts before."

"In that case, please go on. We're still collecting information and we're happy to get all and any background you can give us. Tell us a bit more about what your job is and where it fits into the organisation."

"My job title is Material's Manager, but that's only part of it. It's a strange position because it crosses a lot of boundaries. I'm responsible for procurement, for identifying the best quality of raw materials, and then ensuring we buy them at the best price. From there, there's goods inwards inspection and quality control. Then there's stock control, ensuring we have enough of everything we need without the cost or waste of overstocking. I'm involved in overseeing the production and then, finally, I'm responsible for inventory management of the finished product. I have to be a Jack of all trades."

"You sound a bit resentful."

"No, not really. I wasn't born with a silver spoon in my mouth, not like the Burns family, so I've had to work for everything I've got, but that means I appreciate it. I know what it's like to go without, so everything I have means so much more than it would if it was just gifted to me."

"And what roles do the Burns family have in the business?"

"That sounds a simple question but it isn't really. Up until Mr Daniel stood down, he was in overall control but got involved in every last detail of everyone else's job himself. He also chased after every bit of skirt he came across, so you'll probably find plenty more of his bastards around the country besides me.

"Quentin was in charge of marketing and sales and Hector looked after the office, although Uncle Patrick used to keep an eye on it too, to make sure it ran smoothly. Since Hector took over the reins, nothing much has changed except he didn't know enough to effectively interfere."

"What about other family members?"

"They don't make much impact. Georgie looked after the office years ago, before she was married, and she was really good at it by all accounts. In recent years, she's hardly been involved in the day to day operations. She still attends board meetings though. I get to go to parts of them to deliver my reports, and from what I could see, she's been the only voice of sanity. No, maybe I'm being a bit harsh there, but it's true, she's by far the most able one of the whole family. Her kids, Grant and Henry, have never shown any interest. They've tried coming in to learn what goes on, but they've never lasted more than a few days. They didn't like working when it interrupted their playtime. They're not stupid and I wouldn't rule them out from being able to make a contribution one day, but they've still a bit of growing up to do before that day comes. It's the same thing with Quentin's kids, well not quite. Frank falls exactly into that category, but Samuel is different. Quentin has made him work here almost on a full-time basis and I don't think he minds being here, but the truth is, he's as thick as two short planks. A nice enough lad but he hasn't a clue about anything. He works with Quentin on the marketing and promotions, but that's just so Quentin can keep an eye on him and cover up his mistakes. He's convinced that one day a veil will lift and Samuel will suddenly be competent and ready to take over and run the whole business. There'll be a blue moon in the sky the day that happens.

"Next there's Stanley. The only time we see him is for board meetings, and in his case, they'd be better described as bored meetings, spelt B-O-R-E-D. He doesn't try to follow what's going on and sits dozing or sketching on a pad. He really has no interest and comes along only because he feels he has to so he can collect his fees and indulge in the hospitality. I think his father insisted on him attending and it became a habit, because he still did with Hector in charge. Mind you the reason might have been more so he was able to piss off Quentin. In all the years I've known them, I've yet to hear a kind word exchanged. As for Quentin and Hector, they were as bad, they detested the sight of each other, and Stanley would sometimes get involved just to wind up Quentin even more. It wasn't unusual for Mr Daniel or Georgie to have to keep the peace."

"And where do you fit in with all of this?" Sanjay asked.

"What do you mean? I've already told you what I do."

"That's not what I'm asking. Where do you fit in with the family dynamic?"

"I don't. I'm not considered part of the family. Nobody wants to know my opinion or what I think unless it's specifically to do with the job and not always even then. I've learned to keep my head down and just get on with it."

"What's your relationship like with each of them?"

"I'm tolerated and I tolerate them, what more can I say?"

"How about your true feelings? Give me a one statement summary on each of them."

Callum thought for several moments and then there was the flicker of a smile. "Okay, I'll give it a try. Daniel Burns is a tyrant, a despot really, or that's how he acted until he took ill and he's not too much better now. Hector's a dreamer, or was," he corrected. "Big on ideas, small on ability and application. Georgie is smart and able but not really involved very much now. Quentin would be absolutely brilliant if he was only a fraction as good as he thinks he is. Samuel is a waste of space. Stanley knows nothing and the other boys aren't interested."

"So who'd have a reason to want to kill Hector?"

"What? You don't think it was one of the family do you?"

"I didn't say it was but we can't rule it out, so who do you think?"

"I really couldn't say. Quentin hated Hector with a passion but I couldn't see him killing him."

"And what about you?"

"What? Why would I want to kill Hector?"

"Why don't you tell us?"

"I didn't. I wouldn't. Who's said something?"

"I didn't say anyone had said anything, but what are you afraid they might have said?"

"Nothing. Oh, I don't know. I didn't always see eye to eye with Hector and there might even have been occasions when we had words, but I never wanted him dead."

"So what did you argue about? If you're innocent, then you've nothing to fear by telling us."

"There were plenty of occasions where we didn't agree, but that's what running a business is about – different people with different opinions and then debating them to find the right solution."

"But you just told us they didn't value your opinion."

"They did sometimes. Okay, we did have some arguments, but it was only ever about business and it was only ever talk."

"So tell us more."

"A couple of years ago, not long after Hector became MD, he wanted us to start chill filtering the whisky. He read somewhere that some of the international markets preferred it as it made the whisky clearer, particularly when water or ice was added. I told him he was talking nonsense. It may make the whisky clearer, but it takes away some of the taste and it would lose a lot more business than it stood to gain. He wasn't convinced and the argument went on for weeks. Eventually, he backed down, but only after Georgie took my side. There were other occasions when we had a dispute about the labelling. He approved a printers spec spelling whisky with an 'e' – the American or Irish way. If I hadn't spotted it and corrected it we could have lost a fortune. How could he be a director of a company like this and not know that type of fundamental? Even Samuel wouldn't make a mistake like that."

"Okay, let's move on. You've been away for the last couple of days. I'd like you to tell me about the details of your journey, when you left, where you went, etc."

"I travelled up to Inverness on Wednesday afternoon and stayed at the company flat. I had my first meeting on Thursday morning at ten a.m. I can show you my diary; it's got a note of my itinerary."

"Yes, that would help. On Wednesday, did you meet or see anyone on your journey or when you got there?"

"Not that I can think of. I left here at four; I think I arrived at about seven."

"Did you go for a meal, maybe speak to other customers or staff in a restaurant, or did you make any purchases where we could check your receipt?"

Callum thought for a moment. "I need to confess, I bought a fish supper. There was no receipt. The girl in the shop might remember me because I've been there before and we chatted while I was waiting for the chips to fry up. I'm serious about it being a confession. My wife will kill me if she finds out. I'm meant to be losing weight and chippies are meant to be a no-no."

"Was there anywhere else?"

"I stopped for diesel just before I got there. I bought it using a fuel card, so they'll have a note of my registration and the time."

"What did you do on Wednesday night?"

"After the chippie, I went back to the flat and just watched television."

"So nobody else saw you?"

"I guess not."

"And potentially you still had time to come back from Inverness, kill Hector and get back up there in good time for your meeting."

"Except I didn't. My mileage records will show that."

"There's still the train, or a hire car."

"Check all you like, you won't find anything because I didn't do anything."

"We'll obviously have to check out what you've told us. Now, we understand that you're very interested in politics?"

"Isn't everyone?"

"Maybe, I should have said you're involved in politics and you're passionate about your beliefs."

"Yes, that's true. But don't you think that's a good thing? Shouldn't we all want what's best for our country and be ready to stand up and be counted? That's precisely what we'll get the chance to do next year in the referendum, and I hope you'll agree that we'd be far better off as an independent Scotland, free from the shackles of Westminster. Scotland would be so much better on its own; we have all the resources. It's not just the oil, that's all been mortgaged anyway. We have water, we have green energy, the most advanced in Europe, and of course, there's food and drink. We export salmon and shellfish, but best of all, we have whisky. Scotch whisky exports amounts to four billion pounds a year and Scotland sees precious little of the benefit."

"Thanks for the party political broadcast, but we're not here to speak about our political beliefs and we're only interested in yours to the extent that they might have a bearing on our investigation."

"Why should it have a bearing on the investigation?"

"Well, you've already made it very clear that you're passionate about your country and you feel strongly against it being exploited."

"Yes, we've had more than enough of being raped and pillaged by the English."

"Is it just the English you're against, or are you generally xenophobic?"

"It's not just the English and I'm not xenophobic, but I will fight against injustice. I'm not prejudiced. I just want a fair deal."

"So you admit you'll fight for what you believe in?"

"Yes, that's what I'm telling you, I'll keep campaigning so we get the right answer at the ballot box next year."

"It's not the ballot box we're interested in. You'll fight for what you believe in, but just how far would you go to support your beliefs? If you thought Hector was going to sell out this distillery, a vital part of your precious whisky trade, and he was going to do a deal so it was owned by someone overseas, how far would you go to stop him?"

Callum stopped speaking and his jaw dropped as he assembled his thoughts. "Are you telling me that Hector was really trying to sell us out. I heard the odd rumour or two but I dismissed them as nonsense. I often hear the biggest load of rubbish about everyone and everything so I never pay it any heed."

"You're not seriously telling us you knew nothing about it?"

"I swear to God. If I'd known, I'd have fought him all the way, and by that I mean I'd have tried to reason with him and I'd have enlisted as much support as I could to help me."

"What, from other Nationalists?"

"Not only them, from anyone with any common sense. There are plenty of Nationalists in the company who would fight it, but Quentin's a Tory and I think he'd have fought him as much as me."

"Yes, we're speaking to him too, as you'd expect."

Callum was starting to look worn out and haggard, his shoulders drooped and his eyes looked strained. "Is that all?"

"No, not quite. There's another matter we'd like to discuss with you and it falls firmly within your area of responsibility."

Callum looked up expectantly.

"What can you tell us about the tunnel?"

"What tunnel?"

"The tunnel that runs out of the cask room and through to the other side of the hill."

"I know nothing about it. I've heard stories that in the early days there was some sort of secret operation before the distillery was made legal. I don't know what you've been told but I wouldn't waste your time listening to old wives tales."

"It's not just a story; we've seen it and we've been in it. Surely you must have known about it. You must have come across it when the refurb was done and the shop was built?"

"I'm telling you I know nothing about it. Hector looked after the refurb himself. But why should it matter anyway?"

"Well, that's the interesting part and the one that you're not going to be able to talk your way out of. There's a cave off from the tunnel that's been used for bootlegging whisky. Product has been removed from the distillery, then taken there for storage and bottling in order to evade the duties and taxes."

Callum's face turned chalk white and his hand began to quiver. "I know nothing about it," he uttered in little more than a whisper.

"But you've just being telling us how important your job is and how you control the quality and the quantity of the inventory. You're the Material Controller. How could this be going on without you being aware? You must have been playing a key role."

"I know nothing about it," Callum repeated, slightly louder this time. "How much was involved?"

Ignoring his question, Sanjay continued, "Well, you'd better start doing some quick thinking. We're only here to investigate the murder, but some of our colleagues who are specialists in fraud investigation have already been alerted and they'll want to speak to you, and I'd be really surprised if Her Majesty's tax and duties investigators won't be looking for you as well."

Chapter 19

"Yakimoto can see us right away and I think we need to take the opportunity while we can. He's only in Glasgow until this afternoon as he's already booked on a flight to London, then he's going on to Paris on Monday. He's staying in a suite at the Hilton and he's offered to see us there. I took the initiative to say we'd be there in half an hour. It's close enough, we can walk." Phil blurted out his news the moment Sandra re-entered the room.

"You did the right thing," she replied reassuringly. "What have you told him?"

"I explained we were the police and that we were investigating a suspicious death. I told him Hector was dead and that was why he'd failed to attend their planned meeting on Thursday. I told him we'd picked up Hector's phone and were aware of the messages left."

"Okay, let's make a move. It'll take a good few minutes to get there."

The lobby was quiet when Sandra and Phil presented themselves at the marble clad desk. After first checking with their guest, the receptionist directed them to the bank of elevators and gave them the room number.

A small, immaculately dressed Japanese gentleman held open the door on their approach. He gave a curt nod and held out a business card for each of them.

Sandra and Phil replied by showing their warrant cards for identification and were escorted into a lounge area where they were invited to sit.

"We understand that you don't have very much time and we're grateful for you agreeing to see us," Sandra opened.

"I was pleased to hear from you as it at least allows me to make some sense out of what has turned out to be a wasted journey." He was soft spoken and accented but his voice was clear and precise.

"Was your meeting with Mathewson your only reason for visiting Glasgow?"

"Yes, it was. I have been to Scotland many times and I have visited your beautiful city before. My only reason for coming this week was to see Mr Mathewson."

"Can you tell me the purpose of the meeting?"

"No, I cannot say, it was a private matter."

"Was he offering to sell Benlochy to you?"

Yakimoto's eyes opened wide. "This was meant to be a private matter between the two of us. I was told that I should not discuss it with anyone else at the company or the deal would be off."

"Deal? You'd already reached the stage where a deal was agreed?"

"Not exactly. We had discussed me buying his company and he had prepared a document especially for me. It was a formal 'Information Memorandum' giving key details required to value the business. I had indicated how much I would be prepared to pay and he asked me to fly over to agree a deal. The price was only indicative and was subject to due diligence."

"That sounds fairly advanced. Are you aware of the ownership structure at Benlochy?"

"Of course, but Mr Mathewson told me if we were able to agree a deal, then he was confident that he could deliver it."

"Did he tell you that you were the only company he was considering?"

"Not in those words, but he strongly implied it. He said if I came up with the figure he wanted, then he wouldn't have to talk to anyone else."

"So you didn't know he was already speaking to other companies as well."

A flash of anger shone from Yakimoto's eyes. "He most certainly didn't. I don't like auctions and I don't do business with cheats and scoundrels. It's a matter of honour. I can see now this was always going to be a wasted journey."

"Did Mathewson make mention of wanting to sell anything other than the basic distillery?"

"The memorandum showed the distillery, the land it stands on, some woodlands and other properties and, of course, the brands, the stocks and the sales contracts."

"There was no secondary storage and supply lines?"

Yakimoto looked quizzically. "No, I'm certain."

"Thank you again for seeing us. I believe that will be all, but we have your card in case we have any more questions. I'm sorry your time has been wasted."

Travelling back down in the lift, Sandra felt her phone vibrate. She lifted it from her pocket, switched off the silent, and engaged the call. The display showed Donny's number.

"Sandra, I've had a bit of a breakthrough. I was tracing the other numbers on Mathewson's phone directory, looking at any that we hadn't already identified. There was a mobile number which, when I tracked it down, I found he bought himself. I didn't see any other way to take it forward so I just dialled it. A girl answered. I asked if it was Hector Mathewson's phone and she answered it wasn't but that he'd given it to her. I asked who she was and she replied 'his fiancée.' I was rather taken aback but I tried not to show it. She didn't sound too bright which might have helped. I told her I was from the police and we needed to speak to her as soon as possible. I asked her to come in here. She agreed and said she'd come to the office. I couldn't get through to the Boss, so I thought I'd better let you know straight away."

"You did the right thing. We've just finished with Yakimoto and we'll be back in a few minutes. Did she say anything about Mathewson being dead?"

"No, she didn't and I thought it best not to say anything, not 'till she was here anyway."

"Quite right. Did you get her name?"

"Yes, Alyth, Alyth Spencer, she said. She lives with her parents in Balloch, the one at Cumbernauld, not Loch Lomond. So don't rush, it may take a while for her to get here."

"This could be interesting. Send the Boss a text. No wait, cancel that, I'll talk to him later."

* * *

Sandra and Phil led Alyth to an interview room. She was an attractive girl of medium height with a clear complexion, green eyes, long blonde curly hair and curves in all the right places, but her eyes had a blankness where a sparkle might have turned her prettiness to true beauty. She was aged in her early twenties and dressed in a cotton frock intended more for summer wear, but it was compensated by a wool, thigh-length coat.

Sandra wondered about the accuracy of Anne's speculation but restrained herself from asking Alyth if she had a mole on her breast or a bunion on her toe. The scene of crime team was renowned for its resourcefulness, but the fear that Anne's musings could have been correct might have raised suspicions of witchcraft.

"It was very good of you to come in so quickly, thank you very much," Sandra started.

"That's okay. I've got a moped and I was going to use it but the man said you needed to see me soon and I knew there was a bus due, so I just ran for it and that saved me from having to get changed. I was lucky, I just got to the stop when it arrived and it's only a short walk from Buchanan Street round to here."

"That's good. Well, I'd like to get some information from you. You said on the phone that you were Mr Mathewson's fiancée."

Alyth's face formed a frown and she stared down at the floor. "I'm sorry, did I do wrong? I wasn't meant to say. Hector told me it had to be kept a secret and I shouldn't say to anyone, even my parents. He made me swear. When the man spoke to me on the phone, it just came out. I didn't mean to break my promise." Tears were welling in her eyes.

"There's nothing for you to worry about. We're the police and you're allowed to tell us because it's wrong to keep secrets from the police. We have some questions for you, but I'd like you to excuse us for a moment while I have a word with my colleague."

Sandra and Phil stepped out of the room. "Phil, it's obvious she's not very bright, but I'm worried she's not the full shilling and she might be deemed to have mental health issues. I want to guard against any evidence we collect being deemed inadmissible if we're seen to be taking advantage of her. I think we should arrange for an 'appropriate adult' to be present on her behalf for the duration of the interview."

"Shit, how long will that take? No, you're probably right, Sarg. Let's do it by the book."

As luck would have it, they were all set up and ready to restart within fifteen minutes.

"Alyth, this is Mrs Proctor. She's here to help you and explain anything you don't understand or answer anything you're not sure about. She's not a policewoman. Her only reason for being here is to help you. Is that okay?"

"Yes, I suppose, but I don't need any help."

"That's okay, she's here just in case you change your mind. Now, Alyth, how long have you known Hector Mathewson?"

Alyth smiled at the mention of his name. "I met him a few months ago. I'd gone to a pub near home and I met him there. We got talking and he was really nice and kind to me. He walked me home and he asked to see me again the next night. He took me to his flat and we spent the night."

"Where was the flat?"

"I don't know, somewhere in Glasgow. He picked me up and dropped me home so I'm not sure. I think it was near the river."

"Did you have sex with him?"

Alyth giggled. "Oh yes. It was fun."

"Had you had sex before, or was he your first time?"

"Oh no, I've had sex lots of times."

"Did he force you to do anything?"

"No, no. He's not like that. He's kind and he looks after me. He's good fun and buys me things. He loves me and I love him."

"How do you know he loves you?"

"He makes love to me so he must love me and he gave me a ring, so we're engaged. We wouldn't be engaged if he didn't love me."

"Are you wearing the ring?"

"Yes," Alyth held up her right hand and showed a thin gold band with a heart shaped amethyst on her third finger. "That's my engagement ring. Hector bought it for me, but he told me I couldn't wear it on my left hand because it's our secret. He said he had a lot of things to sort out before anyone else could know and he made me promise not to tell anyone yet."

"Where do you meet him and where do you go."

"Hector works in the Benlochy distillery," she said proudly. "He's one of the bosses. He told me he'd get me a job there so we could spend more time together. He got me a job as a cleaner, but he's made me a special cleaner. I only work three shifts a week but I get paid more than I used to working full-time in my last job."

"When do you work and what do you do? Why is it special?"

"Please only ask one question at a time," Proctor interceded.

"I can answer okay," Alyth cried. "Two nights a week, I go in to clean the offices and the shop. It's every Wednesday and Sunday. On Wednesday, I start work at five in the evening and I work until eleven and on Sunday I work from four o'clock until midnight. I'm special because I'm the only one who works as a cleaner for Benlochy. There are other cleaners who come in every evening from five until seven, but they work for an agency and they just do general work. I have to check that they leave everything right and I'm the only one who gets to clean Hector's room. He says I'm the best cleaner he's ever had."

"You said you worked three shifts. That's only two."

"Yes, the other one can be done whenever I like, but I like to do it on Thursday morning so that I get most of my week's work done at once. It's a really special job. I get to clean a little cottage that's at the end of a road near to the distillery. It's only little and there's nothing much in it, but there's always loads of dust and the floor gets into an awful mess. I sweep it all out and I clean the inside of the windows and I polish all the wood."

"Do you see Hector outside of work?"

"Sometimes, but not very often."

"But you do see him when you're working in the distillery in the evening?"

"Oh yes, every time, twice a week and sometimes he asked me to come in extra times too. That's why he gave me the phone so he could call and tell me where to meet him. I sometimes got paid overtime when I came in for extra work."

"And what happened when you met him?"

"We made love."

"Where?"

Alyth's cheeks burned and she giggled again. "Everywhere. It's so much fun. Hector says the more risk of being caught then the more exciting it is." Alyth suddenly became very serious. "Is that what this is all about? Are we in trouble because somebody saw us?"

"No, you're not in any trouble for that. Did you ever fight with Hector?"

"Sometimes he'd want to wrestle when we were making love."

"No, I mean did he ever hit you or did you hit him?"

"One time he spanked my bottom. Is that what you mean?"

"No, not that. Did he ever get angry with you or did you get angry with him and maybe hit him?"

"No, we love each other."

"Did you make love on Wednesday?"

"Yes."

"Where was that?"

"In the shop."

"What time did you see him?"

"I'd already finished cleaning and he told me to meet him in the shop. It must have been about ten o'clock. Yes, that's when he said to be there but he was a bit late."

"And what time did you leave him?"

"He left about eleven. He said he needed to make a phone call and he left me to clear up before I closed up. I left at about half past eleven."

"Does he always leave you to clear up?"

"Usually he does and I'm meant to lock up, but my memory isn't good and sometimes I forget things. Hector tells me off when I forget to lock doors. It's happened at the distillery and sometimes at the cottage. Oh, I can't remember if I closed the cottage on Thursday."

"You said you have a moped. Is that how you get to and from work?"

"Yes, that's right. Hector bought it for me. It's the only way I can get to the cottage with my cleaning stuff because it's too far to walk. Sometimes if the weather's very bad, I can't drive the moped, and on those days I take a bus or a taxi, but only to go to the distillery. I can't do that for the cottage."

"Did Hector tell you that he was married?"

"Yes, he did. He said he was married a long time ago but he wasn't married any more. He said he was waiting to get papers to show he wasn't married. He said he was working on something to make him lots of money and then we'd be together all the time. I think that's when he wanted us to get married."

"Alyth, I'm sorry to tell you that something really terrible happened at the distillery. Something happened to Hector."

"Where is he? I'll go and see him."

"I'm sorry, you can't do that. I'm afraid that Hector is dead."

Alyth sat quietly, saying nothing looking at each of their faces in turn, tears filled her eyes and started to stream down her cheeks.

It occurred to Sandra that Alyth was the first person they'd spoken to who'd shown genuine regret and loss at Hector's passing.

"I'm going to arrange for someone to take you home. Will any of your family be there when you get back? I'm going to arrange for a social worker to go with you anyway."

A few minutes later Sandra was walking alone, taking a stroll around the police building. She wanted to inhale the cold, fresh air to clear her head. For an instant, she thought she might have preferred to inhale the warm cloudy fumes of a cigarette and imagined the sensation of nicotine drawing down her throat, infusing her being. She dismissed the thought as she'd given up months before and she wasn't prepared to risk the addiction returning. She felt drained after her day's work. She felt heart sorry for Alyth, another poor soul whom Mathewson had exploited for his own gratification. He was a real creep and no loss to the world, yet Alyth's life was being turned upside down by his murder. Her thoughts returned to practical issues. They'd tied up one more lose end but were no closer to solving the case. It was now late afternoon and she realised the football should have ended. Having a moment's privacy, Sandra took the opportunity to call Alex, wanting to hear his voice and so she could tell him what had been happening. The call rang out until voicemail kicked in. Sandra rang off and sent a brief text instead.

Returning to her desk, she noted an unopened email sent the previous night from Anne Dixon. She quickly opened it and read their latest findings on the glass found at the crime scene.

'Glass is consistent with nineteenth century hand blown Italian made, possibly Murano. Would most likely have come from a decorative object, ornament or item with decorative glass finish. One sliver had trace of wood attached, polished oak.'

Chapter 20

At their morning meeting, Alex had consciously let Sandra lead to emphasise to the others that she would be taking charge. He would stay in overall control but wasn't intending to be in attendance again over the weekend. He knew Sandra would have a busy day advancing the case and had complete confidence she would handle everything as he would wish. She could contact him if he was required and would no doubt check in with him later in the day. He left the office and detoured home to get changed and have a better shave before going to collect the boys. He received his normal welcome from Jake and was pleased to see the boys were ready and waiting for him. Helen was out shopping so there was nothing to delay him. He collected their overnight bags and tossed them into the car's boot.

"We can drop into the Laurels for a bite of lunch and then go on to the game," Alex suggested. "Sound okay?"

He drove back down Clarkston Road and found a legitimate space in the midst of a line of parked cars opposite the bistro. It was only about fifty yards along from the Bank where Alex had met Brian the previous evening. Off peak parking was permitted on this side of the street.

The roads were still frosty and it was cold outside; however, a welcoming wall of heat hit them as they walked through the door. The Laurels was clean and fresh with modern furniture and a cool counter displaying an appetising array of gateaux, biscuits and scones. Although it was quite early for lunch, the restaurant was already busy, but they found a table by the window and were welcomed by the owners. Norman was in the kitchen but called a 'Hello' when he saw them walk by. Cathy came over and offered them menus.

"It's good to see you back, Alex. You're looking well. How is everything going?"

"I'm doing fine, thanks. We're just in for a bite of lunch before heading over to Ibrox for this afternoon's game."

"Oh, I'll leave Norman to talk to you about that. He's really upset over what's been happening, what with Rangers going into administration last week. I'll give you a few minutes to choose and then come back for your order."

"Dad, I wanted to ask you about that. What is this administration thing all about?" Andrew asked.

"Well, I'm not an expert so I might not get the technicalities right, but I'll have a go at explaining. Where a company has debts or claims of debts that it can't pay then it is insolvent. One way to deal with it is to be liquidated, that is to close down, sell its assets to pay debts, and then it no longer exists. Assets that are sold can go on trading as a new company so it doesn't always mean an end to everything. Another option is to go into administration and that's what's happened here. The organisation is handed over to a professional business manager who looks at ways of raising finance or selling off bits of the business or of restructuring its debt so that it can try to continue in business. It can sometimes work to save a company, and the receiver will then sell what's left of the company as a going concern. If it doesn't work or if he can't sell it, then it ends up being liquidated.

"In Rangers case, it's about the tax man, that's Her Majesty's Revenue and Customs, or known as HMRC for short, and it's claimed millions of pounds are owed to it. Rangers can't afford to pay, so that's what's brought this all about."

"But why should that be? Rangers were miles ahead in the league only a few weeks ago and now they're miles behind."

"The football side's different to the business but it has an effect. You're right, back in November, Rangers were out in front with a lead of about eighteen points in the league, if I remember rightly. That's when all the stories started and the players lost heart. They were probably wondering whether they'd get paid their wages. They played rubbish and threw away their lead by Christmas, and by the end of the year, Celtic were a point ahead and they've kept in front ever since, although not by much. As a penalty for going into administration, Rangers have had ten points taken away so they're now fourteen points behind and they could also have fines to pay."

"Isn't that a bit stupid?"

"How do you mean?"

"Well, if the administration thing's come about because they've not got enough money, surely it's only going to make it worse to penalise them with fines and to take points off them."

"I can't argue with that. The whole thing sounds really stupid to me. I can't understand how a Club as big and powerful as Rangers can have got into so much trouble. Anyway, you'd better choose what you want to eat or we'll run out of time."

"I'm starving, can I have a soup and a sandwich? Roast beef in brown bread, if that's okay, and a strawberry milkshake," Andrew asked.

"A coronation chicken wrap and I'll have a milkshake too," Craig chipped in.

Cathy returned for their order and Alex asked for a baked potato with tuna and a white coffee. The boys' eyes lit up when two large tumblers, filled to the brim with luminous, bright pink liquid were placed in front of them.

They devoured their lunch with enthusiasm and in no time had empty plates to show, Alex wasn't far behind them. Then Craig and Andrew each tucked into a thick slab of carrot cake while Alex was content with a second coffee. Cathy was bustling about tirelessly, ensuring all the customers were properly attended. Norman found a few moments free and came out for a brief chat.

"Cathy said you're going to the game this afternoon. It should be a good one. Kilmarnock has been playing well, which is more than I can say for the Gers. You can't blame McCoist; he's been an excellent manager and it's a miracle he's managed to hold the team together at all with what they've been going through. For today's game, he says the team are up for it and Rangers are the only team in the Premier League who haven't lost at home, so we don't want that to change now. He's called for the fans to give a show of strength and support so it should be interesting to see the response."

"Yeh, not too sure what to expect, but hopefully it should be entertaining.

"I heard an interesting story earlier on," Alex started. "Apparently Hearts have been having some financial problems and problems with the taxman too. Anyway, there's been a suggestion that, to raise money, Rangers and Hearts should merge with each other and build a single stadium for the two of them so they can sell off Ibrox and Tynecastle. It would raise millions. They're going to call the new club the 'Heart of Midlothian Rangers Club' and the stadium will be the HMRC stadium."

"Oh, groan," Craig and Andrew both replied at the same time.

"You're moaning now but I expect you'll be telling that one to your friends on Monday."

"I don't suppose you'd believe me if I denied it," Craig replied.

"Please excuse me, I'll need to get back to the kitchen. It's too busy for me to be standing talking, but please drop in again so we can have a chance for a proper chat."

"You don't want to come with us to Ibrox then?"

"I'd love to, but I've too much on here. I'll just have to watch the highlights of the game on the box later."

"Let's just hope there's some highlights worth seeing."

Well fed and watered, Alex, Craig and Andrew returned to the car. Alex told Andrew to take the front passenger seat so he'd be better able to talk to him while driving. Craig was happy to sit in the back and didn't pay them much attention as he concentrated on sending and receiving Facebook messages on his iPhone. As they drove, Alex conveyed the news to Andrew about Mr Carpenter and explained that he'd had a nervous breakdown and would not be returning to teaching in the foreseeable future. Andrew's eyes welled up and he had difficulty speaking without his voice breaking. Alex was pleased that Craig was distracted as that prevented him teasing his younger brother. Alex reassured Andrew about Mrs Rankine taking him and the others to the prize-giving and ensuring there would be someone good to continue his maths tuition. To Alex's pride, Andrew was unconcerned with these aspects and his sadness resulted from genuine compassion for his teacher.

They arrived at Ibrox with plenty of time to spare and purchased a programme and beakers of Coke for each of them before going to their seats. The stadium was full with more than fifty thousand spectators. McCoist's plea had been heard, and despite the recent adversity, the fans were in carnival spirit and in full voice ready to cheer on their team, the Warren family amongst them. A rapturous roar greeted the players to the pitch and the game got underway. Rangers made a reasonably confident start and came very close to scoring in the opening phase when an Edu header was cleared off the line, but the optimism was short-lived when, after twelve minutes, Shiel left the Rangers defence in tatters to score for Kilmarnock. From this point, the enthusiasm of the Rangers' support waned. Kilmarnock had the best of the action and both sides had further chances, but Rangers fortunes took a further turn for the worse when Papac was sent off shortly before half time. The second half continued in the same vein with many wasted opportunities, particularly by the visitors. The game ended at the same scoreline of 1-0 with Rangers losing the game and their undefeated home record. Alex and the boys were amongst the stream of dejected supporters leaving the stadium.

"It's been a really crappy day all round," was Andrew's concluding remark.

On the way back to their car, Alex checked his phone and saw a missed call from Donny and a text message left by Sandra. 'Much to catch up on. I still have dessert if you want to come over after the game???'

Alex smiled at the prospect then texted back, 'Still have boys until tomorrow.'

Almost immediately a reply came, 'Bring them too, maybe it's time we met.'

Alex pondered the possibilities. He really wanted his relationship to be in the open and to have his sons get to know Sandra. It would make life much easier and be good for them all, but until the work situation was sorted, it would be too big a risk. It was too soon. With some regret, he texted back, 'Sorry, already have plans, we'll arrange for another time, talk later'.

Seeing the changes in Alex's expression as he was thinking, Craig enquired, "What's that about?"

"Just work, some developments in my case that I'll need to check into later."

Craig's frowned response indicated he hadn't carried off his lie very well.

As they drove home, Alex realised he hadn't made any plans for the boy's dinner. Ordinarily, he enjoyed serving something homemade. When he had time, he'd cook with the boys, involving them in the preparation and treating it as a family activity. When there wasn't time, he's produce something from the freezer that he'd prepared at an earlier time. Today, he'd started his morning at Sandra's then rushed in and out of his own flat before going into his office and he hadn't thought to lift anything for them to eat. By the time they reached home it would be approaching six p.m. and the boys would most likely be ravenous so there wouldn't be an opportunity to cook. Alex considered his options. They could go for a Pizza or a burger, they could pick up a carry-out Indian or Chinese or he could detour to the supermarket and pick up some food to assemble.

Alex put the options to the boys, expecting them to choose Mac-Donalds or Pizza Hut, but to his surprise they wanted to assemble their own supper. He drove straight to Morrisons' Newlands store, only a few hundred yards from his flat. They picked out a trolley and went straight to the deli section.

He recognised the same type of pâté and pie which Sandra had selected from the Partick store the previous evening, but steered the boys first to pick up some pre-prepared salads, choosing coleslaw, potato salad and pasta. They then added various sliced cold meats and some pieces of rotisserie chicken, a bag of chopped lettuce, cherry tomatoes, a red pepper and a freshly baked bloomer loaf. For dessert they selected a large tub of profiteroles. In all, it comprised a very fine feast.

"Can we watch a movie tonight?" Craig asked.

"I don't think I have anything suitable you haven't already seen. Let's have a look in the entertainment aisle and see if there's anything worthwhile," Alex suggested.

As they turned the corner with their trolley, they almost knocked over a young lady who was teetering about wearing impossible shoes. As they watched her recover and totter off into the distance, they realised they had not really been responsible for her instability, but instead it was self-imposed. She was slender with long blonde hair and was naturally of medium height, but this was falsely exaggerated by her platform soles which were about two inches thick and her heels that were six inches in height. She seemed to stagger down the aisle like a tightrope walker, flapping her arms to keep from falling over.

"I reckon she thinks she's Barbie," Andrew whispered.

"More like one of the original Thunderbirds team," Alex responded.

"Who are they?" Andrew asked.

"It was before your time. Before my time even, but I used to watch it on TV. It was an adventure programme using string puppets that moved about with the same staggered steps she was making."

"Hey, there's a DVD with the same name," Craig suggested, but that was as far as their interest went and the boys started working their way through the shelves looking for something that appealed to both. While they were looking, Alex quickly identified some other shopping items he needed. By the time he'd returned, the boys had chosen to buy the recent Bond movie, *Quantum of Solace*.

Ten minutes later, they were back in the flat, setting the table and laying out their purchases so they could eat buffet style. Although both boys ate heartily, there was still plenty of food to spare so Alex carefully stored the leftovers in his fridge.

As Alex set up the film to play, he enquired how the boys wanted to spend Sunday.

"I thought I'd said," Andrew replied, "I'm invited to go snowboarding with Zander and a couple of my other classmates. It's Zander's birthday and his folks are taking us to Xscape at the Braehead Arena."

"If the weather gets much worse, you'll all be able to snowboard in Overlea Park, his folks won't have to pay a fortune for the indoor facility," Craig quipped.

"You didn't say. How are you getting there?" Alex asked.

"His Dad's got a people carrier. It will easily get us all in. I've to be picked up from the house at one. Is that okay?"

"Yeah, sure. What about you Craig?"

"I'm meeting Jenny and the crowd at the ice rink at two. Can you take me there or drop me off early enough?"

"No problem," Alex started the DVD, thinking he'd have Sunday afternoon free after all. While the film was running he slipped through to the bedroom and dialled Sandra's mobile.

"Hi, Sandra, sorry I couldn't really talk before. How was your day?"

"It started really well, as you might remember, but went a bit downhill after that. Nothing bad and I've been very busy, but this morning was a hard act to follow. What about you?"

Alex brightened at the recollection. "Same as you, good start but not so good to follow. I've had a pleasant afternoon with the boys but the game was dire. Are you home now?"

"Yes, I've had a snack and I'm just putting my feet up in front of the box. There's nothing much on, but it's really cosy. Pity you can't be here too. I'm just toying with the idea of opening the dessert you brought. My problem is I know my own weaknesses, and if I do open it, then I'll most likely eat the whole thing."

"A girl's got to do what a girl's got to do."

"Very philosophical. What are you doing anyway?"

"We've just eaten and I've set up the DVD for Craig and Andrew to watch a Bond film."

"In that case, maybe I should come to you and bring the dessert with me."

"There's nothing I'd love more but we need to get the work situation sorted first. If you did come over, then the boys are certain to say something to Helen and I can't be confident she won't say the wrong thing to the wrong person and land me in the shit."

"Do you think she's malicious? Would she do that?"

"I'm not saying it would be out of malice, but there's a strong chance it could happen."

"Following what we were talking about last night, I saw an ad for a coordination officer looking at assembling information about CID's across the country. The job's centrally based, Glasgow or Edinburgh, with travel to each of the constabularies. It's not ideal because it would take me away from the front line, but I've asked for more info and I'll see what it entails."

"That was quick."

"I've not got it yet but I thought I needed to start looking. It could take a while and there's no point in waiting."

"You're right, of course, and I'm pleased but I'm sorry too. I enjoy working with you."

"Well, talking about work, I'd better give you an update on what's happened today."

Sandra ran through all the day's developments from her interviews and from Sanjay's as well as Anne Dixon's email. She finished by advising Alex her plan was to go and see Daniel Burns at about noon and she warned, "There's something else. As we're just about finished seeing everyone and collecting evidence on site at Benlochy, I'd like to give the go ahead to our fraud people to start their investigation. No doubt that will mean bringing in the tax and duty investigators as well."

"Okay, go ahead; give them a call in the morning. As soon as I'm clear of the boys, I'll come out too. I can pick up Sanjay, Donny and

Mary and we can meet at Benlochy, finish off there and clear out all our stuff. That will mean the distillery can get back to normal operation from the start of the week, at least as normal as they can manage after what's already happened and with an ongoing fraud and duty enquiry."

Chapter 21

Sandra slept fitfully. She was still adjusting to her new bed and this was her first night in the flat alone. Following her evening of passion with Alex and her somewhat intense day, she decided to go to bed early. She'd quickly fallen into a light sleep but was awoken only minutes later by the sound of a car horn outside. She stumbled over to the window to check if there was a problem to find it was only a teenager, on his way to a night of clubbing, beckoning to his friends to hurry up. Sandra returned to bed but found it impossible to return to her slumbers. She made the fatal mistake of considering her plans for the day ahead, and it triggered her mind becoming alert, going over and over the various elements of the case trying to focus on any small detail which may have been hitherto overlooked. Thoughts of changing her job entered her thinking, but then it returned to the case. She knew that if she were to decide on a move then she'd be even more desperate to have her current work concluded first.

She tried counting sheep, hoping it might help, but to no avail. First the sheep started to adopt the heads of potential suspects in the case and then her mind wandered to other farmyard metaphors as she contemplated the bull-like physique of Hector Mathewson impregnating Alyth Spencer. Sandra tried to dismiss the vision but it returned every time she closed her eyes. She climbed out of bed and made some tea, hoping the hot drink would help her become drowsy enough for sleep, but it didn't work, and worse still, just when she started to slumber again, she had an overwhelming need to urinate.

Sandra remembered watching the minutes tick by announcing midnight, one o'clock and two o'clock after which it all became rather vague.

At seven-thirty, she crawled from bed. She had a headache and felt groggy as she dragged herself into the shower. Turning the jets on full, she immersed herself under the hot stream hoping she'd be revived. This had limited success and, albeit for a different purpose, she tried Alex's technique of turning the thermostat to full cold. She couldn't tolerate more than a few seconds but she was now wide awake. Sandra grabbed a towel and roughly, almost harshly, rubbed her skin as much to warm her and restore her circulation as to get dry. Her complexion was pale with some areas more red than pink, from the abusive treatment she's administered drying herself. She caught a glimpse in the mirror before quickly dressing and considered some makeup would be required. Knowing she'd again be seeing Daniel Burns, and seeking to guard her legs from his lecherous eyes, she selected a demure but stylish trouser suit. She carefully applied a light touch of cosmetics to give her a modicum of colour and conceal the heaviness of her eyes. Satisfied with the result she locked the flat and drove to her office to prepare for the day ahead.

* * *

On schedule, she and Phil arrived at Burns's house shortly after midday.

As previously, the door was opened by Travers and they were shown to the Drawing Room. "I'll advise Mr Daniel that you're here."

A short while later, Burns was escorted into the room and sat opposite them in his armchair.

"I trust you're here to tell me you've solved the case and we can all get back to normal."

"I'm sorry, Mr Burns, that's not the reason for our visit. We have made significant progress but we're not quite ready to make any announcements yet. We have nearly finished the work which has to be based on site at Benlochy, so from our point of view, the business will be able to go back to normal from tomorrow."

"So why are you here?"

"We have some further questions and I did specifically say 'from our point of view.' As a result of information we have gathered, there is likely to be some investigations of other matters not pertaining to the murder."

"What are you talking about? What investigations?"

"If you don't mind, we'll ask the questions." Sandra was determined to retain control. "When we were here on Thursday, you told us about the tunnel."

"To be more precise, you asked me about the tunnel and I answered your questions."

"Yes, thank you for clarifying that. It serves to emphasise you didn't volunteer the information. What you didn't tell us then was about the cave."

"What cave? There are lots of caves."

"The cave off the side of the tunnel which has been used to store and bottle illegal hooch."

"I don't know what you're talking about."

"We think you do. We think you know exactly what we're talking about. We're talking about the illegal production facility which you set up."

"You're talking rubbish. I know nothing about any such operation. Anyway, even if you have found something, how could I be implicated? I've not been directly involved in the business for more than three years."

"That's our point; some of the barrels we've found are much older than that."

"So what does it matter if they have come from the time when I was in charge or if later? Who's to say Hector didn't steal older barrels and take them in there?"

"So are you trying to tell us it was Hector's fault? We don't think so. The quality of the inventory control system which Callum put in proves that was not possible. If barrels had been stolen after they'd been filled, it would show as a discrepancy on the stock system, so they must have gone missing prior to being registered into the stock control and that makes it your responsibility."

Burns looked shocked. "There's no way you can prove anything."

"We don't need to, all we're trying to do is solve a murder, but some of our fraud investigation colleagues will be having a closer look and we imagine so too will the customs and duty investigation squad, hence my earlier caution."

"You're flying kites. I don't see how you can have any evidence which implicates me."

"We understand that, in the early days, you didn't have any time for Hector Mathewson, but that suddenly changed. We suspect that he found out about your covert activities and he blackmailed you so you would support him in exchange for him keeping his mouth shut. With regard to having evidence to implicate you, we'll leave that to Customs and I'm sure you'll already be aware they don't have a reputation for being gentle."

"There's nothing whatsoever you can pin on me. I can get the media to support me. We are one of the biggest and most powerful businesses in Scotland, so you'll never be able to do anything that can hurt us."

"That's where you're wrong. Maybe you've not been following the news, but I think if you do, you'll find that Benlochy is very small compared with Rangers Football Club, and if the tax man can bring down an organisation the size of Rangers, then I don't think you have any grounds to feel safe."

As Burns digested Sandra's words, his face went red and he started to shake. His hand reached down and grasped one of the heavy Caithness ornaments.

At first, she imagined he was just seeking solace from touching the tactile decorative glass and realised when it was almost too late that he was securing a weapon. Burns's grasp tightened around the heavy ornament and it was to their utter amazement when he lifted and hurled the object with considerable force, aimed straight at Sandra's head.

"Bloody bitch," he yelled aloud.

Sandra's reactions were fast and reflexive. She moved to the left, simultaneously raising her right hand to parry the assault, but not as quickly as she would have liked. The glass flew past her face at great velocity, crashing and then splintering against the wall, but on its way grazing the surface of Sandra's cheek and splitting the skin as it went.

Phil's first reaction was to check to ensure Sandra was not seriously hurt, but then he was out of his seat, bearing down on Burns. "That's quite a temper and a mighty powerful right arm you have there. I wonder what else you've been capable of."

Before he reached halfway across the gap between them, Travers appeared in the doorway, pointing a shotgun at Phil's chest, and he looked as if he knew how to use it. "Get back in your seat," he snarled.

Phil stopped mid-pace. He'd never faced the business end of a firearm before, and not being at all comfortable with the prospect, he followed the instruction.

Sandra was quaking inside, but given the circumstances, she conveyed the impression of being remarkably composed. She was aware of the warm trickle of blood, but she ignored it and the stinging feeling on her face and instead tried to play for time. "I didn't tell you the whole truth when I said we weren't ready to make an arrest. We suspected that you could have killed Hector and now you've removed the doubt. We know that you've hated him for a long time but we need you to help us out here. What was it that made you finally flip?" As she spoke, her hand cautiously slid into the pocket of her trouser suit. Her phone was there; she'd activated the silent button before coming in to start the interview. Her fingers were trembling and she fought to control them. Working solely using sense of touch and based on her memory of the positions of the keys and of the menu system, Sandra coded a search for the last received call and then pressed the send button, knowing if she got it right it ought to connect to Alex. She had no way of knowing if she'd succeeded, but hoping she had, she felt for a paper tissue and scrunched it in front of the earpiece to muffle any incoming sound. She then removed her hand to enable it to be in plain view.

"What difference does it make now?" Burns replied.

"We'd really like to understand what's behind all of this. We know it must have been something significant to make you react after all the time you'd tolerated him." Sandra wanted to keep him talking; the more time she could spin then the more chance of a rescue.

Burns felt assured realising Travers' weapon was restraining his accusers, and knowing it could not make his predicament any worse, he seemed happy to talk and exemplify his current position of power. He wasn't the sort to be relieved to unburden himself with a confession but instead took on the role of a lecturer, flamboyant in his explanation. "I don't see that it matters now, but Hector had already caused so much damage, and left unchecked, he was going to destroy my business. He was talking to a lot of the wrong people. It was bad enough he was trying to offload the company, but the way he was going about it, he was completely undermining its value and he'd have ended up selling it for next to nothing." Burns became more relaxed the more he spoke. He could have been describing a family outing to the park rather than a murderous explosion of anger.

"After his meeting with Holbein, he wanted to talk to me. I didn't want to risk being seen with him and I told him I'd meet him at midnight in the shop. Travers helped me to get in using the tunnel. I arrived early and saw him having sex with some slut."

Burns was about to explain further but saw Sandra and Phil nod and realised they were already aware. "I stayed in the cask room until first he left and then she did before he returned. I told him what I thought of him and his ways. My family had been good to him and this was how he was repaying us. His incompetence was destroying my business. He laughed at me, called me old and useless and said he'd do whatever he wanted and I couldn't do anything about it. He reminded me about the power of attorney and that I had no legal powers and said he wanted me to see exactly how he was screwing everything up because he was enjoying making me suffer. It was deliberate that he'd let me catch him fornicating with that tramp. It wasn't enough for him to fuck up the business; he wanted to rub my nose in it as well.

"I just lost it, 'couldn't do anything about it,' I'd show him. I was using my walking stick for support, it was in my hand and before I even knew it, I'd wielded it round and struck him with its head. It was an antique stick; it had ornamental glass on the top which shattered when it hit him. Hector went down as if he'd been pole-axed. Travers checked him and told me he was dead, just one blow and he was gone. I should have done it years ago. I think I would have if I'd known how easy it would be. Travers tidied up as much as he could so we didn't leave a trail behind, then he pulled apart some of the racking to try to confuse what might be found. He also caused some damage in the shop and pinched a few bottles for good measure. It was all done as a diversion and I thought it worked quite well.

"The big question I have now is, 'What do we do with you?' "

"Don't you think you're in enough trouble already? There are other officers who know we're here and why we came. It would be best if you just give yourselves up." Sandra was quaking but she replied confidently, displaying a composure she little felt.

"Not a chance of that," Burns replied. "I've always lived my life the way I want. I'm not going to end it in a prison cell. Now, if you just do what you're told, you won't get hurt. Travers and I need to get the Hell away from here and I need to keep you out of the way for long enough for us to make our exit. Follow me out into the hall," he commanded.

With Travers' gun barrel pointed at them the whole time, Burns led Sandra and Phil towards an under-stair cupboard and instructed them to get in.

"That's a fine looking gun, a Purdey twelve bore, isn't it? My father used to take me clay pigeon shooting, but we could never have afforded one of those," Sandra observed. She had no way of knowing for sure, but she hoped her call had connected to Alex and he could follow what was going on. She wanted him to know as much as possible about what they were facing.

Burns grew suspicious. He carefully examined her and spotted a bulge in her pocket then rammed in his hand and pulled out her mobile. He slung it on the ground and crushed it underfoot.

"Very smart, but not smart enough," he growled. "Now you," he added pointing at Phil. Phil lifted his phone out for inspection and it was subjected to the same treatment.

"Now get in there."

Phil looked into the confined space. It was small in area, about five feet by two, with a sloping ceiling and it was already packed full of rubbish bags. "You can't put us in there?" he pleaded. Conscious of being claustrophobic, Phil didn't know whether to be more afraid of the gun or of being locked in a tight space. He considered trying to jump Travers but there was no opportunity. Travers, maybe anticipating the risk, was standing at a distance. Phil was perspiring profusely and could feel sweat running down his neck. His palms felt moist and clammy.

"It's your choice," Burns replied. "You seem to have a lot of evidence against me so I don't really have a lot to lose." Burns turned and nodded to Travers who cocked the gun, ready to fire.

"Okay, okay, we'll go in. Just keep your finger away from that trigger," Phil pleaded.

Burns pushed them forward into the cupboard then slammed the door and turned the key.

He and Travers then exited the back of the house and made for the garage. With Travers driving Burns's BMW 735, they shot down the driveway, not at all certain of their planned destination.

Only a glimmer of light penetrated the darkness under the stairs. Sandra and Phil couldn't see one another in the darkness but could vaguely make out the other's outline.

"Well, here's another nice mess you've gotten me into!" Phil muttered trying his best Oliver Hardy impersonation, attempting humour to distract his terrors.

* * *

For Alex, the day had started with a long lie in. He had a pleasant morning, breakfasting with his sons, and then delivered them in time for their planned activities. He'd collected Sanjay, Donny and Mary from the office and was on route to Benlochy when the call came through from Sandra. Using his Parrot system, he pressed the button to accept the call through the hands-free speaker. They were all shocked to hear what was going on, and Alex signalled everyone to stay silent until he had fished out his hand set to engage the mute facility and thereby prevent them from being heard. No sooner had he completed this task than his grip tightened on the wheel and his foot pressed harder on the accelerator. Simultaneously, he barked out instructions, "I'll keep this line connected to follow what's happening. Sanjay, use your own mobile and call for reinforcements. Emphasise it's an emergency and ask for the armed response unit with every support service they can muster."

Following Burns's confession, they heard some noises after the phone was discovered, then the line went dead. They looked at each other with stunned expressions and Alex now floored the accelerator. Although staring at the road in front, Alex couldn't help himself visualising what might be happening to Sandra and Phil. He recollected the image of Sandra's naked body clinging to his in the shower the previous morning and the flicker of a smile touched his mouth but only for a second. Another more sinister recollection came to him, the only time when he'd seen the victims of death by gunfire in the flesh and, try as he might to avoid it, the images superimposed. Alex's hands were trembling and he adjusted his hold on the wheel to a vice-like grip to avoid it showing.

"Take it easy, Boss. There's no point us getting there without the back up or the right equipment," Donny suggested.

"In case you didn't follow what came through on this phone, two of our colleagues are being held at gunpoint, and I consider it our duty to be on hand to provide any help they might need," Alex spat back.

"I understand that, Sir. My first worry is the 'gunpoint.' Does it really make sense to add the four of us as potential targets? My second concern is that driving at this speed, we might not have to worry about guns."

"I've undergone full training as a pursuit driver, so you need have no worries on that score. As for the firearms, thanks to Sandra's comments, we know that they have one twelve bore shotgun. They can fire only two rounds without reloading."

"Just as long as neither of them is aimed at me," Donny whispered.

At that particular point in time, Alex would have been happy to personally discharge both barrels with Donny as a target. "I have no intention of putting anyone in the line of fire. But I do want to be available for Sandra and Phil if they need us. If you're not happy about that, you can get out now. I can..." Alex was interrupted midsentence.

"They're on their way, Boss. One armed unit's already been scrambled and another will follow. Ambulances are being sent just in case and Traffic will be setting up road blocks. The chopper's on its way too, so they can't escape."

Moments later, Alex screeched to a halt a few yards outside the entranceway, then instructed his passengers to disembark and take cover behind the wall. He then sat watching and saw the BMW approach. Alex thought it most likely that Sandra and Phil were locked up somewhere in the house, but even so, he was fearful of the possibility that Burns had changed his mind and brought them in the car. He considered his options, then decided he needed to stop their car, but he wanted to get his timing exactly correct. He could see Travers was driving so knew he couldn't also be holding the gun. Burns was on the far side, in the passenger seat beside him, and Alex knew, even if he had the weapon, he was prevented from being able to effectively use it because of his position and the lack of space. As the car increased in speed, making its final approach towards the gate, Alex quickly advanced the Santa Fe, completely blocking the entranceway. Seeing him only at the last second, Travers stamped on the brake and hauled on the steering, managing by only a few inches to avoid a collision, but it left his vehicle coming to rest against the stone wall. It was exactly as Alex had intended.

Without a moment's hesitation, the other three officers were upon them, pulling the car's doors open, removing the shotgun and then wrestling the two elderly occupants to the ground and handcuffing them.

Alex didn't waste any time looking to follow the outcome. Instead, he sprinted up the driveway and into the house seeking his subordinate officers and calling as he went. He found the key still in the lock of the under-stairs cupboard and, with some relief, opened it to set them free. Desperate to escape the confined space, Phil was first to throw himself through the open door. He shook Alex's hand and they then met in a manly hug as an affectionate thank you. No sooner had their grasp parted than Sandra flew into Alex's arms. They held each other closely and Alex gently caressed the wound on Sandra's cheek before her face turned for their mouths to meet in a full and deep embrace.

It was several moments before they reluctantly separated, but their eyes remained locked on each other as Alex stated the obvious, "I guess our secret's out now."

In the background, Phil stood blinking in the daylight and then chuckled a reply. "What secret? I didn't see anything or hear anything. What with my fear of small spaces and after being locked in that cupboard, I can't be certain of anything. I'm sure it will take me several minutes for my senses to return." Phil then discreetly turned his back to afford them a little privacy to resume their passionate reunion.

A few minutes later, the three clung to each other in mutual support as they staggered back to the main entrance to be met by their colleagues.

The sun was now splitting the sky but a strong wind had whipped up, sending clouds of dust airborne. There was a dull droning sound from an approaching helicopter and a crescendo of approaching sirens.

"Now the fun's over, I'll need to get back to write this lot up," Sandra suggested dismally.

"What are you complaining about? I'm meant to be off today. I'd been planning to try and clear my office last week, before all this blew up, so maybe I'll come back and do it now. If you're working, I've nothing better to do," Alex answered.

"Well, we could take some time to bask in the glory of another case closed, then for good measure we could have a drink to mark the occasion. After what we've been through, you might prefer to stay away from whisky for a while, but I've yet to open the bottle of Remy and we could do it tonight to celebrate."

"You mean closing the case?"

"That too, but regardless of what Phil saw or admits to having seen, I think it's time to accept that we're a couple and I'll put in for a transfer.

The decision was a milestone in their relationship and they exchanged a passionate embrace, ignoring the questioning looks from their colleagues.

End

Author Note

Thank you for reading *A Measure of Trouble*, I hope you enjoyed it. If so, I would be very grateful if you'd leave me a rating and review of the book.

If you have any comments or feedback you'd like to make more directly then please email me at: -

zachabrams@authorway.net

Also by Zach Abrams

Made A Killing

Made a Killing is the first novel in the Alex Warren series.

Scott Stevenson was a despicable character and nobody mourns when his bloody corpse is found with an ivory tusk driven through his torso. DCI Alex Warren and his team are given the challenging task of discovering his killer. They investigate the numerous people Stevenson has harmed, and their enquiries reveal a host of related crimes, motivated by sex and greed. They struggle to close the case before more lives are lost.

A fast moving, gripping novel set in the tough crime-ridden streets of Glasgow.

http://mybook.to/madeakilling

Ring Fenced

If you think your life's complicated, then spare a thought for Benjamin who obsessively juggles and controls his five independent personae, until …*Ring Fenced* is Zach Abrams first novel. A story about power, control and obsession

One man, five lives, ring-fenced and separated,
Bennie, loving husband and father,
Benjie, youngest son of orthodox Jewish parents,
Ben, successful corporate banker,
Benjamin, millionaire author and publisher of pornography
and Jamie, part-time lover of a beautiful musician.

Relying on his Blackberry to keep all his personae separate, his life is perfect.

But what if holes begin to appear in the divisions?

When a sequence of events throws his life into chaos, his separate words collide with explosive consequences.

[This book contains content of an adult nature with use of sexual swear words and depictions of sexual encounters. It is unsuitable for young readers and it may be offensive to some readers of all ages.]

Written to Death

Writing isn't usually considered a dangerous pursuit - but perhaps think again - Sheila Armstrong, a leading member of Eastfarm Writers' group is stabbed to death, on stage, in a school, while rehearsing. The death mimics the plot of the play they'd been rehearsing.

DCI Alex Warren and his girlfriend, DI Sandra McKinnon, return from a short holiday, but hardly manage to step from the plane before he's called to investigate the suspicious death.

Within hours, Sandra is roped into investigating a series of crimes which appear to be mob-related.

Both their enquiries run in parallel as they struggle to make progress while supporting each other professionally and emotionally.

Available at Amazon UK or Amazon US

SOURCE; A Fast-Paced Financial Crime Thriller
A novel investigating financial crime and sabotage within the banking sector

Tom is an accomplished journalist and lead features writer at Global Weekly's London office. He's an unhappily married workaholic seeking to advance his career.

Sally is single, ambitious and independent. Visiting from Australia, she's chasing the same story.

Each is eager to research alleged wrongdoings at Royal National Bank, exposed by a series of whistleblower revelations. RNB is one of the largest and strongest financial institutions in the world, or it was. There have been several incidents within a period of weeks. The effect has rocked the bank to its core, causing its share price to tumble and world stock markets to ripple. International economic stability is at risk.

Both Tom and Sally suspect something or someone must be behind it. It couldn't just be coincidence. They think it inconceivable for such rapid decline to result from merely incompetence and a series of blunders. It must be sabotage. Yet the timing and diversity of location make it improbable. Has someone been powerful and ingenious enough to mastermind such demise? If so who, and why?

Tom and Sally become reluctantly twinned in the investigation looking for the "source' and their trail leads them from London to Glasgow, Manchester, Barcelona and Collioure.

They tread a dangerous path as Tom's life and wellbeing becomes imperilled by strange and cryptic warnings. Through this, Tom struggles to hold everything together. He's hoping to restore his crumbling marriage and uncertain personal finances, yet is distracted by an irresistible attraction to Sally.

They feel daunted by the prospect of an unknown enemy, who seems to have unlimited power and connections. With great fortitude, they tackle the most challenging investigation of their lives, facing threats and hostility countering their every move.

Available at Amazon UK or Amazon US

Released by Zach Abrams together with Elly Grant

Twists and Turns

With fear, horror, death and despair, these stories will surprise you, scare you and occasionally make you smile. *Twists and Turns* offer the reader thought-provoking tales. Whether you have a minute to spare or an hour or more, open *Twists and Turns* for a world full of mystery, murder, revenge and intrigue. A unique collaboration from the authors Elly Grant and Zach Abrams

Here's the index of Twists and Turns -

Table of Contents

A selection of stories by Elly Grant and Zach Abrams ranging in length across flash fiction (under 250 words), short (under 1000 words) medium (under 5000 words) and long (approx. 16,000 words)

- Rhetoric (flash) by Zach Abrams

- Keep It to Yourself (medium) by Zach Abrams

- Lost, Never to be Found] (medium) by Zach Abrams

- Man of Principal] (flash) by Zach Abrams

- Witness After the Fact] (medium) by Zach Abrams

- Overheated] (flash) by Zach Abrams

- Wedded Blitz] (medium) by Elly Grant

- Taken Care] (flash) by Zach Abrams

- The Others] (short) by Elly Grant

- Waiting for Martha] (long) by Elly Grant

Available at Amazon UK or Amazon US

An introduction to Source; A Fast-Paced Financial Crime Thriller - the first few pages

Prologue

There was a loud 'pop' and Tom ducked as the cork flew from the bottle, bounced off the ceiling and ricocheted in his direction. He heard Sally giggle and turned to see foamy liquid spewing out of the opening and running down and over her hand. He proffered a glass to enable her to pour and avoid further waste.

"Don't you think it's a bit premature for a celebration? True, we've made a breakthrough, but we still don't know what it means."

"Don't be such a bore. We've had more than a week of intense work without a break and we deserve a reward. Maybe it's not a major breakthrough, but you can't deny we've made real progress. Besides, I've not gone overboard; it's only Freixenet. It's a decent enough cava but it's not 'Bolly', I'd have gone for real champagne if it was a proper celebration."

Froth was climbing over the top of the first glass and Tom had a second one ready. Sally's enthusiasm was contagious. Her grey eyes sparkled and tears of joy had moistened her cheeks. Her smile was so broad, argument was not imaginable.

"Not for me," Ahmed said, when he saw Tom lift a third glass. "I don't drink alcohol, haven't you noticed already? But I'll happily toast our success with a glass of spring water. I'm sure there must be a bottle in the mini bar."

"The charges this hotel makes, it'll probably cost more than the wine I picked up at the supermarket. Never mind, we can claim it on expenses anyhow," Sally replied.

"What's with the abstinence? I didn't realise you were religious," Tom asked.

"I'm not," Ahmed answered. I was born a Moslem but I don't practice religion at all. I'm actually agnostic. If you really want to know, I'm not an immigrant, I'm third generation. My grandfather came from Karachi and arrived in Glasgow in the nineteen-sixties. We were an archetypical Packy family."

Ahmed saw Sally and Tom's stunned looks. "I reckon I'm allowed to use the term. Packy's only a bad word when directed as an insult by outsiders. I suppose I can say it because I'm talking about myself. It's like Jewish comedians talking about the holocaust, they can be poignant and side splittingly funny, but the same words spoken by a gentile would be in bad taste and offensive. Anyway, like I was saying, Grandad worked as a bus conductor. His son, my father, opened a corner shop and ended up owning three, including a post office. Then, when I didn't want any part of the business, I studied English and Media. I'm about as westernised as it's possible to be. True, none of my family drink alcohol because of their religion, but for me it's more of a health thing. I don't take caffeine, I won't drink tea, coffee or fizzy drinks and I work out at the gym four times a week, when I'm not away from home."

"Sorry Ahmed, we didn't mean to cause any offence, please forgive us. Oh and we've something in common, my father worked for a bus company too, although none of the family ever opened a shop," Sally said.

"Don't worry. It would take a hell of a lot more than that to offend me. Besides, I've got a thick skin. You wouldn't survive long in

Glasgow without one. Ferguson's a Scottish name, is that where your family come from?"

"I think my grandfather came from somewhere near to Stirling," Sally replied, "But like you, I'm third generation although in my case it's English. I was born in Manchester to be more precise."

"Well the name Ferguson will make you popular in Manchester at least, with Sir Alex's past achievements." Ahmed said.

"You might think so, but it's not really the case. Most Mancunians support City. United draws its fans from the rest of the country. And besides I've been away from there for years now.

"Well at least one of us is a pure bred Englishman," Tom interrupted. "My family can trace its roots back to the seventeenth century."

His outburst was met with guffaws from the other two, "Pure bred and English shouldn't be stated in the same sentence," Ahmed claimed, "It's an oxymoron. With the possible exception of Americans, they must be the most bastard race on the planet and you can interpret that any way you like."

Chapter 1

Tom made his way through the fog. It wasn't real fog, at least it hadn't been in recent years, but the clawing atmosphere in Stephan's office hadn't truly cleared after the smoking ban. Prior to it being prohibited, you literally had to part the colloidally imbued air to see your way to a chair. Now there was greater transparency, but no matter how often or how well the office was cleaned or decorated it still felt the same. The smell of stale nicotine and whisky was immoveable and whether real or imagined the smoke was still there.

A career journalist, Stephan Presley fulfilled every cliché associated with the industry. Now aged fifty, he frequently drank to excess and he'd been smoking sixty a day for over thirty-five years. More than three quarters of a million cigarettes in aggregate and his complexion and aroma bore testimony to it. Some years back, Stephan had tried to cost how much he'd spent on tobacco and alcohol in an effort to justify cutting his consumption down or out. His shock at the number of figures in front of the decimal point made him reach for a glass and he didn't feel comfortable drinking without a fag in his hand. So the effect was minimal, a temporary, slight decrease in cigarette intake before resuming his normal level.

When company regulations prohibited him from smoking in his office, he took to using the roof garden for breaks, but it was suspected he more often simply closed his door and opened the window to reduce the evidence of succumbing to his addiction. The smell wasn't too much of a giveaway as the air was already contaminated by the noxious fumes diffusing from his skin and clothes.

It was rare, if ever, for anyone to volunteer to visit Stephan's office, any guests he did have arrived as a result of a summons. But there was no doubting he was good at his job, very good, one of the most respected editors in the business. He had first class instincts and an excellent knack of sniffing out a good story, even if his nose was too damaged to detect his own odour.

* * *

Stephan's yellow-stained forefinger pointed to a chair and Tom reluctantly descended to perch on its edge, praying the fabric's smell wouldn't permeate his favourite Hilfiger chinos. Tom's attention had been on Stephan and only at the last moment he spotted the attractive young lady on the adjacent chair. His attention was immediately distracted by her curvaceous shape and his eyes were drawn to her shapely legs. She was wearing open-toed sandals. He saw her nails were brightly and perfectly varnished confirming his suspicion that her legs were bare and the deeply tanned colour was her skin and not tights or stockings.

Tom's eyes lingered a moment too long for propriety before letting his appraisal move northwards to take in her tight waist, shapely bosom and the flowing curls which framed a disarmingly pretty face.

"Yes is the answer to your question," she said, staring pointedly at him.

"Yes? What do you mean? I didn't ask anything."

"Yes, it is an all-over tan and I'm only telling you because there's no other way you're ever likely to find out. And, trust me, you don't need to open your mouth to ask a question." The girl's eyes were slate grey in colour but were alive with mirth which spread to the rest of her face. The sparkling whiteness of her perfect teeth lit up the otherwise dingy office.

"Www... No, it was only...," Tom stammered. The room's temperature was rising, the heat radiating from his embarrassment.

"Don't bother trying to deny it, Tom. You've been caught red handed, well red cheeked to be more precise. Just accept it and move on. You're starting this game one nil down." The craggy, nicotine stained stumps in Stephan's mouth formed into a hideous smile and although nowhere near as appealing as Sally's it betrayed no less amusement.

Tom resignedly sank back into his chair, his eyes focused downwards.

"Okay, what's this about?" he said hesitantly. He needed to change the subject and try to find a way to regain at least some of his normal, natural confidence and exuberance.

"Well first of all I suppose I'd better introduce you two. Tom Bishop this is Sally Ferguson and vice versa. I think a handshake will do. You've probably already heard of each other. I'd be surprised if either of you weren't aware of the other's by line."

Neither of them followed the suggestion but they both examined each other. This time Tom was careful to keep has gaze above shoulder height and he wasn't disappointed. Sally's face was still aflame with jollity. Her smooth, even complexion was tanned the same shade as her legs and was complemented by the lightest application of cosmetics which showed to their best effect her almond shaped eyes and full mouth.

By contrast, Sally accepted the opportunity to have a long appraising look at Tom, taking in his clean-cut image and powerful form, the cropped, sandy hair topping his slim angular face.

"You scrub up not too bad, a lot better than the photo on your column. You appear younger too. What are you, thirty, thirty-two perhaps?"

Tom was taken aback by her bluntness, but quickly reassessed. After all, what might he expect from a fellow journalist? However, he couldn't remember ever being attracted to one of his profession before.

"You don't look so bad yourself and I'm thirty-four actually, so thanks for the compliment. Maybe I've not worn as badly as I'd thought, but more likely you're needing to see an optician."

"Isn't that a contradiction of terms? If I couldn't see clearly then I wouldn't be able to see an optician."

Stephan cut in, "Okay children, enough of the word games. Let's get down to business." He sank into a chair and lifted and sucked on a pencil, holding it between his fingers as a surrogate cigarette. "I can see I'm going to have my work cut out trying to control you two. As if Tom's not been a big enough pain in the ass for the last five years, now I've got two of you.

"Sally, I'm sure you already know that Tom's been our lead features writer at the London office for some time now. Tom, I know you'll have heard of Sally, but you might not know she took over the lead in Sydney a few months back."

Tom stared back at Sally, "So the tan's real then and I know you're not meant to ask a lady's age, but as you don't qualify I'll ask anyway."

About the Author

Having the background of a successful career in commerce and finance, Zach Abrams has spent many years writing reports, letters and presentations and it's only fairly recently he started writing novels. "It's a more honourable type of fiction," he declares.

His first novel *Ring Fenced* was published in November 2011. This is a crime story with a difference, following one man's obsession with power and control.

After this he collaborated with Elly Grant to produce *Twists and Turns* a book of short stories.

Zach's next novel, *Made a Killing*, is the first book in the Alex Warren series. It follows the investigation after the killing of a much hated criminal where an elephant tusk was used as the murder weapon was. This has been followed by *A Measure of Trouble* where Alex's team are seeking the murderer of a CEO killed within the cask room of his whisky distillery. The third, *Written to Death*, deals with a mysterious death during a writers' group meeting. These are fast-moving, gripping novels set in the tough crime-ridden streets of Glasgow.

Zach's quirky thriller, *Source; A Fast-Paced Financial Crime Thriller* has three investigative journalists travelling across the UK, Spain and France as they research corruption and sabotage in the banking sector while trying to cope with their own fraught personal lives.

Alike his central character in *Ring Fenced*, (Bemjamin Short), Zach Abrams completed his education in Scotland and went on to a career in accountancy, business and finance. He is married with two children.

He plays no instruments but has an eclectic taste in music, although not as obsessive as Benjamin. Unlike Benjamin, he does not maintain mistresses, write pornography and (sadly) he does not have ownership of such a company. He is not a sociopath (at least by his own reckoning) and all versions of his life are aware of and freely communicate with each other.

More in keeping with 'Alex Warren,' Zach was raised in Glasgow and has spent many years working in Central Scotland.

To contact the author mailto:zachabrams@authorway.net

Printed in Poland
by Amazon Fulfillment
Poland Sp. z o.o., Wrocław